DANNY
PLATTEN

CHARLIE
A HULL STORY

BLACK TREE
PUBLISHING

Design and Production by Black Tree Publishing, Hull
Gemini House, Lee Smith Street Hull HU9 1SD
Telephone: 01482 328677

Printed by: Fisk Printers, Hull

CONTENTS

CHAPTER 1
HERE COMES CHARLIE

Charlie Robinson was a Hull lad, growing up on the streets of Hessle Road in the mid-1950s. Now the city at that time was a place of two distinct halves. East of the river Hull lived the dockers and crane drivers who loaded and unloaded the big merchant vessels thronging the busy cargo docks. West of the river was home to the trawling community – not just the fishermen sailing day in day out from St Andrew's Dock, but the engineers, riggers and filleters, the bobbers who discharged the vessels, tipping the baskets of fish into larger kits, the barrow boys who moved those kits around the fish market, and a host of other ancillary workers.

Once filleted, the fish went all over the UK – either boxed, iced and loaded onto railway wagons stationed close to the trawlers, or smoked or frozen in the local fish houses and dispatched by lorry. This work continued day and night, employing many families in the Hessle Road area. Cars were few but the streets were always alive with buses, trolleybuses and bicycles – as well as the horse-drawn carts that moved the boxes used to pack the fish. Even handcarts were common. You could hire them by the hour for just a few pence.

At the weekend the huge shire horses were a sight to behold, walked down to Corporation Pier by the young lads who looked after them, then down the stone slipway to be washed in the Humber. Steam ferries ran regularly across the estuary from there to New Holland to meet the train for Grimsby and Cleethorpes – a good day out at the seaside for many families.

People kept the same friends and neighbours for life and knew each other inside out. They were always there to help – in good times and bad. Local women attended births, helping the midwife during labour and keeping an eye on mother and baby afterwards, though new mothers were often up and about within hours, caring for their older children or doing the housework. Neighbours would even lay out the dead.

In 1954 the city was thriving. The deep-sea trawlers coming and going from the Arctic were landing plenty of fish, and jobs were plentiful. Everyone was willing to work, but the pay wasn't great and many families struggled. Every penny had to be accounted for. From my earliest youth, I watched families get by on very little. As a lad I had to attend school with paper filling the holes in my boots to stop the water getting in. My parents just couldn't afford to buy me a new pair.

When my story begins, Charlie is just fifteen years old. He's spent all his life in these cramped terraces off Hessle Road – in tiny houses with no bathroom and just an outside toilet in the yard, usually backing on to next door's. Sharing bedrooms is common in larger families. Things don't change much here. Boys play football in the road; dogs run barking after bicycles; little ones upset the neighbours and are called inside; women stand outside gossiping, scrub their front step, sweep the pavement outside, push prams full of clean linen back from the wash house – hair in curlers, wanting to look their best when their men get home from a trip.

Most families follow a similar routine. Each morning dad sets off for work and the kids go to school, while mum cleans the house inside and out, then cooks something for them all to enjoy when they get home again at night. Charlie lives happily with his dad Mike, a foreman in one of the fish houses, his mum Mary, and older sister Eileen. They have a decent home, kept spotless by Mary, but like their neighbours they live from day to day, with no luxuries. Life has certainly improved in that respect in the last sixty years.

The local school wasn't great – and nor was the education – but children were taught respect. Most of the teachers were men and fear of swift retribution deterred anyone from answering back or misbehaving in class. Braver souls sometimes smoked in the outside toilets at break time, but anyone caught by the master on yard duty would be hauled straight off to the headmaster's office for 'six of the best', or three whacks of the cane on each hand, not pleasant at all.

On his last day at school, Charlie walks through the gates with his pals Joe Harrison and Bob Watson. Charlie and Joe live in the same terrace – more or less opposite each other – while Bob's house is a little further down the street. The lads have been friends since long before they started school. None of them is any great shakes academically but Charlie definitely has the edge. If you want to know anything, ask Charlie: that's their motto. They're all pleased to be leaving and – even at fifteen – prepared to start earning their keep. Their families are working hard enough already. They can't be expected to do it all.

This is Charlie's story …

CHAPTER 2
SCHOOL'S OUT

'Well, lads!' says Charlie. 'Our last day. Great, isn't it?' He puts his arms around his pals. 'Don't look so worried, you two. We'll be fine next week once we've started work.'

'I'm off down the dock Monday morning,' says Joe. 'Uncle John has a friend in one of the fishing companies. He's taking me to meet him.'

'I can't believe you wanting to go on trawlers,' says Charlie. 'Not when you lost your dad at sea.'

'Me neither,' says Bob. 'Good luck, though. Give it a couple of trips. You can always try something else if it doesn't work out.'

'Gone for weeks at a time,' says Charlie. 'That's not for me. It's decent money in the fish house, and I want to be out with the girls, enjoying life.'

'I'll be all right at the shoe factory,' says Bob, with a wicked grin. 'There must be at least thirty lasses working there. I'll be able to take my pick.'

Charlie slaps Bob on the back. 'You must be joking, you ugly sod. The lasses will run a mile before you get anywhere near them.'

'Very funny. They definitely won't entertain two smelly prats like you, stinking of fish.'

They carry on laughing and joking until Charlie and Joe turn into their terrace. 'See you after tea,' says Joe. 'Usual spot.'

Charlie goes inside and walks straight into a hug from his mum.

'Poor bairn,' says Mary Robinson affectionately. She dotes on her only son. 'Give us a kiss. I can't believe you've left school.'

'Come on, Mam,' says Charlie, rubbing his cheek. 'I'm not a baby any more.'

'Course you are,' she says, kissing him again. 'You'll always be my baby.'

'Don't let my mates hear you say that. I'll never live it down. What's for tea? Smells good.'

'Just you wait and see.' Humming happily to herself, Mary returns to the kitchen and the pans bubbling away on the stove.

Then Mike Robinson walks in. 'Hi, sweetheart,' he calls to his wife. 'How's the big man, then?' He puts Charlie in a headlock and ruffles his son's dark curls. 'You're going to have to work for a living now, lad.'

'Dad,' sighs Charlie, vainly attempting to smooth his hair down again. 'You're just as bad as Mam.'

Mike grabs the paper and settles into his favourite armchair. 'God, that's good. I'm bloody knackered. This'll be you next week, Charl.'

'Bob and Joe, too. Fancy Joe going on trawlers. I don't think his mam'll be too happy.'

'Too damn right,' says Mike, shaking his head. 'I don't know how in hell anybody could think about going on them bloody things.'

Last home is Charlie's sister Eileen, who also gives him a big hug and a kiss. 'Poor lamb. Remember you'll have to start paying board now you've left school.'

'Not you too?' he sighs, pretending to push her away.

The kids normally gather in the schoolyard, and that's where the lads head after tea. A few girls and boys are there already, some puffing at cigarettes sneaked off their parents or begged from the older lads. Everyone is laughing, joking and discussing the latest Top 20 stars, Frankie Laine and Johnnie Ray. The girls are practising the jive while the lads look on. A couple of the boys are trying to sing.

'Don't take it up for a living,' jokes Bob.

Everyone is pleased to see them – Charlie in particular. His dark curly hair and excellent physique make him a favourite with all the girls. He has a crush on a very pretty blonde called June, who blushes and smiles when she sees him eyeing her up.

Joe and Bob are chatting to their friends about work next week. Charlie, however, has other preoccupations.

'Hi, June,' he says. 'I was wondering. Could I maybe take you to the pictures one night?'

June's pals are green with envy. 'Of course, Charlie,' she says quickly. 'When?'

'How about Monday night? See you outside your house at six?'

'That's fine,' she says. 'See you then.'

Tomorrow is a Saturday and one lad suggests a bike ride to Hornsea. 'It'll be a laugh,' he says. 'I bet half of us don't make it.'

Charlie is all for it. 'Sounds good,' he says. 'I'll borrow my dad's bike.'

'Me too,' says Bob.

'I haven't got a bloody bike,' moans Joe.

'No problem,' says Bob. 'You can borrow our Sarah's old one. Might need a bit of work, though.'

'What about you, George?' asks Charlie.

George Sutherland only moved to the area a few months ago. Although a year or so older than the lads, he soon became a good friend. He and his dad are rag-and-bone men, going round town with their horse and cart collecting scrap to sell. He's a bit of a character, too. He likes to be the centre of attention and just hates to be outdone.

'I'll be there bright and early,' he says, 'properly attired and suitably equipped for the epic journey.' He runs his fingers through his hair – a habit that always makes Charlie smile.

'Is your bike a good 'un? asks Bob.

'Good 'un. Are you kidding, Bob lad? It's the best – three gears, a bottle carrier. It's got the lot.'

'I'm impressed,' says Charlie. 'I can't wait to see it. Sounds like we'll have a job to keep up with you.'

George gives them the thumbs up. 'You'll certainly need to be fit,' he laughs.

They agree to meet at the top of the street at nine o'clock, then disappear to sort out their bikes.

Next morning Charlie and Bob arrive together, both in regular shirt and long trousers, turn-ups tucked inside their socks. Some of their pals are properly kitted out, and a couple of the girls really look the part in their shorts and flimsy blouses. Then Joe rides up on Bob's sister's old bike, rear mudguard dangling and an old tammy covering the springs where the saddle used to be.

'Sodding hell,' says Charlie, shaking the bike experimentally. 'Is this thing safe to ride?'

'Hope so,' laughs Joe, 'otherwise I'm in trouble. My arse will be sore as hell by the time we get to Hornsea though.'

Charlie turns to Bob. 'And you're on a right sit-up-and-beg job. Are you sure you can see over the handlebars?'

'Of course I can,' replies Bob. 'At least I won't be crouching down like you. Watch you don't end up with a bad back.'

Last to arrive is George, in baggy brown shorts, white vest and black kneesocks, plus plimsolls all dried and cracking with layer after layer of whitener.

'Who the hell got you dressed?' asks Charlie. 'Where did you get those shorts?'

'I think my granddad wore them in Burma,' says George.

'What have you got in here?' says Bob, tugging at an apparently World-War-I-vintage haversack. 'Corned beef and a frigging gas mask?'

'My refreshments,' says George proudly. 'Jam sandwiches and a bottle of water.'

Some of the girls have also brought drinks, carried in string bags fastened to their saddles. Not that it stops them taking the mickey, mind.

Charlie starts laughing too. 'And where did you get this old crock? What happened to the gears and the bottle carrier?'

'To be honest, me and mi dad picked it up on our round,' says George. 'But, hey, it'll do the job.'

Everyone is laughing.

'You do exaggerate,' says Joe, giving him a push.

George jumps on his old boneshaker. 'Well I'm ready,' he shouts.

June climbs on her bike, too. Good looks, slim figure, and very tight shorts – she certainly stands out from the crowd.

Mmmm, thinks Charlie appreciatively. Nice legs.

'Come on,' she shouts. 'Are we going or not?'

'Let's go,' everyone yells back.

George leads the way, his bike making an ominous grinding sound with every pedal stroke. Behind him comes Joe, rear mudguard swinging wildly, then the rest follow single file, passers-by staring as they thread their way through town, dodging cars and trolleybuses.

An hour or so later they're well out into the countryside, but George is struggling.

'OK, there?' asks Charlie, dropping back to join him. 'Any slower and you'd stop dead.'

'Of course,' pants George, soaked in sweat. 'It's just this bloody wind.'

Even the girls ride past them. 'We're stopping in the next village for a rest,' shouts one.

Charlie tries to shelter George from the wind, but they're still last to arrive. The others have already laid their bikes flat against the verge and are stretched out on the grass, relaxing or having a drink.

George pulls out his water bottle and flops down too. 'I must admit, I am a bit bushed.'

'Bloody hell,' sighs Joe. 'How much further?'

'What was that?' says Charlie, absently. He's too busy watching June.

'Dirty devil,' says Joe. 'I know what you're up to. How much bloody further? I'm knackered already?'

'Not far,' says Charlie. 'Only another twenty minutes or so.'

'What's that smell?' asks Bob suddenly. They regard each other suspiciously.

'Uuugh,' moans George, jumping to his feet. 'My arse feels damp.'

'That's because you're sitting in dog shit,' says Charlie.

'Oh God,' says George. 'It's all over my shorts.'

The girls run off, grabbing their bikes as they go. Meanwhile George discards his jam sandwich and uses the wrapping paper to try and clean himself up. 'Any better?' he asks.

'No,' says Joe. 'You're just making things worse.'

'Get back on your bike,' says Charlie. 'The stink should fade a bit. We'll ahead of you and keep you downwind.'

Out on the road the wind is stronger still, filling the legs of George's baggy shorts and hindering him even more. Soon they have to stop again.

'This wind is freezing my privates,' says George.

'Why not tie up the legs of your shorts?' suggests Bob helpfully.

Grudgingly, George borrows an elastic band and a safety pin from two of the girls. 'This won't do anything for my image,' he grumbles.

'Shut up,' snaps Charlie. 'It's that or your bits'll drop off.'

When they get to Hornsea, George heads to the public conveniences to have another go at the stain, and the lads all follow him in. 'My sodding leg's completely numb,' he says, removing the elastic band. 'That bloody thing has cut my circulation off.'

'Make sure you put it back on later,' says Bob. 'You'll never get home otherwise.'

Eventually they go and rejoin the girls – George still gazing ruefully at the nasty brown marks all over his shorts. The drizzle sends them into an amusement arcade to put a penny or two in the slot machines. George starts to play, but the woman next to him is most unhappy. Pulling a face, she sniffs, then sniffs again. She leans back and surveys George's backside, then grabs hold of her son and stalks off to the far side of the arcade. Not that this bothers George, who just shrugs and carries on playing the machine.

Outside it's still wet and miserable, so they decide to call it a day and head for home. By now the rain is hammering down and they're more strung out on the return journey. Charlie and Bob are riding heads down, pedalling hell for leather. Then June cycles past, hair dripping, her sodden shorts nearly transparent. She turns and gives Charlie a come-hither smile. He likes what he sees and, eyes glued to her rear, pedals even harder to catch her up.

'Not far now, thank God,' he says.

'I can't wait to get home,' she replies. 'I'm soaked.'

'I can tell,' he says with a grin.

A slow smile spreads across her face. She knows exactly what he's looking at.

Bob is on his own now, laughing at Joe wobbling past with water streaming in a rooster tail over his back. Last in line is George. 'Get a move on,' calls one of the girls, but he can't keep up no matter how he tries.

'I'll bloody give her "get a move on",' he snarls. 'Hell's bells, I can't go any faster. I'm knackered, wet through and ruddy freezing. I've dog shit all over my shorts, my bike's crocked and my left leg's gone to sleep. Last time I ever get on a bike. Bus and train for me in future.'

The bunch of drowned rats who finally make it back to Eton Street soon split up and go their separate ways. Poor old George is last home – on foot. To top off a perfect day he suffered a puncture coming into Hull.

Charlie returns his dad's bike to the yard and nips in the kitchen door. 'You're soaked,' laughs Eileen. 'Have you been for a swim?'

'Ha ha, very funny,' he replies. 'You should see the others. What a day! George sat in a load of dog crap. You could smell him a mile off. No one would go anywhere near him.'

'The water's running off you. Go and get changed.'

'Good idea. All I want now is to put my feet up for a week.'

The following evening they're back in the schoolyard, messing around and talking about the ride. Some couples pair off and go in search of a quiet corner, while the rest soon head for home.

June lives in the next street and agrees to let Charlie walk her back. Joe and Bob are jealous as hell. 'That Charlie,' says Bob. 'How does he do it? What's he got that we haven't?'

'No idea,' says Joe. 'But I wouldn't mind some of it. He's a good pal though, isn't he?'

'Course he is. But I hope he tells us what happens.'

Meanwhile Charlie and June aren't talking much. Hesitantly, he takes her hand. Then, meeting no resistance, he pulls her closer and kisses her on the cheek. June responds by kissing him on the lips and within seconds they're ducking out of sight down a passageway. He runs his hands all over her. No girl has ever let him get this far before. But suddenly she stops him dead in his tracks.

'No, Charlie,' she says, forcing him away. 'I've got to get home.'

'Just a bit longer, June,' he pleads.

'No,' she repeats, pushing him more firmly still. 'We shouldn't be doing this.'

She straightens her clothes and marches off, Charlie in her wake. Before he knows it, they're at her front door. 'Goodnight, Charlie,' she says, giving him a chaste peck on the cheek. 'See you tomorrow.'

Grinning, he turns for home. He can't wait.

Early next morning Charlie heads to the fish house with his dad. The cold and the smell are incredible. 'You'll soon get used to it, lad,' Mike reassures him. 'I promise you won't notice it after a while.'

Mike stays on constant guard, checking that his son does exactly what he's been told and fervently hoping he makes no mistakes. Eventually he sets Charlie to work alongside a big chap called Norman.

'Hey, Charlie!' shouts Norman. 'Get your arse over here, lad. Stack these boxes properly so we can get 'em on the barrow and move 'em. I'll leave you to it.'

Charlie scurries to obey. He's still a bit scared of Norman.

Some of the girls are taking the mickey. 'Hey, Charlie!' calls Big Maggie. 'Are you and me off out tonight?'

'Are you kidding?' says Charlie. 'You'd smother me.'

'Cheeky little sod. I'll get you later. Just you wait.'

Better watch out there, thinks Charlie.

Late in the day, while they're all hosing down the working area, a group of girls stroll casually towards him. As soon as they're close enough, a couple grab hold of him while Big Maggie pulls down his trousers. She reaches for a hose and sticks it down his pants, spraying his private parts. 'Here, girls!' She sticks the hosepipe in even further. 'What a little willy! Come and look at this!'

Charlie struggles but they won't let go. Everyone else is watching and egging them on. Finally he breaks free and walks away blushing, pulling his trousers back up again.

Maggie saunters over and gives him a big kiss. 'It's just our initiation ceremony, Charlie. We do it to everyone. And don't worry, we won't tell anyone your little secret.'

'What did you expect with all that icy water?' laughs Charlie. 'It'll be a while before my you-know-what recovers.'

Everyone is still grinning as they put on their coats, Mike included. 'Come on, lad,' he says. Time to go home.' Charlie's sodden trousers are sagging at the crotch. 'Why are you walking bow-legged, son? They didn't stick a couple of cod fillets down there, did they?'

Very funny, thinks Charlie, trying to hitch up his trousers. Hope June doesn't hear about this. *Bet the lads'll think it's a laugh, though.*

Back home Mary is no more sympathetic. 'I just hope you were wearing clean underpants,' she giggles.

Charlie cleans himself up with a strip wash at the kitchen sink – the normal routine, except when the tin bath is brought out and filled with water boiled on the stove – then heads off for his date.

The front door opens just as Charlie is going to knock. 'I'm off now, Mam,' June is calling over her shoulder. She's obviously pinched some of her mother's lipstick and perfume and blushes when she sees him.

'Hi, June!' says Charlie. 'You look lovely. Is the Regis all right with you? It's Judy Garland in A Star is Born?'

Hand in hand, they set off down the street. Hessle Road has several cinemas, some better than others. With little else for entertainment, all the teenagers go regularly – if only in search of a place to smooch. Charlie has borrowed four bob from his dad, promising to pay him back from his first wage packet. He reckons two bob for the tickets, bus fares and maybe an ice cream in the interval.

Once inside, Charlie steers June to the thinly populated rear of the auditorium. They take their seats, and as the lights dim and the film begins to roll, he edges closer, snaking his arm around her. He can't concentrate on the screen – the film is dull and June's perfume is much more exciting. They start to kiss and his hands begin to wander.

'No, Charlie, please,' she says feebly.

He lifts her skirt and slowly starts working his fingers up her legs. Stocking-tops – that's a first! But the flash of the usherette's torch soon puts a stop to all that. They jump apart, and June pulls down her skirt and straightens her hair.

Charlie tries his luck again but now June has changed her mind. 'Stop it,' she says, grabbing his hand and forcing it away. 'Someone might see.'

Eventually he resigns himself to the inevitable and they spend the rest of the evening just holding hands. But outside her front door she checks carefully for witnesses, then gives him a big kiss.

'I suppose I'd best get inside before Dad comes looking for me.'

'Bye, June,' says Charlie, squeezing her hand. 'See you during the week sometime.'

On Wednesday night Charlie and Bob go round to see Joe. It's been a couple of days since they last got together. Joe's mother answers the door. 'Hello, you two,' she says. 'Come on in. Joe's just finished his tea.'

'Thanks, Mrs Harrison,' says Charlie, with a grin. He has a sneaky crush on Pat Harrison. She's in her late thirties, with long black hair and a voluptuous figure.

'The terrible twins are here, Joey.'

Joe looks up. 'Where have you two been? I thought you'd moved house.'

'Working for a living,' says Bob. 'How are things with you? Did you go down the fish dock?'

'Yes. I'm sailing tomorrow as galley lad on the *Lord*

Middleton.'

'Nervous?' asks Charlie.

'No, not really. I just hope I'm not too seasick. How did you two get on?'

Charlie and Bob both burst out laughing. 'Well ...' says Bob. He already knows about the hosepipe incident.

Charlie jumps in quickly. 'Not in front of Mrs Harrison,' he pleads.

'What is it?' asks Pat.

'Please don't embarrass her,' says Charlie.

'For heaven's sake,' says Joe. 'Just get on with it.'

Bob tells them the tale. 'Has that Maggie still got her claws into you?' asks Pat, giggling.

'No, thank God,' sighs Charlie.

'She'd better not have,' says Joe. 'He's going out with June from the next street.'

'I've only taken her to the pictures once,' protests Charlie.

'Don't tease him, Joe,' says Pat. 'I could tell them plenty of tales about you.'

'What do you fancy doing this evening?' Charlie asks his pals, trying to change the subject. 'How about a stroll?'

'Fine,' says Bob.

'Be good,' says Pat. 'And don't be late.'

'We won't, Mam,' says Joe. 'See you later.'

As soon as they're outside, Joe demands the full details. 'Did Big Maggie grab hold of your dick, then?'

'No,' says Charlie. 'Just touched it. She told everyone it's tiny. What did she expect with all that cold water?'

'No girl has got anywhere near mine,' says Joe ruefully. 'I wouldn't care what she looked like.'

They buy a fish supper from the chip shop at the top of the street and stand around eating and chatting. It's quiet on a weekday night. On a Sunday all the young 'uns would be promenading up and down Hessle Road, pairing off or hoping to find a new partner.

Several girls walk past them. 'How about a date?' the lads shout every time. But all they get is a two-fingered response – the girls just carry on walking.

'They don't know what they're missing,' says Joe. 'What about the shoe factory, Bob? Any initiation ceremonies there.'

'No, I'm sorry to say. There's some lovely girls, and some of the older women aren't half bad either. If one of them tried pulling my trousers down, I'd let 'em get on with it. I'd enjoy it. In fact, I'd pull 'em down myself. How did you get on with June, Charlie? Anything juicy to report?'

'I'm saying nothing,' says Charlie with a smirk.

'Come on,' says Joe, winking at Bob.

'Nothing happened,' maintains Charlie doggedly. 'Just a bit of kissing, that's all. You do right to consult the expert, though. I bet neither of you have got your leg across yet.'

'Not for want of trying,' says Bob. 'Tell you what. How about a bet? Three bob each for the first to get his leg over. What do you reckon?'

'The way our luck's going it'll be years before anyone gets a pay-out,' says Joe disconsolately. 'Do near misses count?'

The following night the lads are back at Joe's to walk him down the dock.

'Take care,' says Pat, tears rolling down her cheeks as she kisses him goodbye. 'You don't have to do this, you know.'

'I've made up my mind, Mam,' says Joe. 'I want to go. You take care now.'

Charlie reaches for Joe's kitbag, slings it over his shoulder like a proper trawlerman, and the three pals set off for the dock. Three trawlers are sailing on this tide – each with a crew of twenty – so spotting Joe's ship isn't easy. Some men have walked to the dock like them, while others are arriving by taxi.

'There's the *Lord Middleton*,' says Charlie finally. 'Shit, what a bloody tub. You'd never get me sailing in that rust-bucket.'

'Uncle John said I might get a better ship after a few trips,' says Joe. 'Come on. Let's see what it's like on board.'

Eyes everywhere at once, they clamber on deck, then enter the accommodation.

'Now then, young'uns,' says a deckhand standing chatting to his mate. 'Where do you lot think you're going?'

'I'm the new galley boy,' says Joe.

'Right then, follow us.'

They take the lads down to the mess room, with its central table, seating round the walls and cupboards above. The lads just stand and stare. 'Your bunk's in here,' the deckhand tells Joe.

Then a tall, dark-haired bloke walks in. 'Which one of you is the galley lad?'

'That's me,' says Joe.

'I'm Jim, the cook. What's your name, son?'

'Joe, Joe Harrison.'

'First trip, Joe?'

'Yes.'

'Here's your bed.' Jim walks over to one of the cupboards and pulls back a sliding door to reveal the mattress inside. 'Put your stuff at the end of the bunk there. I'll see you later. Your friends had better be going now. We're sailing shortly.'

The lads all return to the deck. 'Shit, that smell,' says Bob. 'I couldn't stand it. I'd be sick before we even sailed.'

'I suppose you just have to get used to it,' says Joe.

Charlie and Bob shake hands with their friend and wish him all the best, then they climb down to the dockside and wander across to the lock-pits. One trawler leaves, then another. Quite a crowd have gathered to wave off their menfolk. Now it's the turn of the *Lord Middleton* and they scan the decks for Joe.

'There he is, Bob,' yells Charlie. 'Stood with them men.'

'See you, Joe,' they shout, frantically waving their arms.

Joe waves back – rather apprehensively, they think. They watch the trawler until it disappears from view, then slowly make their way home.

'Three weeks on that tub,' says Bob. 'Shit, it's not for me.'

'Me neither,' says Charlie firmly.

On Friday evening Charlie collects his first pay packet. He joins his workmates in the queue, everyone delighted it's payday. They each walk up to a hatch, state their name and are handed a small packet. Then they wander off, opening the envelope and checking the payslip. Charlie can't wait to see how much he's earned. £3 3s and 6d. *Great*, he thinks. *At last money of my own.*

Back home, he draws the packet from his pocket with a flourish. 'How much do you need for my board and lodging, Mam?'

'£1 5s, son.'

Charlie counts out the money and hands it over.

'That's not fair,' complains Eileen. 'I have to give you £1 10s.'

'He'll pay the same as you when he starts earning a bit more,' says Mary.

Charlie turns to Mike. 'And here's the four bob I owe you, Dad.'

'No problem, Charl. Give me two bob now and the other two next week.'

That suits Charlie. *Wow, a whole £1 16s 6d to myself.*

'Any plans for tonight?' asks Eileen. 'Who are you going out with? June or Bob?'

'Don't know. Bob, probably. What about you? Still seeing old Loppy Lugs?'

'Don't call him that. His name's Howard. And his ears aren't that big.'

'Don't be daft. I've heard he wants to join the Air Force. He'll be like Dumbo, an elephant that can fly.'

'Not funny, Charl,' says Mary, chuckling quietly to herself.

I wonder what June's up to tonight, thinks Charlie, opening his front door and walking straight into Bob. 'Oh hi, Bob! How's things?'

His pal jangles the coins in his pocket. 'Pocket full of cash and nowhere to go.'

'Let's go and see if anyone's around.'

In the schoolyard June is talking with her friends. She smiles at Charlie and gets a big beam in return. George is there too, a dedicated follower of fashion in his drainpipe trousers and crepe-soled shoes.

'Look out,' he shouts. 'Here come the workers.'

'Nice haircut, George,' says Charlie.

George runs his hand through his heavily Brylcreemed locks, preening himself as usual. 'It's a DA, Charlie. The latest thing.'

'DA?' says Bob. 'What the hell do you mean?'

'Don't know really. Duck's arse, some say. Can you see how it's cut at the back.'

'Means nothing to me. Never examined a duck's arse close up.'

Charlie feels pretty shabby by comparison. 'Where did you get those trousers, George? I really fancy a pair. Great shoes as well.'

'From the club man,' says George. 'That's best. Then you can get 'em straight away. You don't have to wait and save up.'

Bob starts chatting with some of the other lads, but Charlie makes a beeline for June.

'Sorry I've not been in touch,' he says. 'I've been working. Haven't really been out this week, except to see Joe off on his trip.'

'That's OK, Charlie. I understand. Was he nervous?'

'A bit. No more than we'd have been. It's a tough job on trawlers.'

'You've never fancied it, then?'

'No,' says Charlie quickly. 'It's not for me.' But deep down he isn't quite so sure. *Do I really mean that*? he wonders.

'How about clubbing together for a few beers?' suggests George.

Everyone likes that idea, so they all put some money in the pot and send one of the older lads round to Pop's beer-off. Pop knows most of them are nowhere near eighteen, but he's quite happy to sell beer and spirits to under-age drinkers, or after hours.

'We can take it back to my house,' says another lad, Alec. 'Mam and Dad are spending the night at Gran's. We'll have to keep the noise down, though. I'll be in the shit if the neighbours start complaining.'

When they get to the house, George winds up the gramophone and starts riffling through some 12" records. 'How about some Rosemary Clooney,' he says. He sticks the record on the turntable and the music begins to play.

Quite a few couples are pairing off, so Charlie pulls June towards him and holds her close. He can't really dance, but he's seen the Hollywood stars – all they do is stand still and sway. 'Hey there,' he croons in time to the music. 'You with the stars in your eyes.'

June gazes up at him adoringly. She really has missed him during the week. His kisses turn her to jelly. 'Oh, Charlie,' she says, closing her eyes and kissing him back.

They go into the hall in search of a bit more privacy. His hands are everywhere, then he slides them under her top and starts fondling her breasts.

'No, Charlie, please. Not here.'

'Where then?' says Charlie. 'Come on, June.'

'No,' she says, pulling down her top. 'I want to go home.'

'Are you sure? It's not that late.'

'You stay if you want to,' she says huffily. 'I'll be fine on my own.'

'No, no,' says Charlie. 'That's all right. I'll walk you back.'

Elsewhere the others are happily smoking, drinking and pairing off – but Charlie and June say goodbye and set off home in silence.

Charlie doesn't know what to think. *What on earth gets into her?* 'I don't understand,' he says at last. 'First you will, then you won't. You lead me on, then stop me dead.'

'Oh, Charlie,' says June. 'I like you a lot, but I don't want to go too far. I'm frightened of getting pregnant.'

'What if I took precautions?'

'I don't know, Charlie. I'd have to think about it.'

Back at her house, June makes it clear that's it for the evening. 'Night, Charlie,' she says. 'When will I see you again?'

'Don't know,' says Charlie shortly. 'I'm off out with the lads this weekend.'

June gives him a look, then turns and marches straight inside.

Instead of returning to the party, Charlie heads straight home. *Don't think I'll bother with June again*, he thinks. But come

Saturday he's wavering – *perhaps I might ... in a few days or so.*

He's also thinking about fashion. 'I need some new clothes,' he tells his mum. 'It's embarrassing when I'm out with my friends.'

'Why?' says Mary.

'Everyone is better dressed than me,' says Charlie. 'Do you think I could use the club man? It'd take me ages to save up for something.'

'Sure, son. I'll ask Dad if we can get you a club cheque. Then you can buy yourself something new and pay it off each week.'

'That would be great, Mam. Do you think Dad will say yes?'

'I think so. We've used the club man ourselves when we've been really desperate for something. How much would you need?'

'I don't know, Mam. Enough for some clothes and shoes.'

Mary asks Mike the first chance she gets. He's reluctant at first – the club man, like the rent man, has a nasty habit of walking into the house uninvited – but Mary eventually persuades him, and a few days later Charlie heads into town with his club cheque.

'Let's have a look, Charl,' says Eileen, grabbing his bags as soon he gets home. 'What have you bought?'

'Let me get inside first,' says Charlie. 'I'm going upstairs to change.'

'Ta da,' he says, reappearing a few minutes later, resplendent in new shirt, drainpipe trousers and crepe-soled shoes. 'What do you reckon?'

'Irresistible,' says Mary proudly, spinning him round and looking him up and down.

'Pains me to say it, but you look great,' says Eileen.

'Glad you like 'em,' says Charlie. 'All I need now is somewhere to wear 'em.'

CHAPTER 3
ON THE TOWN

Back at the shoe factory Bob has settled in well. He's made plenty of friends and loves all the quips and the banter. The girls are always kidding him and playing around. 'Hey, Bob!' shouts one. 'Where's that good-looking pal of yours?'

'Not telling,' he calls back. 'Anyway, what's wrong with me?'

'Nothing, Bob. You're great, too.'

'Thanks, that's nice of you.'

'Don't mention it. Still prefer your mate Charlie, though.'

All the girls are laughing, but Bob doesn't mind. He has his eye on a cute little blonde called Pam. He reckons he might even be in with a chance of a date there!

Later in the week he goes round to Charlie's for a catch-up. 'What happened between you and June?' he asks. 'You seemed to be doing all right there.'

Charlie hesitates but eventually he relents. Bob is a friend, after all.

'I know just what you mean,' says Bob. 'Same thing happened to me. I'm in here, I thought. But a quick feel of her breasts and she carried on like I'd done something terrible.'

'So the six bob's still safe, then?' laughs Charlie.

'If we stuck it in the bank we'd earn a fair bit in interest before either of us gets any sex. And poor Joe has no chance, stuck away on that bloody rust-bucket.'

'I wonder how he's doing. He should be home in a week or so. I don't envy him at all.'

'Me neither. I hope he's OK. I see his mam every now and again. I bet she worries all the time after losing her husband at sea like that. She's a good-looking woman, too – and not really that old.'

Charlie says nothing. He doesn't want to admit to his crush on Pat Harrison. To change the subject, he suggests they team up with George and go to a dance at City Hall on Saturday night.

'I can't bloody dance, Charl.'

'Nor me, but there'll be plenty of girls around. George says it's great.'

'OK, we'll give it a try. I'm off now. I'm knackered and I need my beauty sleep.'

'Me too,' says Charlie, slapping Bob on the back. 'See you, mate.'

'Wow!' says Bob, when Charlie appears at his door on Saturday night. 'You smart prat. How did you get hold of that rig?'

'Dad got me a club cheque,' says Charlie, brushing imaginary fluff off his trousers.

'I could do with one of 'em myself, Charl. I don't have anything like that to wear. Come on in and say hello to the rest of the family.'

Bob's mum Barbara, dad Jim and two sisters, Denise and Sarah, are all sitting round the table. 'You look smashing, Charlie,' says Denise. 'I just love those crepe-soled shoes.'

'How do you think I'd look in a pair of them trousers?' asks Jim.

'You couldn't fit your arm in one those legs,' jokes Barbara. 'Twenty years ago, maybe. But it'd have been a tight squeeze even then.'

'Are calling me fat?'

'Not fat exactly. But if we rendered you down, we wouldn't need any dripping for a while.'

'She's pulling your leg, Dad,' says Bob. 'Come on, mate. Let's go.'

En route to the dance they meet up with George. 'Hi,' he greets them, preening himself as usual. 'Been splashing out, Charlie boy?

'You could say that,' laughs Charlie.

'Got to look good for the girls. You won't pull otherwise.

Let's get in there.'

They just stand and watch for a while as the dance hall fills up. A group of girls are dancing together, spinning around, their flared skirts rising up, teasing the boys with glimpses of bare flesh and stocking-tops. Bob nudges Charlie. 'What do you think of them lot, then?'

'Very nice. Wouldn't say no to any of them.'

'Just watch the master at work,' says George, homing in on a tiny brunette sitting quietly with a couple of her friends. He strides over to the girls. 'How about a dance, then?' he asks her.

She smiles, stands up and accompanies him on to the dance floor, pulling a face at her pals as she glances back over her shoulder. The band – piano, saxophonist, bass and drummer – starts belting out a rock'n'roll number and George starts bopping, throwing the girl every which way.

All eyes are on them. 'Where the hell did George learn to dance like that?' Bob asks Charlie.

'Don't know. Wish he'd teach me, though.'

The band swings into a slower number and George brings his partner over to meet them. 'These are my mates, Bob and Charlie,' he tells her.

'Nice to meet you,' says Gwen.

'How about introducing us to your friends?' continues George smoothly.

'Of course,' she says. 'Come and say hello to Wendy and Elaine.'

They walk over to the other two girls. Wendy is quickest off the mark. 'Would you like to dance?' she asks Charlie.

'I would,' says Charlie. 'I'm not that good, though.'

'Well, this is your chance to learn.'

Wendy takes Charlie by the arm and leads him on to the dance floor. Then she places his hand around her waist and demonstrates a few steps. It's another slow dance and the lights have dimmed. As Charlie gains confidence he starts to relax and soon he's rather enjoying himself.

That just leaves Bob and Elaine.

Bob is trying to look good but he stumbles and treads on her toes. 'Sorry,' he mutters. 'I tripped.' They carry on dancing together, but Elaine takes the precaution of holding him at arm's length for the rest of the evening.

Meanwhile George and Gwen couldn't get any closer. Bob looks across and winks at Charlie. With the difference in height George seems to be bent right over her head. He has his eyes tight shut: he's either in a world of his own or fast asleep.

The last dance is always a waltz. Charlie can feel Wendy's breasts against his chest and her perfume is very arousing. He pulls her closer so he can kiss her neck and she makes no move to draw away.

'Can I walk you home?' he whispers.

She nods yes.

While the girls are in the cloakroom, the three boys get together. 'Go to it, lads,' says George, digging Bob and Charlie in the ribs. 'Give it everything you've got.'

While telling Charlie where she lives, Wendy slips her arm through his. It's too far to walk, so they end up on the trolleybus. Approaching her stop, she takes hand and yanks him to his feet.

'Is it far?' asks Charlie, dubiously. *God*, he thinks, *it's a bit rough round here.*

By now she's fairly dragging him along. 'No,' she says. 'Just round the corner.'

When they reach her house, she pulls Charlie into the doorway and starts kissing him. He does what he can while he can, deploying all his best moves, and Wendy starts groping him in return. *This one's a bit forward*, he thinks. *Not that I'm complaining.* He lifts her skirt and she's just begun work on his fly when suddenly the front door slams open.

Framed in the doorway is a big woman, hair in curlers, cigarette clamped between her lips. 'So that's why my step's always so bloody filthy,' she roars, smoke curling from her mouth. 'Get yourself in here now, my girl. And as for you, lad, piss off before I call my husband.'

Frantically buttoning her blouse, Wendy disappears inside while Charlie stumbles off down the street, trying to fasten his fly and stop his trousers falling down, all at the same time. He looks back to see Wendy's mum still standing there, waving her fist.

'If I see you round here again, you little sod, I'll cut your dick off.'

Once he's safely back on the bus he starts to see the funny side. *Shit*, he thinks. *Could have been worse. At least my trousers were still round my waist.*

When Charlie meets Bob the following day they both have a good laugh about it. 'What about you?' he asks. 'Any luck?'

'We walked for ages,' says Bob. 'Then – would you credit it? – her old man was only waiting for her on the front step. All I could do was say goodnight and trail all the way home again. It really pissed me off. I bet George got his leg across, though. Lucky sod, he amazes me.'

'Wait till we tell Joe,' splutters Charlie. 'He'll call us a right pair of useless prats.'

The next week is all work and no play for them both. Charlie sees nothing of June and to be honest he hardly spares her a thought. He's working lots of overtime and getting home knackered at the end of the day, so he and Bob decide to stay in at the weekend, gathering strength for another tough week to come.

Living right opposite Joe, Charlie often bumps into Pat Harrison and they always stop for a chat. 'I'm expecting Joe back next Thursday,' she tells him. 'I'll be relieved to see him home again.'

After work on Thursday evening Charlie and Bob go down the dock to join the crowd of friends and relatives waiting for the *Lord Middleton* to come alongside. The crew are passing mooring ropes to the men on the jetty, while the skipper leans out of the bridge window shouting orders.

Charlie is first to spot Joe. 'There he is,' he tells Bob. 'Hi there, you old sea dog!'

Joe waves back eagerly. He can't wait to be back on dry land. Once the trawler is secure, he tosses down his bag and jumps ashore. The lads greet each other and head off the dock, Charlie and Bob quizzing Joe ten to the dozen.

'Was it what you expected?' asks Charlie. 'Did you enjoy it?'

'God, it was hard work,' says Joe. 'Very long hours, too. And the bloody weather was terrible at times. I was sick as a dog for the first two days but I still had to work. The crew were great but you don't get any sympathy. They just tease you instead. They kept asking me if I fancied a nice greasy rasher of bacon. You get used to it after a while, though.'

'How do you get paid?' asks Bob. 'Do you get a share of the catch?'

'No. The galley boy just gets a wage and what they call backhanders from the crew. I clean the fo'c'sle where they sleep and help them out on deck after I finish in the evening, even in shitty weather, so they each give me a treat.'

'Are you going back, then?'

'Yes, if I don't get the sack. I got on fine with the cook, though. Jim's a laugh a minute, a very funny man. But he won't stand any backchat. He clips you round the ear.'

'Bloody hell,' says Bob. 'You'll never get me going to sea. What about you, Charlie?'

'Definitely not. Wait till you hear our news, Joe.'

'About what?'

'A girl called Wendy.'

'Do I know her?'

'No, and you don't bloody want to either.' Charlie slaps Joe on the back. 'Tell you more later.'

Back at the terrace Bob opens Joe's front door. 'Here is the sailor,' he shouts, 'home from the sea.' He turns to Joe. 'See you after work tomorrow then.'

Pat rushes to hug her son. 'How did things go, Joe? Were you seasick? Did the crew treat you all right?

'Everything went fine, Mam.'

'Your wages are in the dresser drawer, love.'

'I thought I told you to take it all for the housekeeping.'

Life has been hard since Joe's dad died. Although Pat has a job in a clothes shop nearby, she doesn't earn much. 'I can't take all this,' she says. 'Just pay me board and lodging like we agreed.'

'Please, Mam.' Joe puts an arm around her. 'You deserve it, you know.'

'Thanks, love.' She gives him a kiss. 'Just this time, then. I really do appreciate it.'

Once the 'bobbers' have discharged the trawlers in the early hours, the catch is auctioned off on the fish market, then the crew come down the dock at lunchtime to collect their share of the trip. Joe goes to stand outside the office where they'll soon be arriving for their cash. The trip was a good one and he's hoping they'll slip him a few bob in appreciation of his efforts. He finds it a bit embarrassing but that's how things have always operated.

The crew start turning up on foot or by taxi and one by one they make their way into the office. The first man to emerge comes over to say hello and hand Joe some silver. 'Here's a few bob, young'un.' Some give him five shillings; others, ten. Jim gives him a ten-bob note and soon Joe's pocket is full. Finally, the skipper walks over and gives him a pound. He used to sail with Joe's dad and holds him in high regard.

Most trawlermen head next for the Hessle Road or town centre pubs. Many of the younger ones are under age but that doesn't stop them downing a pint or two, despite the threat of a court appearance and a fine if the police catch them.

Joe can't wait to show Pat his earnings, but first he has to report to the ship's runner – the man who signs on the crew. The *Lord Middleton* is sailing again on Monday – three days in dock instead of the usual two. Apparently it needs some extra time for repairs. *Great*, thinks Joe. *More time at home. And chance for a weekend out with the lads*.

As he leaves the dock, counting his cash, a young deck learner pulls up in a taxi alongside him. 'Here, Joe. Get in. Coming for a pint?'

'No thanks, Ben. I'm heading home first.'

'I'll drop you off, then. Where do you live?'

'Eton Street, just round the corner.'

'Climb in.'

Joe's dinner is ready when he walks through the door. Pat has been spoiling him rotten ever since he got home, trying to persuade him not to go back.

He sits down at the table and slowly counts out his

money. 'How much have you got there?' asks Pat incredulously.

'£14 15s.'

'You'll have to put some of it in the bank.'

'You weren't listening to me properly, Mam. I want you to have all of my wages.'

'I can't do that, Joe. You've worked hard for that money.'

'Buy yourself some nice clothes, Mam. You've always put me first. Think of yourself for a change.'

'Thank you, sweetheart.' She gives him a hug. 'Are you going back next trip?'

'Of course. They're doing some repairs so we're not sailing again till Monday. That means I can have a weekend out with the lads.'

'That's good. Go and enjoy yourself with your friends.'

On Saturday afternoon the lads decide to catch the bus into town, buy some records at Sydney Scarborough, then head back to Bob's house to listen to them. His gramophone is one of the latest models and you can stack several records on it at once.

They jump on the bus and immediately start chatting to a couple of girls. 'We've heard all about you lot,' says one.

'Nothing bad, I hope,' says Charlie.

'I wouldn't say that. Especially him with the DA.'

The girls start laughing and whispering together. 'What's this, George? asks Charlie. 'Do they know something we don't?'

'They've probably heard how sexy I am when I get a girl alone in the dark,' he replies smugly.

'It'd have to be in the dark with you, you ugly prat,' jokes Charlie

Soon they're browsing the latest records, trying before they buy in the listening booths and jigging around to the music.

'I thought you couldn't dance, Charlie,' says Joe.

'I'm learning, Joe. I'm learning. Wait till you see me tonight.'

They buy a couple of records, then George suggests they go for a pint. They look at each other, wondering whether to risk it. 'Let's do it,' says George. 'We'll go to the King's Head. It's OK there. They aren't bothered about you being under age as long as it isn't too obvious.'

They head for the back room and the barmaid follows them in. 'What can I get you, lads?'

'Four pints of mild, love,' says George confidently.

She smiles. 'You are all eighteen, aren't you?'

'Course we are,' says Bob in his deepest voice.

As soon as she leaves the room they start laughing. '"Course we are,"' parrots Charlie. 'Bloody liar.'

The barmaid soon returns with their drinks. 'Who's paying then?' she asks, surveying each of them in turn.

Charlie, George and Bob all point towards Joe. 'He is,' they chorus.

Joe hands over some cash. 'And get yourself a drink too, love.' He's heard the crew saying that they sometimes treat the barmaid.

'Thanks, love,' she smiles, handing him his change, less the price of her drink.

'Last of the big spenders,' jokes Bob. 'Do you fancy her, then? She's not bad for fifty!'

'Fifty,' says Joe. 'You're kidding. She must be sixty plus.'

'Beggars can't be choosers,' sniggers Charlie.

Downing two pints has no ill effects on George – he's used to drinking – but the other three are all distinctly the worse for wear when they hit the fresh air. They tour the shops, buying a few things and making a general nuisance of themselves.

'Who fancies going and having their photo taken at Jerome's?' asks Joe.

'Good idea,' says George. 'I'll autograph mine and give them away. I might even be able to sell one or two.'

That makes them all laugh. 'You cocky bastard,' says Bob. 'Don't you just love yourself?'

'With good reason, Bobby lad. With good reason.'

Jerome's window is packed with portrait photos, but George isn't impressed. 'God, look at these. Snapping some handsome shits like us should make a nice change for them.'

'How about a group photo?' says Joe.

'Fine,' says Charlie. 'Let's do it.'

Inside the studio, the photographer struggles to get them

organised. 'You there, tall lad. Go stand at the back, please.'

'But I want to sit at the front,' says George. 'Bob, you go stand at the back.'

'Just do as you're bloody well told,' says Charlie. 'We're all going to be in it.'

'OK,' says George. 'Just wait while I comb my hair.'

'Are you sure you don't want to put some make-up on too?' asks Joe.

The photographer is getting impatient. After all he has other customers waiting. 'Are we ready then, gentlemen?'

'Well I am,' says George. 'I don't know about the rest of them, though.'

The photographer just shakes his head. 'So we're all set?'

'Just shoot and have done with it, mister,' laughs Joe. 'We'll be here all night otherwise.'

A quick flash and it's done. 'Come back in an hour,' says the photographer, hastening them out. 'I take it you'd like four prints?'

'Please,' says Charlie politely.

'You could cause trouble in an empty house,' Joe tells George as they leave the shop.

'I just didn't want a shit photo,' he replies. 'You know I always like to look my best.'

They decide to pass the time in Marks & Spencer, mooching around in search of some good-looking assistants.

'God,' says Bob, as they wander into the lingerie department. 'Fancy taking some bird home and seeing her in that.'

'I'm sure you'd be a very happy chappy,' says Joe.

'A lucky sod, too,' says Charlie.

A young assistant approaches them while George is examining some very skimpy underwear. 'Can I help you at all, sir?'

'No thanks,' says Charlie. 'Just window shopping.'

'Wow,' whispers George. 'She could help me by modelling these for us.'

When the time comes to collect the photos, it's Joe who takes them out of the envelope. The others fight for a look. 'Give us a peek,' says George.

'No way!' says Joe. 'You look shocking.'

Eventually he hands them over. 'Rubbish,' says George. 'I look great. Shame about the rest of you, mind.'

'He's unstoppable,' laughs Charlie. 'Come on, lads. Time to get home.'

In the evening they meet up again, ready to hit town. George suggests they try a couple of pubs and then go dancing. Their first stop is the Paragon. It's packed and smoky, the music so loud you can scarcely hear yourself speak. The lads look round warily. 'First round's on me,' says George, pushing his way to the bar. 'What are you having? Pint of mild as usual?'

Charlie is staring at a group of four heavily made-up women – dressed like sixteen-year-olds but fifty-odd if they're a day. He digs Joe in the ribs. 'Just look at that bunch over there.'

'God,' shudders Bob. 'I wouldn't want to wake up next to one of them.'

Just then George reappears with the beers. 'Don't tell me you fancy one of 'em, Charlie.'

'Are you kidding? Only if I'd something wrong with my eyes.'

Laughing, they see they're being watched. One of the women blows them a kiss.

'Shit, Bob, you've scored,' says Charlie.

Bob looks away quickly. 'I'd rather shoot myself first.'

'Ladies of the night, boys,' whispers George. 'Ladies of the night. Would you believe they charge for a jump.'

'No wonder they don't come out in daylight,' laughs Charlie. 'They'd have to pay me and I wouldn't come cheap.'

The lads sit laughing and chatting, taking it in turns to buy a round and slowly getting sozzled. Eventually one of the women totters over in her high heels, wriggling her bottom to readjust her skirt. It's so short and tight, it scarcely covers her thighs. 'Hello, boys,' she says, putting an arm around Bob. 'Are you going to buy me and my friends a drink?'

'Drink up, lads,' says Bob, pushing her away and making for the door. 'Time we got going.'

'Sorry, love,' says George. 'We're off now, but him over there is definitely interested.'

They don't know the lad from Adam, but the woman looks across and smiles at him. She's missing two of her front teeth and the rest are all lipstick smudged. Sensing the danger, the lad plonks his glass down and runs for it, closely followed by his pursuer.

'Shitbag!' says Joe. 'I bet I've bad dreams about her.'

'Don't you mean wet dreams?' says Bob.

They decide to go straight to the dance hall and arrive alongside a whole gaggle of girls.

'I'm in paradise,' says Charlie. 'You can take your pick.'

'I think I preferred them lot in the Paragon,' laughs George.

'You must be barmy,' says Joe.

The dance floor is packed – the girls in flared skirts, the boys in trendy knitted ties, drainpipe trousers and crepe-soled shoes. But first the lads have to go to the toilet.

They all line up, urinating in the trough. 'Don't piss on my new shoes,' says Charlie, edging away from Bob.

George is staring at his feet. 'Now listen here, my friend. Don't start embarrassing me if I'm dancing close to some honey.'

'Who on earth are you talking to?' asks Joe.

'My dick,' says George. 'What did you think?'

'That's it,' says Joe. 'Now I'm sure you're barmy.'

'Come on, lads,' says George, putting his arms round Joe and Charlie. 'No time to lose. Let's go get them lovelies!'

The lads rush on to the floor and quickly put themselves among the girls. George is still the star, attracting a lot of attention when he throws his partner around, but Charlie is improving all the time and the girls are queueing up to dance with him. Bob has bumped into Pam from work and is very excited at the chance to hold her close. Meanwhile Joe is getting friendly with a dark-haired beauty called Mavis. They take a break from dancing and sit kissing and cuddling in the corner.

'Where do you work?' she asks.

'On trawlers.'

'That's a dangerous job.'

'I know, but my dad was a fisherman.'

'Is he still sailing?'

Joe stops dead in his tracks. 'No, he was lost at sea.'

Mavis doesn't know what to say. 'I'm so sorry, Joe.'

'That's okay. I'm sailing on Monday.'

'That's a pity!' She can't hide her disappointment. 'I was hoping I might see you again.'

'Of course you can. Perhaps I could walk you home later.'

'Yes, I'd like that.'

Joe moves closer and kisses her. The music has slowed right down now. He takes her hand and leads her on to the dance floor. Then they just cling to each other, swaying gently to the music.

Every now and then the lads get chance to compare notes. 'Look at our Joe,' says Bob to Charlie. 'He's doing all right for himself there.'

'Good on him.'

They both smile and carry on dancing.

'Taking anyone home?' Bob asks Charlie and George later.

'All in hand,' says George, cocky as ever. 'Just haven't decided who yet.'

'I've got my eye on a girl I danced with earlier,' says Charlie. He threads his way across the floor to ask his intended for the last waltz and soon they're dancing cheek to cheek.

'Can I walk you home?' he asks.

'Yes,' she says. 'But I don't know your name yet.'

'Charlie. What's yours?'

'Joan.' She pulls back slightly and studies him more closely. 'Don't I know you? Aren't you the lad who took Wendy home a few weeks ago. She's a friend of mine. She lives near me.'

'W-Wendy, y-yes,' stutters Charlie, recalling the girl's fearsome mother. 'You say you're neighbours?'

'Yes, she lives a few doors down from me.'

Not sure about this, thinks Charlie. *Could be making a big mistake here.*

George has finally made his move. He's holding his

partner so tight she can hardly breathe. 'What's that I can feel sticking into me?' she asks.

'Only my torch, darling. Don't worry about it. How about me walking you home tonight?'

'If you want,' she laughs. 'But it's very dark down our alleyway. You might need that torch of yours if you know what I mean.'

'Sure do,' laughs George, pulling her tighter still.

When the music stops the lads go for their coats, then stand around waiting for the girls to come out of the cloakroom. Laughing, they agree to meet at Bob's house the following afternoon. Meanwhile Charlie has decided discretion is the better part of valour. 'I'm not hanging around,' he says. 'The girl I fancied is a friend of that Wendy I told you about. I don't want to chance meeting her mother again. Good luck, lads. See you tomorrow.'

'How did you get on?' George asks Bob the next day.

'All right. I like Pam, she's a nice girl. No sex, but I'm planning to see her again.'

'I think I'm in love,' says Joe, throwing his hands in the air.

'Come on,' says George. 'Tell us more.'

'No details. Sorry, mate.'

George digs him in the ribs. 'So you didn't get your leg across, then?'

'I said no details.'

'No six bob for you then,' says Charlie. 'How many times did you do it, George?'

'Just a couple,' he smiles, running his hand through his hair.

'Lying shit. I bet you didn't get a thing.'

'Shush,' says Bob. 'Keep your voices down. I don't want Mam and Dad to hear. How about I put some records on?'

That quietens them down a bit, then Denise sticks her head round the door. She has a real crush on Charlie – the family are always teasing her about it.

'What's going on in here?' she asks. 'What are you all

laughing about? Oh hi, Charlie.'

'What about the rest of us?' asks George, running both hands through his hair. 'Aren't you going to say hello to us, too?'

'I might,' she says cheekily. 'None of you are as good-looking as Charlie, though.'

Slowly she closes the door again, leaving Charlie blushing furiously.

'I'm going round to see Mavis for an hour tonight,' says Joe, as he and Charlie walk home together.

'OK, mate,' says Charlie.

They get to the terrace and shake hands. 'You take care.' He pats Joe on the back. 'See you in three weeks.'

When Joe climbs aboard the *Lord Middleton* on Monday evening, he feels like he's never been away. Never mind, at least he knows what to expect this time.

Some of the hands are out on deck drinking beer, typical of fishermen whatever time they're due to sail. 'Hello, Joe!' calls Jim the cook. 'Fancy one?'

'Thanks,' says Joe.

'Get your leg across this weekend?'

'No,' laughs Joe. 'Still a virgin, I'm afraid.'

'Don't worry. Maybe we can arrange something next time you're home. One of those lovely ladies from the Paragon, perhaps?'

'Not if it's anything to do with me,' says Joe hurriedly. 'I know all about that bunch of tarts.'

Over the next three weeks Bob and Pam start going out together, while George is dating the girl he took home from the dance. Only Charlie isn't seeing anyone. He hates owing money, so he's working as much overtime as possible to pay off his club cheque in double quick time. It's always so cold and wet in the fish house. Everyone else seems hardened to it, but he finds it hard to motivate himself each morning. *How has Dad managed to put up with this all his life?* Bantering with the girls helps pass the day and, of course, the weekly pay-packet comes in handy.

On his way to work, he watches the children going to school. *Not so long ago since this was me*, he thinks. Now he feels grown-up. Generations of Hessle Road families have lived like this and he expects to do the same. *The only way out is trawling*, he decides. *That's the only job where you can really work your up through the ranks. But God, could I really go on trawlers*?

CHAPTER 4
BLACKPOOL ROCK

The girls at the shoe factory are planning a weekend trip to Blackpool. 'Would you like to come, too?' Bob asks Charlie the next time they meet. 'There'll be around twenty all told, but only three men. Four with you. I bet it'll be a laugh. Pam can't make it, lucky for me.'

'Book me in,' says Charlie. 'Just tell me when and how much.'

'That's great,' says Bob. 'We're going this Friday. It'll cost £2 15s and we're leaving at seven from outside the factory. You get the bus, plus two nights B&B and meals. It'll be late when we get there, so we'll be going straight to the guest house.'

'I'll get you the money to book my seat. I'm looking forward to it already. I've never been to Blackpool.'

'I went once years ago. I was only young at the time so I can't remember much. It's probably changed a lot.'

Charlie can't wait to tell his mum and dad about the trip. 'I'll sort out your clothes for you,' says Mary, practically. 'I'm sure you won't have any idea what to take.'

'Just don't get into any trouble, son.' Mike winks knowingly. 'Don't do anything I wouldn't do.'

Charlie gives him the thumbs-up. 'Of course not, Dad,' he grins.

On Friday night Bob is waiting with a gang of factory girls, young and old. 'All ready?' he asks, picking up Charlie's bag. 'Bloody hell, what on earth have you got in there?'

'Mam packed it,' says Charlie. 'I don't have a clue.'

'Meet Clive and Alan,' says Bob, introducing him to a couple of older men.

'Looking forward to this,' says Clive, rubbing his hands

lasciviously. 'Hope there aren't too many blokes roaming bloody Blackpool. The fewer there are, the better.'

They all laugh.

'All aboard,' calls the driver. The single-decker is pretty cramped and they stow their bags wherever they can find room. Then the banter starts.

A few of the women know Charlie already. 'You can share a room with me, love,' shouts Dot.

Charlie blushes.

'Dirty old biddy,' calls Bob.

'Make hay while the sun shines,' she replies. 'That's my motto, love.'

'How about me?' asks Alan, rather an ugly mug with his bulging eyes and big nose. 'I'd be happy to share with you.'

'Like hell,' says Dot, to more laughter. 'I wouldn't give you a bite of my corned beef sandwich.'

As the bus makes its way along the A63, some of the women are nattering while others take a nap. They've been working hard all day and know the journey will be a long one.

Charlie enjoys watching the countryside roll past the window, but the towns and villages all look the same to him.

'What do you think the guest house will be like?' he asks after an hour or so.

'Six to a room, I hope,' says Bob. 'Five girls and one man.'

By the time the bus is crossing the Pennines, three of the girls are lined up near the driver, legs crossed and faces flushed. 'We need a toilet stop,' says the tall blonde at the front.

'Is that right?' says the driver. 'Sorry, you'll just have to wait.'

'That's no good,' she says. 'Please stop. I need a pee now.'

The driver just laughs.

'It's no bloody joke. Stop the frigging bus.'

Everyone else is enjoying their plight, but the driver eventually relents and pulls up at the side of the road. It's very dark out there – no houses or buildings visible, just hills and open countryside.

'No peeking,' shouts the blonde as she opens the door and

jumps down on the grass. A strong wind lifts her flimsy dress as she squats to do the necessary.

'God,' she says. 'My bottom's freezing.'

A second girl is holding grimly on to her dress, trying to preserve some semblance of modesty. 'What's that?' she squeaks. 'Someone's watching. Over there, look!'

Her friends turn to see two eyes gleaming in the moonlight. Hastily they pull down their dresses, run to the bus and clamber back on board.

'It's only a bloody sheep!' shouts Bob.

The girls aren't bothered about him taking the mick, they can relax. But now the lads have decided they need to go too. Backs to the bus, they stand in a line. 'Give us a flash,' the girls shout through the open windows.

Clive does up his fly, then turns and gives them a V-sign.

'Spoilsport,' they shout. 'You could have given us a quick peek.'

'Fair's fair,' he jokes. 'I'd have shown you mine if you'd shown me yours.'

Eventually they pull up outside a transport café, where the irresistible smell of frying bacon soon has them queuing up for a mug of tea and a sandwich.

'I'm starving!' says Bob. 'Bacon butty for me. What about you, Charl? I'll get 'em.'

'Same for me, please. I'm hungry too. I'll pay for mine, though.'

They sit down to eat at a big communal table. 'Fancy a lift, love?' a lorry driver asks one of the girls.

'No thanks, mate,' she quips. 'I'd prefer something with a bit more room.'

Charlie and Bob both laugh. The girls always have an answer.

At last everyone returns to the bus. 'OK, ladies and gentlemen,' shouts the driver, closing the door. 'Next stop, Blackpool.'

Charlie and Bob nod off for the rest of the journey … until suddenly Clive is shaking them awake. 'Almost there, lads.'

They sit up and rub their eyes. They're on the front, the trams festooned in lights, crowds pressing into the clubs, pubs and amusement arcades. They stop outside a row of boarding houses just behind the prom, retrieve their bags and climb off the bus. 'Quiet everyone,' calls a woman armed with a clipboard. 'I'll call your name and tell you where you're staying. Your landlady will hand out your room numbers and keys.'

Charlie and Bob are staying at the Paradise Guest House.

'Welcome to Paradise,' barks a scarily big woman as they pack into the narrow hallway. 'We have two bathrooms, one for the upstairs rooms and one for the downstairs. No guest of the opposite sex is allowed in your rooms, gentlemen. And that goes for you too, ladies. The doors are locked at eleven thirty prompt. Any later and you won't get in.'

'God,' whispers Clive. 'It's like a bloody army camp.'

The landlady glares at him. 'Bathrooms fifteen minutes maximum. Think of those who are waiting, please. Breakfast is at eight until nine, lunch at midday, dinner six to seven thirty. Finally, ladies, any women's necessities must be discarded in the appropriate bins.'

She starts giving out keys and room numbers. Charlie and Bob are down to share a twin room. '"Paradise!"' splutters Bob. 'Hell's teeth, Charl. It's tatty as hell. "No guest of the opposite sex is allowed in your rooms!" I bet the girls soon break that rule. We should too, if we can.'

'"Eleven thirty prompt",' says Charlie. 'It'll be a ruddy miracle if I'm still awake. I'm usually tucked up in bed by that time.'

'Wha's the time?' asks Charlie blearily next morning. 'I can hear people outside the door.'

'Don't know, Charl.' Bob opens his eyes. 'Don't have a watch.'

They roll out of bed and Charlie heads for the bathroom. He tries the door but finds it locked.

'It's occupied,' calls a woman's voice.

Charlie is desperate. 'How long are you going to be?' he shouts.

'Bloody hell,' she says. 'I've only just walked in here.'

Then Bob turns up. 'What's up, Charl? I'm not standing around out here. I can't wait. I'm off downstairs.'

'I think I'll stay,' says Charlie – a decision amply rewarded five minutes later when the door opens to reveal a beautiful girl wrapped only in a bath towel. She's about to give him a mouthful but changes her mind as soon as she claps eyes on him.

'All yours, sir,' she says winsomely, brushing past him on her way out.

As she tries to open the door to the room opposite, her towel starts to slip, giving him a tantalising glimpse of bare flesh while she struggles to grab the towel with one hand and cover herself with the other.

Charlie watches the whole thing with some amusement, then rushes for the bathroom.

Just as he emerges, Bob is coming back up the stairs. 'Best get ourselves down there pronto,' he says. 'Don't want to miss breakfast. I'm starving.'

They throw on some clothes and hurry to the dining room. 'Too late,' shouts the landlady, putting out her arm to bar their way. 'Breakfast is over.'

'But it's only two minutes past nine!' pleads Charlie, looking at the clock on the wall.

The dragon is unmoved. 'I told you last night – breakfast is served from eight until nine.'

'You must be bloody joking. We're only two minutes late.'

'I think you'll find I'm not.'

Charlie and Bob trail despondently up to their room. 'I'll give her bloody Paradise bloody Guest House!' says Bob. 'Come on, let's go out for breakfast instead.'

They soon find a café and sit down to eat. 'I've had no time to tell you what happened earlier,' says Charlie. 'There was a girl in the bathroom. What a body! Want to know how I found out?'

Bob is all ears. 'You lucky shit, Charl,' he laughs. 'If that'd been me, she'd have turned out to be some big fat bird.'

Breakfast over, they decide on a bit of sightseeing,

starting with the Tower.

'God,' exclaims Charlie. 'I've seen it in photographs but I can't believe how big it is in real life. There's a bloody circus in there, too. Shall we go and have a look?'

Just then they spot Alan and Clive with a bunch of factory girls. 'What happened to you two?' calls Clive. 'We didn't see you at breakfast.'

'Got there at two minutes past nine,' says Bob. 'The old cow wouldn't let us in.'

'Miserable biddy,' says Alan, shaking his head. 'I'd have just pushed past her. You didn't miss much, though. Breakfast was shit. '

Everyone laughs, and they decide to set off round town together. Alan and Clive are good fun, and it turns out Alan has quite an eye for the girls. Unfortunately, however, they don't seem to fancy him.

They walk quite a long way, then eventually decide to head back to the guest house for lunch. Bang on twelve o'clock, they're lining up outside the dining-room door. The dragon is there again, looking daggers at Bob as he leads the way in.

'I wonder what's for starters?' laughs Charlie.

'Vegetable soup according to the menu,' says Bob, as an elderly waitress staggers in and plonks a bowl down in front of him. He takes his spoon and gives the liquid within an experimental stir. 'Call this vegetable soup? he says. 'It's just warm water with some bits of carrot and a few peas.'

'I don't suppose you've any bread to mop it up, have you?' says Clive, trying hard not to laugh.

'Bread's extra.'

'Extra!' splutters Clive. 'What the hell do you mean extra?'

The waitress puts her hand on her hip. 'You have to pay for it separately.'

Clive is getting more and more annoyed. 'Take this so-called soup and tell her by the door to stick it where the sun don't shine.' He shoves his bowl towards her, then jumps up and stomps from the room. The rest of them follow, the girls giggling as they walk past the angry landlady.

'I bet we've not seen the last of that soup,' Bob whispers ruefully to Charlie. 'What are the odds it turns up again at dinner?'

They decide to seek refuge in a local pub and after a few drinks they're all enjoying themselves. The girls are teasing the lads a little, sitting on their laps. Charlie is having a good laugh with the girl on his knee. She keeps ruffling his hair, kissing him and telling him how nice he is – much to the envy of Alan and Clive. 'Get used to it,' says Bob. 'All the girls love Charlie. It happens all the time.'

They leave the pub in favour of a stroll along the front. A couple of the girls buy kiss-me-quick hats, pointing them out every time a good-looking lad walks past – some of whom are only too ready to oblige.

Around four Bob suggests it's time to rest up and gather their strength for the evening. 'God, I hope I haven't had too much to drink,' says Charlie, flopping down on his bed. 'An hour's kip will sober me up a bit. I wonder if my friend from this morning will be down for dinner?'

'Hope so,' says Bob, 'particularly if she has a good-looking friend. I've definitely drunk too much. I fancy a kip, too. But we must remember to be up in good time for dinner – always assuming it's edible, of course.'

When Charlie wakes up, he goes downstairs to check the time. *Nearly half past five already, incredible*! On his way back he bumps into the girl he met that morning. 'Bathroom's clear,' she says, grinning.

'Thanks,' laughs Charlie. 'That's my next port of call.'

'No problem,' she says.

'Might I ask your name?' says Charlie.

'Janet,' she says, her Welsh accent strong. 'What about you?'

He gazes deep into her eyes. 'I'm Charlie.'

Then another girl appears on the staircase. 'Who's this then, Jan?'

'This is Charlie, Sheila. I told you about meeting him earlier. I was just going to ask him where he's off to this evening.'

'I'm going for a drink with my friend Bob,' says Charlie. 'Then probably the Tower Ballroom.'

'Is this Bob as good-looking as you are?' asks Sheila.

'Better,' says Charlie, colouring up.

'In that case we should definitely meet later,' says Janet. 'All right with you, Charlie?'

'Fine. Where do you suggest?'

'How about the Watering Hole? It's a bar near the Tower. Around eight o'clock?'

'See you there.'

'Make sure you tell Bob I'm looking forward to meeting him,' says Sheila.

Back in their room Bob is snoring away. 'Get up, you dippy shit,' says Charlie. 'It's nearly quarter to six. I've just fixed you up with a date.'

'Who with?' says Bob, yawning and stretching.

Charlie pulls him off the bed. 'Those two girls in the room opposite. We're meeting them around eight.'

Bob stands up in his baggy underpants, rubbing his private parts. 'Better get to the bloody bathroom before the rest of them, then. What's this friend like? I bet she's nuts and bolts.'

'You remember the women in the Paragon.' Bob turns pale. 'Well, she's nothing like them. In fact, she's a very nice Welsh girl called Sheila.'

'Welsh?' says Bob. 'Can she sing? I bet she's in a choir.'

At six o'clock they head for the dining room, joking about the meal to come. Everyone else is ready and waiting.

'Are you all having having the starter?' asks the same sour-faced waitress. 'It's liver pâté on toast.'

'Have you anything else?' asks one of the girls. 'I don't like pâté.'

The waitress smiles thinly. 'Vegetable soup.'

'From lunch,' whispers Charlie, nudging Bob in the ribs.

'Probably in the same sodding bowl,' chuckles Bob.

'No thanks,' says the girl. 'I think I'll give it a miss.'

The waitress soon returns and places a small plate in front of each diner.

'Pâté be blowed,' says Alan, picking up his toast and taking a bite. 'It's bloody potted meat!'

They're all in stitches. *What's next*?

'Toad in the hole with mash and peas,' announces the waitress.

Clive extracts a lump of burned sausage from a leathery Yorkshire pudding. He holds it to the light and starts waving it about. 'Looks rather over-cooked to me – more turd than toad.'

Meanwhile Bob is sampling the mash. 'This is repulsive.' He pulls a face. 'It tastes of disinfectant.'

'Perhaps it's meant to cleanse your palate,' laughs Clive.

They all sniff the potatoes suspiciously, then one of the girls flicks a spoonful at Alan. He looks round to see what happened to it.

'It's stuck to your forehead,' says Charlie helpfully.

Alan scrapes it off and is just about to return the compliment when the landlady appears. 'I understand you're not happy with the food,' she snaps.

Silence falls.

'Just try these spuds,' says Clive bravely, offering her a spoonful. 'They taste of disinfectant. You'd be better off using it on the floors.'

'They taste fine to me,' she says, grimacing. 'If you've any complaints you can record them on the sheet of paper you'll receive on departure.'

'Are you sure one will be enough?' says Bob. 'Two or three would be more like it.'

Everyone laughs, and the woman walks away chuntering to herself.

They decide to abandon dinner and go straight to one of the bars instead.

'We're off to the Watering Hole,' says Charlie.

'Can we join you?' ask Clive and Alan.

'Of course,' says Bob.

It's a popular place, full of young people, but they manage to bag a table for six – Bob and Clive with their backs to the door, Charlie and Alan facing them.

Jan and Sheila arrive while Bob is in the toilet.

'Over here!' shouts Charlie, standing up and waving.

'Who's that sitting next to Charlie?' whispers Sheila.

'Surely that's not Bob? I think I feel a headache coming on.'

'Shush,' laughs Janet. 'He's not that bad.'

Forcing a smile, the girls sit down and just then Bob reappears. 'Meet my mate, Bob,' says Charlie. 'And this is Clive and Alan.'

Thank God, thinks Sheila.

Soon the evening is going with a swing. Sheila and Bob are getting on well, and Charlie and Jan also seem to have hit it off. The girls have already spent a week in Blackpool and are going home in the morning. They sympathise when they hear about the food.

'We haven't eaten there at all,' says Janet. 'A friend of ours told us the food's rubbish.'

'Wish we'd known,' says Bob. 'We could have saved a bob or two.'

'Don't let on we've no money,' laughs Charlie.

'Well, we haven't,' says Bob. 'We're bloody paupers!'

'Aren't we all?' says Janet.

The club is very noisy, the dance floor packed and the music deafening. 'What did you think of the view this morning?' murmurs Janet, pulling Charlie closer as they dance.

'Beautiful,' he whispers back. 'I can't get it off my mind.'

She nibbles his neck. 'If you're lucky, you might see it again later.'

'Can't wait.'

Bob gives Charlie a grin and thumbs up as he and Sheila swing past. 'They seem to like one another,' says Jan. 'Sheila panicked a bit when she saw Alan. She thought he was her blind date. She wanted to make her excuses and leave.'

'Poor lad,' says Charlie. 'Looks aren't everything, you know.'

'Perhaps,' laughs Jan. 'They are a help, though.'

The night flies by and they decide to stay put for the evening. Clive is getting friendly with one of the factory girls, and even Alan is trying his luck with one of the older women. Some of the younger lasses have also found a partner. They don't need their kiss-me-quick hats any more, they're doing just fine without them.

Slowly the club begins to empty and they haul themselves back to the guest house, singing and messing around. They have to be back before the dragon locks the door.

'Quiet,' says Jan, as they giggle their way upstairs. Motioning Sheila to go with Bob, she leads Charlie into her room. She pulls him close, putting her arms around his waist. He kisses her and starts fondling her breasts, then she draws him over to one of the two single beds.

'Just going to the bathroom,' she says, tiptoeing from the room.

Great, thinks Charlie, unbuttoning his shirt. Alone at last with a beautiful girl.

She comes back and lies down next to him.

Time to make my move, he thinks, sliding his hands south, but she grabs hold of them at once.

'Sorry, Charlie, you can't.'

'Can't what?' he says, confused. 'What have I done wrong?'

'Nothing, Charlie. It's a girl thing. It's just, you know, I'm sorry.'

Eventually light dawns. 'Do you want me to go?' he asks hesitantly.

'No,' she says, returning his hands to her breasts and kissing him hard on the lips. She runs her hand down his body, unzips his trousers and takes hold of him.

'Is this OK, Charlie?'

'Oh yes,' he says. *God, she knows what she's doing*.

He feels her hand tight around him, shutting his eyes as she moves faster and faster. Her tongue enters his mouth. She seems to be enjoying herself as much as he is. Soon he can restrain himself no longer. He calls out.

'You OK?' she asks, coming slowly to a halt.

He pulls away, a little embarrassed. 'Sorry,' he mumbles.

'No need to apologise, Charlie. Could you just hold me?'

He pulls her close and soon they're fast asleep, wrapped in each other's arms.

Returning from the bathroom early next morning, Charlie

peers into his room to find Bob and Sheila sleeping soundly.

Closing the door quietly, he goes back to Janet and climbs into bed. She looks at him sleepily, slides an arm around him and kisses him. Then she shuts her eyes and nods off again.

Next thing he knows, Jan is waking him up. 'Morning, sleepyhead. It's seven thirty. I've just given Sheila a call. Time to go, love. The dragon might be on the prowl.'

Charlie jumps up and gives her a hug. 'Will I see you again before we leave? We'll probably try breakfast. Surely she can't make a balls-up of two boiled eggs?'

They laugh.

'I bet she can,' she says. 'I'll see you downstairs.'

He opens the door just as Sheila is emerging from his room. 'We're just ships that pass in the night,' she smiles, pulling down her top.

Yawning, Bob is dragging himself out of bed. 'Good night, Charl?'

'Could say that, Bob. Looks like you've been enjoying yourself, too.'

'Can't grumble, Charl. Gentlemen don't tell, so I won't say too much. She wouldn't go all the way though.'

They pack their cases, making sure they get downstairs in plenty of time for breakfast. As usual the dragon is in position by the door, glaring when Charlie points meaningfully to the clock.

The others trail in one after another – some looking pretty ropey. Clive and his girl have obviously paired off. He winks as they sit down together. Meanwhile Alan comes in alone, looking uglier than ever.

'Did you get lucky last night?' asks Bob.

Alan shakes his head, blowing his big nose and wiping it with a handkerchief. 'No, the woman I was with told me she preferred women. She went off with another girl. I saw them kissing outside the club. What do they call them?'

'Homo–sexuals,' laughs Charlie.

'Don't be daft,' says Bob. 'They're lesbians. Or you might say just plain unlucky.'

'Why so?' asks Alan.

'Because they'll never have sex with a red-blooded male like me,' says Bob. 'I was at school with a lad who didn't like girls, you know.'

'Get away,' says Alan. 'Did he, like, go with men?'

'No,' chuckles Bob. 'He didn't just like girls, he loved them – particularly any who'd say yes!'

After breakfast Charlie and Bob collect their bags and go to wait outside. They're leaving at half past ten, about thirty minutes after Jan and Sheila.

'I don't suppose we'll ever see each other again?' says Charlie to Jan.

'Let's be honest, it's not very likely.' She kisses him on the cheek. 'We live such a long way apart. Let me know if you come into any money, though! I've enjoyed your company and I'm sorry about last night. Nature got the better of us, I suppose.'

Alan is standing a little apart from the others, watching the taxis come and go, when a very pretty girl walks up to him. 'Can you take me home?' she asks. 'If you're not otherwise engaged, that is?'

'Sure,' he says, eyes popping. *I'd get the bloody train back if I got a chance with her.* He smiles and puffs out his chest. 'Where do you live?'

'Poor sod,' Bob whispers to Charlie. 'He thinks he's hit the jackpot here.'

"Wiltshire Road,' says the girl. 'About two miles away. Can you point out your cab?'

'I'm not a bloody taxi driver,' he shouts.

'Oh, sorry,' she says, disappearing rapidly up the road.

Poor Alan looks so dejected, Bob and Charlie just have to laugh.

At last Jan and Sheila climb aboard their bus, waving goodbye to them all. 'You never know,' Jan calls to Charlie. 'We might meet again some day,'

No chance, he thinks. *Shame, I did rather like her.*

Finally the Hull bus appears. 'Hope you've all had a good time,' calls the driver.

'You bet,' shout the girls.

The journey home is uneventful and soon they're back outside the shoe factory. *That was fun*, thinks Charlie. Back to work tomorrow, though. *More of the same old, same old.*

CHAPTER 5
FEMMES FATALES

A week or so later, Bob and Charlie meet up with George. 'Come on, you two?' he asks them. 'Tell me more about Blackpool. Did either of you get a bit, then?'

'We nearly did,' laughs Charlie.

'Nearly did, what do you mean?'

Charlie looks at Bob.

'Well, we slept with two birds,' says Bob. 'But mine wouldn't go all the way and as for Charlie ...' He chuckles. 'Well, let's just say it was the wrong time of the month.'

'Can you only get it up at a certain time of the month then, Charl?'

'No, you silly shit,' says Charlie, giving him a push. 'It's a woman's thing.'

'I know that,' laughs George. 'Listen here. I've got a right bloody story to tell you. You won't believe this.'

'Is this one of your whoppers, George?' asks Charlie sceptically.

'No, straight up, Charl. The old man had flu, so I took the cart out. I went to one of the posh areas on the outskirts. I was going along this road with loads of big houses. There's some rich bastards live out there, I can tell you. Well, Betsy stopped outside this real mansion.'

'Who the hell's Betsy?' asks Bob. 'Your new girlfriend?'

'No, you silly fool. Our bloody horse. Anyway Betsy wouldn't walk on for some reason. I was calling as usual – rag-a-bone, rag-a-bone – and I spotted a woman in the front garden. In her forties probably. She was wearing a big hat and looked very posh. I think she was cutting flowers. She looked up and walked towards me.

'"Hello, young man," she said. "I've got some old clothes for you if you're interested."

'I jumped off the cart and followed her.

'"Where's Tom?" she asked.

'Well, that's my old man. I was bloody gobsmacked. "He's got flu," I said. "I'm his son."

'She just nodded. Then when we got to her back door she invited me in. "Tom always pops in," she said.

'Well, what a house. Her old man must be a bloody millionaire or something. She disappeared for a bit, then came back with a bag of clothes. I had a glimpse inside and they looked brand new. Some silky underwear in there, too.'

'Come on,' says Charlie impatiently. 'Get on with it.'

'Well, she handed me the bag and asked if I'd like a drink.

'"Yes," I said, so she told me to sit down and brought me a glass of water.

'"Back in a minute," she said in this really posh voice.

'I sat there looking round, thinking what a place. Then when she appeared again, wow!'

'Keep going,' says Bob, trying to hurry him up.

'Well, she was only wearing this see-through bloody dress. It left nothing to the imagination, I can tell you. Boy, was I excited. I nearly spat out my drink when I saw her.

'"You're much better-looking than your dad," she said.'

'That's not saying much,' says Charlie, and they all start laughing again.

'No, listen. She walked over to me and ran her hand through my hair. I was frozen to the spot. I didn't know what to do next.'

'Never,' shouts Bob. 'Come on, what happened then.'

'She sat down on my knee and put my hand on her leg. That was it, I was in like a shot. God, she liked it rough. She was all over me. She took me upstairs. "Shit," I thought. "I'm not wearing my good underpants." It didn't matter, though. They were off in a shot. We were at it like two dogs on heat, when all of a sudden she got up, went to the dressing table and opened a drawer. She took out a little whip. Then she sat me on the end of the bed, handed me the bloody whip and laid herself across my knees.

"'I've been a bad girl," she said. "I need a good spanking.'"

Charlie looks at Bob, then back at George. 'She never.'

'She did,' says George indignantly. 'I smacked her lightly a couple of times.

"'No," she said. "Harder. I've been a really, really bad girl."

'Better not tell her I've been a bad boy,' I thought. No way was she smacking me on the arse! I was knackered by the time we got down to it again, but the sex was wild, lads, really wild. Then when we were done she said, real cool, "I think you'd better get dressed now before my husband comes home.'"

The lads sit there, stunned into silence.

'She never told me her name,' says George. 'And she never asked for mine. All she did was to tell me to whack her harder. When I got out, poor old Betsy had decided to go for a walk and I had to spend a couple of hours looking for her. She was stood in a field eating the bloody grass. Then when we finally set off home I'd no ruddy scrap and of course I'd forgotten the bag of so-called rags.

'*You dirty old man*, I thought when I saw mi dad. "Mucky git," I said. "You've been seeing Madame Whiplash, haven't you?"

'He just laughed. "Don't tell me you've been there too, George."

"'I have," I said. "And it was some bloody experience, I can tell you. Why did Betsy stop at her bloody house?"

"'Because she always gives her an apple or something.'"

The lads can't stop laughing.

'Are you sure that isn't one of your porkies?' asks Bob.

'No, straight up,' says George. 'It did happen.'

'Wait till we tell Joe. Where is this bloody house anyway?'

'Not saying. You'd only want to go straight round.'

Things quieten down somewhat over the next few months, and Joe gets several more trips under his belt. The lads have the odd night out, taking their chances in the pubs and clubs, but often they're too tired to bother – even when Joe's at home.

Walking down the terrace after one night out, Charlie bumps into Pat Harrison, smartly dressed and nicely made up. *That's funny*, he thinks. *Joe's mam isn't usually one for socialising.*

'Hi, Mrs Harrison!' he calls. 'How are you?'

'Fine,' says Pat, fluffing her hair up. 'Oh dear, I think I've overdone it a bit.' She throws an arm around Charlie's shoulders to steady herself. 'Just help me to my door, Charlie lad.'

'Sure, Mrs Harrison.' *God*, he thinks guiltily. *Joe's mother has her arm around me. I'm close enough to smell her perfume. I really do fancy her as well. She's a stunner.*

'Call me Pat.'

Charlie grabs her round the waist and walks her slowly to her front door. She slumps against him, sending his hand slipping to her lovely soft breasts. 'Joe seems to be enjoying himself,' he says awkwardly.

'He is, I'm afraid. I'm petrified every time he sails.'

'I'm sure he'll be fine, Mrs Harrison.'

'I told you, Charlie. It's Pat.'

'Sorry … Pat.' His face is very close to hers. He half turns, embarrassed by his very obvious state of arousal.

She opens the door. 'Thanks, Charlie. I knew I shouldn't have drunk so much. Never again, eh.'

'I'm no drinker, either. Are you OK now, Mrs … Pat?'

'Fine, thanks.' As she leans back against the doorframe, she notices his condition. 'Would you fancy a coffee or something?' she says seductively.

Charlie hesitates momentarily. Why not? he thinks. 'Yes, sure.'

'Come in then, Charlie. I really could use the company.'

Eyes glued to her tight skirt and slender figure, Charlie follows Pat into the house. She kicks off her shoes and smooths down her skirt. 'God, my feet are killing me. You men have no idea what we go through to look good for you.'

'You men', he likes that. 'I'm sure it never takes much to make you look good, Mrs ... Pat.'

She smiles. 'That's a nice compliment, Charlie. You're a real charmer, aren't you?'

Oh God, he thinks. *Hope she doesn't think I'm coming on*

to her.

'Sit down and make yourself comfortable,' says Pat, slurring her words slightly. 'I'll make us some coffee.'

Charlie perches in the armchair, very much on edge. Pat walks in from the kitchen with exaggerated care, trying not to spill the drinks. She passes him a cup, then sits down opposite him. 'How do you like your job, Charlie?'

'Very much, thanks.'

'Joe and Mavis are seeing a lot of each other. Have you got a girlfriend yet?'

What kind of question is that? 'Not really, no.'

'No girlfriend, a handsome young fella like you. What are you waiting for, Charlie Robinson?'

Tipsily, she leans forward to put her cup on the floor, giving Charlie a good view straight down her blouse. He can't tear his eyes away from her breasts. Then she flops back, legs apart, brazenly flashing her stocking-tops. He's trying not to stare but he knows his cheeks are burning.

'I get so lonely since my husband passed away, Charlie.' She gazes at him.

What gorgeous eyes, he thinks. *She's beautiful*. 'Have you ever thought of remarrying … Pat?'

'Why, Charlie Robinson! Are you offering?'

He turns pale.

'Only joking,' she giggles. 'I haven't met anyone who fills the bill yet. I'm not ruling it out, though.'

Charlie hesitates. *Perhaps I ought to be going*, he thinks. Then Pat walks over and holds out her hand. *Now what*?

'Your cup, Charlie. Pass me your cup.'

Shit. He hands it over. *I thought she was coming on to me*.

She puts the cup down and moves closer still, swaying slightly as she strokes his face and runs her hand through his dark curly hair. Silently, she pulls his head to her stomach, leans back and closes her eyes. He sits motionless, terribly conscious of her perfume. She lifts his head and sinks to her knees, gazing at him intently. When their faces are level, she strokes his cheek and kisses him long and slow.

He no longer cares whether she notices his excitement. He takes a deep breath and hesitantly puts his hands on her breasts, squeezing them gently.

'Oh, Charlie! It's so long since I've been with a man.'

She starts to unbutton her blouse, then reaches round to loosen her bra. Seconds later she's sitting on his knee. As they kiss he opens his mouth to touch tongues. He caresses her buttocks, afraid she might say no. Moaning, she pushes his hand underneath her skirt. He feels stockings and suspenders, then the smoothness of her thighs. Now his fingers are exploring further, moving inside her panties, feeling her warmth and moistness. She undoes his fly and grips him tightly, amazed at the size of him.

Soon he's laying naked beside a gorgeous mature woman. He's never been with a woman before, and for the first time he realises the beauty of the unclothed female form. He wants to explore every inch of her body as she lies back, eyes closed. *This woman has everything*, he thinks.

He hesitates again, uncertain how to proceed. But Pat takes the lead, pulling him closer, placing his penis between her legs and then guiding him inside her. He's never felt like this before. He kisses her breasts, her neck. By instinct, he moves slowly and Pat responds, touching him where no woman has ever ventured before. 'Yes, Charlie. Yes.'

He moves faster and faster, the wonderful sensations building until it feels as if he's about to explode. The final eruption makes him shudder and catch his breath. For a brief moment, his body seems no longer to be his own. Then slowly the feeling evaporates.

'Oh Charlie,' cries Pat, holding him tight and kissing him hard. 'Charlie, Charlie.' They lie quiet for a time, then she whispers, 'Are you OK?'

'Yes, Pat.' *What a feeling.*

She moves closer. 'Maybe we … maybe I shouldn't have let this happen. What was I thinking of? I'm so sorry.'

'What for?' he replies hotly. 'You're the most beautiful woman I've ever met. I've never been with anyone like you before. In fact ... I've got to own up, you're my first. I'll remember this moment as long as I live.'

'Charlie, you angel! That wasn't bad for a novice. I'd like to do it all over again. How about you?'

'Do you even have to ask?'

This time they take things more slowly. Charlie wants these new feelings to last for ever. They make love for what seems like an eternity, with Pat always ready to guide him. Eventually Charlie looks at the clock. 'It's two in the morning. I'll have to go.'

'Sorry, Charlie. I lost track of time.'

'I hope no one's up when I get in.'

Pat leaves her dressing-gown loose as she accompanies him to the door. Charlie slips his hand inside it and kisses her, then reluctantly turns away. 'Night, Pat.'

'Night, my love.'

Pat watches him slip across the terrace, open his front door and sneak into the house.

Inside he stands and listens. *Hope everyone's asleep*, he thinks. *Dad would definitely want to know what I've been up to*. Then he tiptoes quietly upstairs, tumbles into bed and dozes off, his mind besotted with Pat.

'Come on, Charlie lad,' calls Mike the next morning. 'Time you were up and doing.'

'Coming,' replies Charlie, aroused again by his memories of last night. It all seems like a dream. He closes his eyes … and Mike's exasperated voice interrupts his reverie.

'I'm not telling you again.'

Charlie jumps out of bed, tugs on some clothes and rushes downstairs. The family are all eating breakfast. 'My, you look rough, lad,' says Mike, peering across the table. 'When did you get in? I never heard the door.'

'Late,' mutters Charlie. 'I was round at Bob's. We lost track of the time.'

'Well, I'm off now. I'm not waiting for you. I bet that bloody saddle's freezing.'

'Watch it,' says Mary. 'You don't want your piles playing up again.'

'Oh Mam, please,' pleads Eileen. 'Not at the table. Not

while I'm eating.'

Muffled against the cold, Charlie walks to work dreaming of Pat. *Was it just a one-off?* he wonders. *She was tipsy after all. She never said anything about seeing me again.*

'Hi, Charlie!' calls one of the shoe-factory girls. 'Doing 'owt this evening?'

He gives her a wave and keeps on going. At work he struggles to concentrate, and at home that evening he's a bag of nerves, prowling from kitchen to front room, checking Pat's house across the terrace. *Should I go round? What if she gives me the brush-off?*

Eventually he makes up his mind. 'Just going out for a while,' he shouts to no one in particular.

There are no lights on in Pat's front room so he decides to check round the back. He makes sure the coast is clear, then ducks down the alley. Again he hesitates by the back gate, then he finally screws up the courage to go in the yard and knock.

To his surprise, it's Joe's girlfriend Mavis who opens the door. She gets on well with Pat and often pops round for a chat while Joe's away on a trip.

'Hi, Charlie!' she says. 'What do you want?'

'Er … I … I just wondered if Mrs Harrison wants me to bring her some fish.'

Mavis is mystified. *He only lives just opposite. Why's he coming round the back?*

'Who is it?' calls Pat from the kitchen.

'Charlie. He want to know if you'd like some fish.'

Pat comes to the door. 'Thanks, Charlie.' She gives him a wink. 'That's kind. I'll be in tomorrow night. Could you bring it round then?'

Charlie grins. *Maybe it wasn't a one-off after all.* 'Fine, P–Mrs Harrison,' he says, loud enough for Mavis to hear. 'See you tomorrow, then.'

'Bye,' says Pat, blowing him a sneaky kiss.

Next day Charlie leaves for work, dreamily anticipating the evening to come. Soon Mike comes wobbling past, waving at him to hurry up. 'Come on, son. Get a move on. We'll be late.'

Charlie laughs at his dad pedalling off up the road, dodging horse-drawn carts and fellow cyclists alike. He hates the fish factory on these cold winter mornings – the filleters, noses dripping with dewdrops, and the girls in their turbans, all wet sleeves and baggy overalls, standing in freezing water to box up the fish. *It's no sort of life*, he thinks, though no one ever seems to complain. *I've got to find a way out if I can.*

Going home that evening Charlie spots his father pushing his bike.

'Wait, son, wait,' says Mike. 'I've got a bloody flat tyre.'

They walk home in silence. *Charlie seems a bit quiet*, thinks Mike. *Hope there's nothing worrying him.*

Back at the terrace they bump into Pat. 'Hi, Pat,' calls Mike, giving her a smile. 'Hard day's work?'

Charlie can't bring himself to look at her.

'You bet,' she replies, ignoring Charlie too. 'A girl's got to earn a living somehow.' She turns the key in the lock and goes inside.

'What a bloody waste,' says Mike. 'A woman like her with no man. She always looks so damned lonely.'

'How well did you know Joe's dad?' asks Charlie.

'Pretty well. Mam and I used to go out for the odd drink with them when you were a kid. His ship went down with all hands. It was a real tragedy. I'm sure one day she'll find someone. He'll be a lucky man. Who wouldn't want a woman like her?'

If only he knew, thinks Charlie. He eats his tea, then goes to get washed and changed.

'Where are you off?' asks Eileen. 'Somewhere special?'

'No, just round to see my mates.'

Avoiding Pat's front door, he sidles once more to the end of the terrace, slips down the passage, hurries into the yard and closes the gate behind him. Pat answers his knock immediately and he stands transfixed, bewitched again by her beauty.

She grabs his hand. 'Come in, my darling Charlie. I can't stop thinking about you.'

Passion wells up inside him. He kisses her neck, her lips.

'This way, my darling,' she purrs.

She leads him upstairs and pushes him onto the bed.

Eyes trained upon him, she slowly removes her clothes. By the time she's down to her stockings and suspenders, he's completely mesmerised. Then she undresses him, quickly learning that he's fully aroused already. She lies down next to him and within seconds his hands are all over her. She guides him again to her most sensitive areas, encouraging him all the time. Then she starts kissing him, using her tongue on his chest before slowly moving down to his stomach. His eyes are closed, his face suffused with pleasure.

Charlie arches his back so she can take all of him. *Is there anything she doesn't know about lovemaking?* he wonders.

She moves to kiss him on the mouth, then pulls him on top of her. 'I want you, Charlie. Do it to me. Do it to me now.'

She guides his manhood inside her, wriggling to accommodate him. They're both panting and perspiring. 'Slowly, Charlie,' she whispers. 'Slowly, darling.'

They do their best to prolong the moment but eventually neither can hold back any longer. They start moving faster and faster, Pat arching her body and digging her nails into Charlie's back until an inner burst of warmth erupts into a raging fire that makes them both cry out. They lie there exhausted, touching and caressing each other, finding different ways of pleasuring each other until their strength deserts them and they fall asleep.

Well after two o'clock, Pat shakes him awake. 'It's getting late, Charlie.'

'I've got to go,' he says, kissing her and fondling her breast.

'You're insatiable, Charlie Robinson,' says Pat playfully. 'Better be off before you tempt me again.'

Charlie knows he must be back before his family is up and about, but still he struggles to drag himself away. Lurking in the gloom of the passage, he spots two figures across the street. Mrs Brady – clad only in underskirt and bra – is kissing a man who is definitely not her lorry-driver husband. *Good God*, thinks Charlie. Six kids and still game for a bit on the side. *I bet her husband's off on an overnight run somewhere*. He smiles to himself and waits for the man to leave. Mrs Brady looks right and left, then turns and disappears inside.

Charlie rushes across the terrace and enters the house as quietly as he can. Creeping upstairs, a sudden creak stops him dead in his tracks. 'Bloody hell,' says Mike, opening the bedroom door. 'What kind of time do you call this?'

Shit, I'm for it now. 'Three o'clock, Dad. Sorry to wake you.' No way is Charlie going to admit where he's been. Fortunately Mike asks no more questions.

'Three o'bloody clock. Get yourself to bed, lad. It's work in the morning. You'll be knackered.'

Bound to get a grilling tomorrow, thinks Charlie. *Don't care though. I'd do it again in a flash.* 'Sure, Dad. Goodnight.'

'Bloody good morning more like,' grumbles Mike, closing the door behind him.

At breakfast Mike says nothing, while Mary and Eileen seem to have slept right through. Charlie is tired and Mike watches him even more closely than usual at work. Still, it's tea-break before they get a chance to talk.

'You OK, Charlie?' asks Mike, putting an arm around his son's shoulder.

'Course I am, Dad.'

'Look, son. Don't forget I was young once. I did everything you're doing now. But you have to get some sleep, otherwise you'll be knackered at work. You could end up getting the bloody sack. Just be careful, OK?'

'I will, Dad,' says Charlie sheepishly.

After several more encounters, things start to quieten down between Charlie and Pat. She's beginning to realise there's no future in their relationship. The sex is great but she needs a long-term partner, someone to care for her and rebuild her confidence, and she'd hate Joe to find out what's going on.

Charlie makes several attempts to see her while Joe's away at sea, but she makes an excuse every time. He tries again one evening, desperately hoping Pat will let him in.

'Hello, Charlie,' she says, glancing anxiously over her shoulder. 'I wasn't expecting you.'

He tries to step inside but she moves to block his way.

'No Charlie, not tonight.'

'Why? What's wrong? I haven't seen you for weeks. What have I done to upset you?'

'I'll explain later, Charlie.' She looks round again. 'Just go now, please.'

A man's face appears at the kitchen door. 'Everything OK, love?'

Pat blushes. 'Fine, I'll be with you in a minute.' She shoos Charlie away. 'Sorry, I have to go.'

She closes the door, leaving Charlie on the doorstep. He turns and walks home, feeling like a naughty child. *Those nights I spent with her were the best of my life*, he thinks tearfully. *I can't live without her. She can't end it now. She just can't.*

He pulls himself together and walks into the house. Eileen is sitting reading, the radio playing quietly in the background.

'You're very quiet, our Charl? What's wrong? You've not been yourself for a while.'

'Nothing, our lass. I'm OK.'

'Come on, you can tell me. Is it girl trouble? Who's the mystery woman?'

'There is no mystery woman.'

'I think there is. There's plenty of fish in the sea, Charl. Just you remember that.'

'I will, Eileen. Thanks.'

Charlie often sees Pat and her new man coming and going. *How could she change her mind so quickly*? It really hurts to see them arm in arm together.

One day Pat spots him leaving the house and runs to catch up with him. 'Charlie!' she calls. 'Can I walk with you.'

'I suppose so,' he says grudgingly.

'Look, Charlie. I'm sorry if I hurt you but we couldn't carry on as we were. You're so young. I'm sure you'll meet someone your own age. I don't want to fall out with you – for Joe's sake, if nothing else. You're his best friend.'

'Don't worry,' says Charlie miserably. 'I'm fine. Who's the man?'

'His name's Vince. I met him in the shop. He reminds me a lot of my husband. I'll never forget you, though. You're a wonderful lover. You'll make a marvellous catch for some lucky girl.'

She holds out her hand. 'No hard feelings.'

'If you say so.'

She leans towards him and kisses him on the cheek. 'See you around. Joe'll be home next week by the way.'

Charlie is still besotted. *What a woman*, he thinks as he watches her walk away.

'I think I've found someone special,' says Pat, when Joe is next home. 'I've been seeing a lot of him. I'll try and introduce you while you're here.'

'That's great,' says Joe. *She's been on her own too long*, he thinks. *I just hope he's a good 'un.*

Joe isn't happy at work, though. The last trip was poor. Prices are down on the fish market, and when he goes down the dock to settle the crew are getting next to nothing. 'Sorry,' says one man after another. 'No backhander this time.'

Joe makes up his mind. 'I'm not going back on the *Lord Middleton*, Mam.'

'I don't blame you,' says Pat. 'Three weeks away is ridiculous for that tiny wage.'

'I still want to go to sea, though. I'll try to sign as deck learner, hopefully on a better trawler.'

'You know I'd rather you didn't, love. Still, you've got to do what you want. Are you going out with Mavis tonight? I've not seen her for a while.'

'Strange she hasn't been in touch. She must know I got home last night. I think I'll call on Charlie and then go round to see her.'

'Joe, mate,' says Charlie. 'How are you doing?'

'Okay, Charlie. Shit trip, though. Hardly caught a thing. I've decided to chuck in the *Lord Middleton*.'

'Is that you done with fishing?'

'No, I'm going to find a better ship and try sailing as a

deck learner. I'm just off round to see Mavis. I haven't heard from her at all since I got back.'

Hell, thinks Charlie. *She's been seen with another lad. Best say nothing.* 'Fancy going out this weekend?' he asks Joe.

'Why not? Unless Mavis has plans. See you later, Charlie.'

Half an hour later Joe is back, spitting blood. 'What's wrong?' asks Charlie apprehensively. *Hope Mavis hasn't mentioned me and Pat.*

'Would you believe it?' says Joe. 'The little cow has dumped me.'

Phew, thinks Charlie. *What a relief.* 'What did she have to say?'

'Just that she was seeing someone else. Never said sorry or 'owt. She can kiss my arse.'

'Not much chance of that now,' says Charlie, trying to cheer him up.

They both burst out laughing.

'I was getting sick of her anyway,' says Joe. 'You and Bob both owe me three bob, by the way.'

'Dirty sod! Did you give her one, then?'

'More than one, actually.'

'You lucky SOB. You kept that quiet. Wait till we tell him. More than one, bloody hell.'

On Saturday night all four lads decide to hit the pubs and clubs.

'If Pam's not happy about it, tough,' says Bob. He's decided it's time to cool things.

'How about going to see the good-time girls in the Paragon?' asks George.

'No,' says Charlie. 'Let's go to the Punch. Then we'll be right for City Hall later.'

As usual the pubs are full and the girls are out in force. The Punch is packed, but George forces his way through the crowd and snags some seats. 'Come on lads,' he calls, waving them over.

The girls at the next table are all a little tipsy. 'Hey, big boy!' says one, tapping George on the backside. 'Mind your arse.

You'll have our drinks over.'

'Steady, lass!' laughs George. 'Hands off. What would you say if I touched your arse.'

'You never know, Lanky. I might like it.'

The girls start laughing and flirting with them. However, one has a bad attack of hiccups.

'Are you a-a-all going to City Hall later?' she asks.

'Yes, darling,' says Bob. 'Do you want to join us?'

'Yes, h-h-h-hope you can all dance.'

'Darling, the place comes alive when we hit the dance floor,' says George, waggling his bottom.

'So you're a h-h-hot lot,' she stutters.

'Hotter than hot, my love,' says George, with a wink to the lads. 'In fact, we're boiling.'

'Let's stick with them,' says Charlie. 'They're a good laugh. Which do fancy, Joe?'

'Little Miss Hiccup,' says Joe. 'She couldn't say no.'

'I don't give a toss,' says George. 'Any will do for me.'

When they get to City Hall, the girls start dancing in a group and the lads rush to join them. Joe grabs Little Miss Hiccup and the other three all find themselves a partner.

'Come on, love,' says George, pulling a girl towards him. 'Come to daddy.'

He preens himself as usual, then licks his finger and runs it across his eyebrows. She slaps him playfully on the cheek, then he starts throwing her round the dance floor. City Hall is so noisy they can hardly hear themselves speak. The sweat is dripping off them and Charlie gestures for them to take the girls for a drink in the café.

'Bloody hell, it's hot in there,' says Joe, mopping his forehead. 'All right, sweetheart?'

'Yes, I-I-I-I'm okay.'

'Hellfire, have you still got the bloody hiccups?'

'Yes, c-c-c-can't stop.'

'Try holding your breath,' shouts George helpfully. 'They say that cures it.'

'How l-l-l-long for?'

'Try ten minutes for a start, love.'

'Very f-f-funny.'

'Just going to the toilet,' says Joe. 'Won't be long.'

Charlie, George and Bob all decide to follow him. No alcohol is allowed in City Hall, but a couple of older lads are passing a half-bottle of whisky from hand to hand, necking it straight down. Another lad staggers in and throws up in the corner. A third is peeing anywhere but the toilet.

'Let's get out of here,' says Charlie, heading for the door.

'Shall we go back to the girls or do you want a look around?' asks George.

'Bugger it,' says Joe. 'Back to the girls, I suppose. It's getting late.'

'How are you going to kiss yours?' asks Charlie.

'She'll be fine, Charl. I still might get lucky. I'll just have to put up with the hiccups.'

Back on the dance floor, George asks his partner if he can take her home. 'Yes,' she replies. 'It's quite a long way though.'

'Don't worry, darling. I'll get a taxi. Where do you live?'

'Manchester.'

'Frigging Manchester? You're joking, aren't you?'

'Of course I am,' she replies, taking George by the arm. 'I live on Beverley Road.'

'Thank God for that.'

At the end of the night all four lads get to take their partner home.

Bob's girl lives in a block of flats. 'Want to come in?' she asks outside her door.

'Love to,' says Bob. *Hell, she seems to be up for it.*

'Come on then,' she says, grabbing his hand and pulling him inside.

There's a light on in the kitchen, but she takes him straight into a sparsely furnished bedroom – just a bed and small chest of drawers.

'Come and give us a kiss,' she says, dragging him closer.

She starts undressing and Bob removes his clothes as well. *Could be in here*, he thinks happily. She pushes him on to the bed, then jumps in beside him and kisses him. Suddenly she stops and sits up. 'Would you mind three in a bed?'

'I wouldn't say no,' says Bob. *Bloody hell, I really have scored here. Hope she's nice, too.*

'Come here, Jack,' she calls.

Bob doesn't like the sound of that. 'Hang on a minute,' he says, ready to make a run for it. Then a Jack Russell terrier bounds in and jumps on the bed. 'Thank God for that,' he laughs. 'I thought you were talking to a man.'

'Just pulling your leg. I knew you were expecting another girl. It'll take you all your time to satisfy me, mate. Let's see what you're made of.'

She's on him in a flash, completely uninhibited, but Bob gives as good as he gets. Meanwhile the terrier sits and looks on quietly from the end of the bed.

Joe signs on as deck learner on the *Lord Stanhope* – a much better trawler than the *Lord Middleton*. No more backhanders, either: now he gets a cut from the sale of the catch. The other lads are working hard all week and enjoying themselves on a weekend. Nobody has a regular girlfriend. They're just relishing their freedom in the pubs and clubs of Hessle Road.

George has just turned eighteen, a year or so older than his friends, and one Saturday afternoon he makes an announcement. 'Bloody National Service,' he says, as they sup a quiet pint. 'I've just got my call-up.'

'First thing they'll do is cut your bloody hair,' says Bob.

Charlie laughs but George doesn't find it funny. 'No chance,' he says, running his hand through his Brylcreemed locks. 'I think I'll do a bunk. Go somewhere they can't find me.'

'Don't talk rubbish,' says Charlie. 'It can't be as bad as all that.'

'What about Keith Mason down the next street?' says Bob. 'He was a nice lad. He was sent to Korea and got killed out there. He was only nineteen.'

'No one's sending me to bloody Korea,' says George, blanching. 'I won't let them cut my hair, either.'

'Don't worry, the war's over now,' says Charlie. 'Keith was just unlucky, that's all. A year younger and he'd have missed it completely.'

'If I had to … you know … to die,' says George, 'I'd like to be killed in action like Keith. Did he get a medal?'

'No point in a ruddy medal if you're dead,' says Bob roughly.

'Look at Joe, though,' says George. 'Lucky sod. No call-up for him. Being on trawlers, he just does a couple of weeks a year in the Royal Naval Reserve.'

'I'd much rather join the army than go on a bloody trawler,' says Bob. 'By the way, I've got some good news.'

'Seeing Jack again?' jokes Charlie, reminding him of his encounter with the terrier.

'No, I'm climbing the ladder at work.'

'Get away,' says Charlie.

'No really, they've taken me off soles and 'eels and moved me upstairs ... to uppers!'

They all laugh.

'Daft shit,' says Charlie. 'We thought you'd been promoted.'

They make their plans for the evening and then head for home. As Charlie turns into Eton Street, he sees June walking towards him. They haven't spoken for ages but now he can't avoid her.

'Hi, June,' he stammers. 'How are you?'

'Fine thanks, Charlie. What about you?'

'Good, good. Just been out for a drink with the lads.' *What can I say next*? 'You're looking nice.'

'Thanks, Charlie. That's sweet of you.' *He's filled out a lot*, she thinks. *And he's better looking than ever*.

'Perhaps I shouldn't ask but would you like to go out one night?'

June smiles – she'd just about given up hope. 'I'd love it. Come round to our house one evening during the week. We've got a television set now.'

Like the sound of that, thinks Charlie. *Might get lucky there*. 'Great, will it be OK with your mam and dad?'

'I'm sure it will.'

'It's a date then. Just let me know when.'

'I will. See you, Charlie.'

Charlie opens the door and hears Mike shouting. *That's strange*, he thinks. *Dad hardly ever raises his voice.* 'What's up?' he asks. 'What's going on?'

'Nothing to do with you,' snaps Mary.

Eileen's eyes are red with crying. 'Are you OK, our lass?' he asks protectively, making her sob even harder.

'We may as well tell the lad,' says Mike. 'He'll find out soon enough. She's expecting.' He thumps down in his chair and picks up his newspaper.

'You can't be, Mam. Aren't you too old to get pregnant?'

'Not me, you daft beggar. Our Eileen. I can't believe it. What are we going to do? You know how they gossip round here.'

Charlie takes Eileen's hand. 'Don't worry, sis.' *Who's the father, I wonder. Don't want to upset her even more, though.*

'This is all Howard's fault,' snorts Mary.

'What, old Loppy Lugs?' says Charlie. *The little shit doesn't look strong enough. Our Eileen would make two of him.*

'I'd like to strangle the little bugger,' says Mike. 'Not that it will help much.' *Why the hell aren't they more careful?* he thinks. *Why do they never consider the consequences?* 'Did he say anything about marrying you?'

'Not really, Dad, no,' she replies.

'What do you mean not really?' shouts Mike.

'He never mentioned it,' sobs Eileen.

'Well, get the little sod down here and let's get it sorted out.'

'I think he's scared of you, Dad.'

'Scared, don't be daft,' says Mike. 'Get him down here tomorrow afternoon.'

'I will, Dad. I will,' says Eileen. *At least I hope I will.*

Charlie goes to get washed and changed. *Fancy our Eileen not taking precautions*, he thinks. *I know I didn't, but I'm sure Pat always looked after that side of things.*

Charlie has a good night out with Bob and George. After visiting so many pubs and clubs without problems, they never bother now about being under age. Charlie looks eighteen and Bob can just about get away with it.

The following day Charlie can't wait to see what happens. Mike sits pretending to read his Sunday paper, while Eileen keeps glancing anxiously at the clock. She runs to answer the knock at the door. Then she and Howard walk into the room holding hands, both of them looking scared stiff.

'Hello, Mr Robinson,' mumbles Howard, staring sheepishly at the floor. 'Mrs Robinson, Charlie.'

'Just look what the wind's blown in,' says Mike. 'Come on, lad. What have you got to say for yourself?'

'Nothing,' squeaks Howard, tugging at one of his big lugs. 'I can only apologise.'

'Apologise! Bloody hell, lad. Are you going to marry my daughter or not? There's a baby on the way, you know.'

'Yes, I know.'

The poor lad's scared out of his wits, thinks Mary. *He's terrified of saying the wrong thing.*

'Have you asked her?' barks Mike.

Charlie smiles to himself. His dad is behaving completely out of character.

'No,' says Howard, in confusion. 'I mean yes, sure.'

'It'll be a register office wedding, I suppose. And of course you'll be keeping the baby?'

'Of course, Mr Robinson,' mutters Howard.

'What did you say, lad?' Mike shakes his head. 'Speak up, for God's sake.'

'Yes, we'll get married at the register office. And of course we want to keep the baby.'

Poor mite, thinks Charlie. *Hope it doesn't look like its father.*

'Well, you'll need to get a move on,' says Mike. 'Do it in the next couple of months before our Eileen gets too big.'

Too big! thinks Charlie mischievously. *Bloody hell, she's enormous already. How much bigger can she possibly get*!

'Well, I think we've got that sorted,' says Mike, as the two lovebirds sit holding hands. 'What do you think, Mother?'

'Perfect,' says Mary.

74

Whenever the lads want a proper soak they go to the local swimming baths, which has eight baths for men and eight for women on opposite sides of the building. The whole place is spotlessly clean, with highly polished brass fittings in each cubicle. The taps, though, are outside. The men's attendant does the filling, and the bathers shout for more water as they need it: 'Hot in Number Two', 'Cold in Number Five'. Fair enough in principle, but in practice plenty of scope for practical jokes. All the lads like to request cold water for one of their pals. 'Bloody hell,' shouts the victim. 'I didn't ask for any cold.'

Now though Charlie is enjoying his usual strip wash in the kitchen before he goes round to see June. Suddenly the door opens. 'Mam,' he shouts, grabbing a towel to cover himself.

'Sorry, Charlie,' she laughs. 'Nothing I haven't seen before. Don't forget I used to powder your bottom.'

Bloody hell, he thinks. *No sodding privacy in this house.*

He sets off rather apprehensively. He's never met June's parents before and he's wondering what they'll be like. He knocks at the door and June answers it. 'Hi, Charlie!' She smiles at him. 'Come on in.'

The house is in a better part of Hessle Road and much nicer than his. Charlie follows her down the hall and into a comfortable lounge. 'Mam, Dad,' she says. 'I'd like you to meet Charlie.'

'Nice to meet you,' says June's mum.

'Nice to meet you, too,' says Charlie politely.

June's mum reaches for her coat. 'We're just going out for an hour or two. Enjoy yourselves, you two.'

June's blue eyes are sparkling – she can't wait to be alone with Charlie. She switches on the black and white TV and Charlie sits transfixed. He doesn't have a telly in his house and he can't drag his eyes away from the screen.

'Never mind the telly,' she pouts. 'What about me?'

'Sorry,' Charlie gives her a desultory kiss and a cuddle, eyes still glued to the TV.

'Are you going to pay me any attention at all, Charlie Robinson?'

'Of course.' He pulls her closer and kisses her again, then his hands start to wander.

She makes no move to stop him. 'Turn the light off, Charlie,' she orders him.

Having finally torn himself away from the telly, Charlie does what he's told, returning to the settee to find she's unbuttoned her blouse and removed her bra. He lies down beside her and tentatively lifts her flared skirt. Then to his surprise she lowers her hand and feels her way into his trousers. *God, she's changed*, he thinks.

She moans when she touches him. 'Oh, Charlie!' she whispers. 'Do you really love me?'

He has no intention of answering that one. *I like June a lot*, he thinks, *but that's all*. Still, she lets him carry on where he left off. 'What if your mam and dad come back early?'

'They won't,' says June, still moaning gently. 'I've missed you so much.'

Just as he's on the point of entering her, she stops him. *Not again*, he thinks. But, no.

'Let me do it,' says June. She takes hold of him and guides him inside her. 'You do love me, don't you?

Again Charlie says nothing: he doesn't want to commit himself.

He starts making love to her, gently at first, then deeper and deeper with every thrust. He can feel her muscles tighten around him with each stroke. Pat has taught him to be slow and precise and June can feel his every movement. Eyes closed, body trembling, she grabs hold of his shirt and digs her nails into his back, calling his name and screaming with pleasure. His whole body stiffens just before he reaches a climax – then he withdraws. He doesn't want to get her pregnant.

They lie together quietly for quite a time. Then June kisses him. 'Won't be long,' she says, getting up and leaving the room.

Better tidy myself up and check the settee, thinks Charlie. *Don't want her parents to suspect anything*. He sits down and wipes his brow. *My, that was a surprise.*

Arms around each other, they spend the rest of the

evening watching television – an opera singer with a piano accompaniment. Eventually Charlie stands up. 'I think I'd better be off now.'

'When will I see you again?'

'Not sure,' he replies. 'I promised to go out with the lads this weekend. Perhaps next week sometime.'

Strange how quickly things change, he thinks. *I thought I really fancied June but now I don't feel anything for her – not like I did with Pat.*

June follows him to the door. *I should never have let him go that far*, she thinks. *I'm sure he's going to forget me again.*

'I'll be in touch.'

'OK, Charlie.' She kisses him once more, then slowly closes the door as she watches him walk away.

CHAPTER 6
CARRY ON, PRIVATE

George has got his call-up papers, ordering him to report to Catterick Camp the following week. 'Don't worry,' jokes Charlie. 'You'll be fine. Just think of it as a new set of free clothes. Perhaps not your style or cut. Still free, though.'

'Bloody baggy shit-brown uniform,' grumbles George. 'No girl will go for me in that.'

'Do you get a gun as well?' asks Bob.

'Better not or I'll shoot myself,' says George, 'especially if they make me get my hair cut.'

'Let's change the subject,' says Charlie. 'We've been planning a farewell party for you. We're going to take you round the town.'

The pubs are quiet midweek, not too many girls around, and they start off at the Paragon. The usual ladies of the night are there – ladies of the day as well when it comes down to business.

'How about joining that lot for a laugh?' says George.

'I think we need a drink first,' says Charlie. 'They might look a bit better with some alcohol inside us.'

They find a table and Bob goes to the bar. A couple of drinks later and the pub is filling up. The new arrivals all seem to be fishermen, smart as ever in their distinctive stiff-collared white shirts, narrow ties, wide-bottomed trousers and jackets with pleated backs.

A couple of deck learners come across to sit at their table. They've already had a skinful. 'I'm off to do my National Service next week,' says George.

'Enjoy yourself while you can,' says one. 'My mate frigging hated it.'

'How bad was it?' asks George anxiously.

'Dreadful. Up at five, ten-mile run, then a compulsory cold shower – in bloody mid-winter too. Two slices of toast for breakfast and a cross-country exercise till lunchtime. Quick break, then off again on an obstacle course all afternoon.'

'Did he get through it?' asks George.

'No,' says the lad, straight-faced. 'It killed him.'

George turns pale.

'Just kidding, mate.' He slaps George on the back. 'You really fell for that one. Even your pals were taken in.'

'Lousy shit,' says George, laughing along with everyone else.

The drinks are coming fast and furious, then a couple of the Paragon 'girls' saunter over.

'Fancy taking me home?' the skinnier of the two asks George, revealing uneven, nicotine-stained teeth. With her heavy eye-shadow and black mascara, she could be wearing sunglasses. She winks at Charlie, who immediately ducks for cover behind Bob.

'How much, love?' asks George.

'Ten bob for a quickie. Quid for a full night.'

'Ten bob's worth will be fine,' says Bob. 'He never lasts long.'

'Has he dipped his dick before? I'll give him a discount if he hasn't?'

'What are you talking about?' says George, running his fingers through his hair. 'I've quite a reputation for my sexual exploits, I'll have you know. You should be bloody well paying me – and a damn sight more than a quid.'

'Tight-arse.' She gives Charlie a tap, flashing her less-than-pearly white teeth. 'Fetch us another drink, you little bugger.'

At the end of the evening the women go to call a taxi, clinging tipsily to the arms of the two deck learners.

'Those lads must be really hard up,' says Charlie. 'Come on, George. Time to get you home.'

George can hardly stand. 'I do feel a little inebriated,' he says, grabbing hold of Charlie.

'A little?' says Charlie. 'You must be kidding. Hold on to me and Bob, you bastard.'

None of them are feeling too clever, especially once they hit the fresh air. Charlie and Bob lay George out on the back seat of the trolleybus and they need the conductor's help to get him off again. Eventually they plonk him down on his doorstep, then knock on the door and scarper. They'd rather not be around when his parents find him.

Head pounding, Charlie topples into bed. *Never again*, he thinks. Then he starts to feel sick and hurtles downstairs in his underpants to use the backyard toilet. It's freezing out there, the wind whistling through the gaps around the door. Shivering, he finally drags himself back to bed, pulls the covers tight and falls sound asleep.

All too soon Mike's voice bursts into his dreams. 'You getting up, Charlie?'

Charlie ignores him and drifts off again. Then the voice comes louder still. 'Time to move.'

Charlie can hardly lift his head from the pillow, never mind struggle out of bed. *Oh shit, my head. Never, ever again.*

Outside it's cold and damp, and he walks along collar up, hands in pockets, shoulders hunched, trying to keep warm. All he can think about is how to escape from all this. Passing one of the terraces, a woman from the fish house comes to join him – a dark-eyed beauty called Rose.

'Hi, Charlie, she laughs. 'Not looking too good there. What've you been up to?'

'Rough night, Rose.' Charlie loves listening to her Irish brogue, but they've never exchanged more than a few words before.

'Somehow you don't look like the same happy young chappy that first started working with us.'

Charlie looks at her. 'Is it that obvious?'

Rose nods her head.

'To be honest, Rose, I'm thinking of leaving. I want to do something where I can better myself, but the only prospect seems to be trawlers.'

'My husband went to sea. He was called Charlie too.'

'I didn't even know you were married.'

'Not any more. I lost him twelve years ago. I came to

England a couple of years later and I've been on my own ever since.'

'I'm so sorry, Rose. It must have been terribly hard.'

'It was. I was only fifteen when I met Charlie and I've never looked at another lad since. We got married at eighteen – it was the best time of my life. We lived in southern Ireland – just a handful of scattered cottages outside a place called Castletown. Charlie had a share in a small fishing boat with two of his friends. They'd go out for a couple of days at a time. I used to stand on the jetty and watch 'em sail every time. And I'd be there waiting for him to return. I remember everything as though it was yesterday. They'd been away for three days, and we were all getting anxious because nothing had been heard from them. The days passed and boats went out searching – but no joy. The weather was dreadful and we all knew something terrible must have happened. The search was abandoned – not a scrap of wreckage ever found. I just had to accept that my lovely Charlie would never return to me.'

Charlie can see the anguish etched on her face. 'How did you cope?'

'I don't know. And to make it worse, soon afterwards I lost the baby I was expecting. That was when I decided to come to England. I'd never tell you what to do, Charlie. Trawling's a dangerous business, but the decision has to be yours. You're a bright lad. You'll do what you think best.'

'Thanks, Rose. I'm glad I've had the chance to talk to you. Please don't mention it to Dad, though. I'd rather tell him in when I've made a decision.'

George, too, spends most of the day recovering from the exertions of the previous night.

'If you can't do the time, don't do the crime,' jokes his dad Tom.

Charlie and Bob go to wave him off and wish him all the best. 'Don't worry about taking your Brylcreem,' says Bob. 'You won't be needing it where you're going.'

'Ha ha,' says George. 'I really don't want to go, you know. Nothing for it, though. They'd put me in gaol if I didn't turn up.'

The next time Joe's home between trips, he hears all about George's farewell do.

'Wish I'd been with you,' he tells Bob and Charlie. 'I'd like to have seen George before he left.'

They're meeting to discuss a possible holiday – a week at Bob's uncle's caravan in Withernsea. 'How much would he charge?' asks Charlie.

'About ten quid a week,' says Bob.

'Ten quid?' Charlie can hardly credit it. 'Is it like some posh hotel?'

'More of a train carriage,' laughs Bob, who's been there before. 'Well, a converted train carriage.'

'With a bloody steam engine?' asks Joe.

'Don't be daft,' says Bob. 'It's great – three bedrooms, a kitchen, all mod cons.'

'I'll bet,' says Charlie. 'Could you manage a trip off, Joe? We could have a great time, the three of us.'

'I think my trawler's due a survey in a couple of trips. I should be home for a week or more. Get it organised and we'll hope for the best.'

'Fine,' says Bob. 'That's settled, then. Do you think George might have any leave due?'

'Who knows?' says Charlie.

Joe is enjoying life as a deck learner but he's worried about his mum. He's been out for a drink with Pat and Vince, but he really didn't like the man. He seems a moody so-and-so, a fella with a bit of a chip on his shoulder.

'What do you reckon to your mam's new boyfriend?' Charlie asks him as they walk home together.

'Don't know, Charlie. She's changed a lot recently. She seemed much happier even before they met. Vince is OK, I suppose. He just seems a bit touchy to me. I think he'll be moving in with her soon. She's dropped enough hints about it. Just to see how I take it, I reckon. I may be wrong. If she's happy, I'm happy.'

'If they care for each other, I suppose they should be together,' says Charlie reluctantly. He can't bear the thought of the woman he adores being happy with another man.

'We'll see how it goes,' says Joe. 'See you, Charlie.'

'Night, Joe.'

Pam and Bob are no longer on speaking terms. Not that he's worried – he's happy to play the field.

'Why not try an older woman?' advises Charlie.

After some careful research Bob reckons Lucy might be the one. Seeing her round the factory one day, he decides to try his luck. 'How about a date?' he asks, with a wink.

'You're too young, love,' she says coolly. 'They'd do me for baby-snatching.'

'Come on, Luce,' he pleads. 'I'll take you out for a drink this weekend.'

'Where to?' she laughs. 'A Peter's Café for a lemonade?'

With their workmates are listening in and egging him on, Bob is getting desperate. 'It'll be a night to remember, I promise.'

'Tell you what, Bob. Let me think about it.'

She walks away, bottom swaying. 'Hrrrr,' he growls, letting her know he likes the view. *Might be in there after all.*

As everyone is leaving at five o'clock, Bob spots Lucy going out the door. 'Luce, Luce,' he shouts, running after her.

She turns. 'Oh no, not you again.'

Grinning, he falls into step alongside her. 'How about Saturday night then?'

'Persistent little bugger, aren't you? OK, Saturday night outside Rayners. Don't be late and remember, I'm not buying.'

'You won't regret it, Luce,' he says, tapping her on the bottom.

She smiles and carries on walking. 'Watch out, love,' she calls over her shoulder. 'You might find me a bit too much of a handful.'

On Saturday night Bob arrives early at the pub. Then he sees Lucy coming down the road – big boobs, high heels, long dark hair. *Mmmmm, nice*, he thinks. 'Hi, Lucy. You're looking good.'

'Not so dusty yourself, Bob Watson. We going in, then?'

'Yeah, if it's OK with you. Back room all right?'

'Fine,' she says, putting her arm through his. Her high heels make him taller than he is, compelling him to smile up at her. They find a seat, then the barmaid totters over, looking well past retirement age.

'What can I get you?' she asks wearily.

'Pint of mild for me,' says Bob. 'How about you, Luce?' *Hope it's something cheap.*

'Large gin and tonic, thanks.' Bob forces a smile. 'And easy on the tonic.'

The barmaid wanders from the room. It's very quiet, only a few people around.

'Lively, isn't it?' says Lucy sarkily. 'Is it always this busy?'

'Just wait,' says Bob. 'It's early yet. It'll soon fill up.'

Their drinks are taking an age to arrive. 'Do you think she's gone to the pub up the road?' asks Lucy.

Eventually, the barmaid returns. 'A pint of mild and a large gin, light on the tonic. That'll be four shillings - please.'

The barmaid holds out her hand while Bob counts out the money. She looks at him, then back at the cash. *What now?* wonders Bob.

'Bloody hell,' says Lucy, grabbing her drink and downing most of it in one gulp. 'For God's sake, buy her one or she'll be here all night.'

Bob gives the barmaid an extra shilling, getting a filthy look for his pains before she turns and strolls nonchalantly away.

God, he thinks, eyeing Lucy's glass. *I hope she's going to make 'em last longer than that.*

Lucy takes out a packet of cigarettes, puts one to her lips and lights it. 'Want a fag?' she asks, blowing smoke in his face.

Bob turns away, coughing. 'No thanks,' he says. 'I don't smoke.'

Conversation soon dries up and reluctantly he orders two more drinks. Lucy just sits there, smoking and drinking, then two women walk in. 'Hi, Luce!' they shout, laughing. 'Who's this, then? Your lad?' They turn to Bob. 'All right if we sit with you, love?'

At least their singing and dancing liven things up a bit.

Meanwhile Bob is worrying whether he can afford another round, sneakily trying to count the coins in his pocket without it looking like he's playing with himself.

Two men come over to join the party, and Bob spends the rest of the evening listening to everyone talk.

'Last orders,' calls the barmaid from the doorway, then – much to his relief – disappears before anyone can respond. By now Lucy is three sheets to the wind, putting her arm around him and kissing him on the cheek. He just wishes she wouldn't keep blowing smoke in his face at the same time.

Eventually they all leave the pub together – Lucy clinging to him, singing and waving her fag around.

'Let's go back to your house,' suggests one of her friends. Bob hasn't a clue where she lives but he decides to tag along. *You never know, might get lucky.*

The house is sparsely furnished and not that clean. It also contains a boy of around twelve. 'Meet my son Roger,' says Lucy, kissing the lad on the head. 'Get yourself upstairs, love.'

Roger drags himself off to bed with a baleful stare, while Lucy finds some music on the radio. Soon everyone is pairing off and dancing. She fetches six bottles of beer from the kitchen and they all help themselves. 'When's your old man due back, Luce? asks one of the women. 'Seems like a long trip.'

God, thinks Bob, *she's married. And to a bloody fisherman, too. Someone might have seen us together. I think I'd better get out of here.*

Just then Lucy beckons him into the kitchen. He knows he shouldn't follow her but the lure of sex trumps all common sense. The light is off in there. She closes the door, gets him in a clinch and grabs his crotch. She squeezes hard, then again, harder still. He almost squeals with the pain but it has the desired effect. He lifts her dress and places her arms around his neck. Then she raises her legs and wraps them round his waist. His hands are inside her bra, trying to grab a feel of her breasts.

What the hell's this? Bloody cotton wool! She's virtually flat-chested.

What a passion-killer! Lucy is gagging for sex but much to his embarrassment Bob can't oblige. 'Frigging hell,' she shouts, feeling for him. 'You haven't come already, have you? Or couldn't you get it up to start with?'

She thrusts Bob away. But what with her bad breath, smoking and false breasts, he's already had enough. He starts heading for the door. 'Where in hell do you think you're going?' she shouts.

'Home,' he calls back. 'Bye!'

Cotton wool? Bob smiles to himself. *I couldn't even swear that was her own hair. Wait till I see that Charlie. Him and his frigging older women.*

A couple of days later Eileen arrives home in some distress. 'What's up, love?' asks Mary, putting an arm around her shoulder, and Eileen starts to cry.

Here we go again, thinks Charlie.

'It's Howard,' she sobs.

'What about him?' asks Mike.

'He doesn't want to marry me. He's left home. His mam says he's gone to his auntie in Scotland. He hasn't even left a note.'

'Little sod,' says Mike. 'I'll kill him if I get my hands on him.'

Although Eileen is a big girl, her pregnancy is starting to show. 'There's nothing we can do about it now,' says Mary practically. 'The neighbours are bound to find out soon. We'll just have to brave the gossip.'

'And who's going to look after the baby?' says Mike.

'I am,' says Eileen.

'You, young lady? And how do you plan to do that? Where's the money going to come from? It's hard enough now, without a baby to care for.

'Mike,' says Mary, trying to pacify him. 'This is our grandchild we're talking about.'

'I know, love. I know. But Eileen will have to keep working. You'll be the one looking after the baby. We'll just have to pull together, I suppose, as usual.'

'Thanks, Dad,' says Eileen, drying her eyes. 'I really am sorry.'

'Just take note, lad,' Mike whispers to Charlie. 'Don't let this happen to you. Get something on the end of it. You know what I mean?'

'I do, Dad.'

God, thinks Charlie. *I just never remember. Perhaps I ought to get some Durex in case I get another chance with someone.*

The next time Bob sees Charlie all the talk is of Lucy. 'She's been taking the piss ever since,' says Bob sadly, 'telling everyone I can't get it up. My reputation is shot. I'll never get a date again.'

'Don't worry,' laughs Charlie. 'They'll soon forget about it. Just be a bit choosier next time. Find someone with her own tits.'

'And you know the worst thing about it?

'What's that, mate?'

'I'm only bloody allergic to cotton wool.' They collapse in fits of laughter. 'What about you? Are you still seeing June?'

'Sort of,' says Charlie.

'Sort of?' says Bob. 'Still in love?'

'Never have been. She's a nice girl, but I've never wanted us to get too serious.'

'Why not? Is she too nice, if you know what I mean?'

'Not at all! I'd rather keep that to myself though. I just want to keep my options open.'

'Fine with me, mate.'

'Look, Bob. You're bound to find out eventually. Our Eileen's pregnant.'

'Get away, really? Who's the father? Not that little fella with the big ears?'

'Yeah. You wouldn't think he had it in him, would you? The little shit promised to marry her, but now he's cleared off to bloody Scotland or somewhere out of reach of my old man.'

'What's Eileen going to do? Is she keeping the baby?'

'Yeah, she is.'

'Shit,' laughs Bob. 'You'll be an uncle, Uncle Charlie.'

'Just say nothing for now.'

'Of course, mate. Not a word.'

'My old man warned me to get something on the end of it,' says Charlie.

'What did he mean?' laughs Bob. 'A nice girl who will? Definitely not an older woman, though. Hope no one has said anything to Lucy's husband. I might have to run off to Scotland, too.'

CHAPTER 7
BY THE SEASIDE

Nothing has been heard from George, but Charlie and Bob have booked a week off while the *Lord Stanhope* is in for survey, so at least there'll be three of them going to Withernsea.

The day after Joe gets home, they drag their battered suitcases down the street to catch the bus into town.

'Can we come too?' asks Charlie's neighbour Mrs Booth, gossiping outside her front door as usual.

'Sodding hell,' laughs Charlie. 'We're only going to Withernsea, not bloody Australia.'

Sweating, they push their way on to the crowded bus, stand wedged in by their cases, then force their way off again when they reach Paragon Station.

'Thank God for that,' says Bob. 'A fat woman's arse was crushing me all the way. I could hardly breathe.'

They find their train, choose a compartment and settle down. They're like small boys again, thrilled to be going on holiday on their own. They're sharing the compartment with an elderly couple who sit silently for most of the journey, then the woman turns to Charlie.

'Going on holiday are you, love?

He glances round. *Is she speaking to me*?

'Yes,' he replies politely.

'How long for?' She leans closer to catch his reply.

'Just a week.'

'In a caravan?'

'Not a caravan exactly, more of an old railway carriage.'

'A what?' she shouts, cupping a hand to her ear.

'A railway carriage,' sighs Charlie.

'You can't stay in a railway carriage, love.'

'Yes, we can. It's been converted into a caravan.'

She nods. 'Been there before?'

Charlie is already bored with her questions. 'Not really. Just for the day.'

'Just for the day? Why do you need a caravan?'

'No,' says Charlie wearily. 'I said I'd been before for the day. We're stopping a week this time.'

The old lady nods again.

'Fish and chips,' says her husband dreamily.

'Pardon?' says Charlie. *What is he on about?*

'Sullivan's,' says the old man. 'The best. Lovely fish.'

'Really?' says Charlie. *God, will these two never shut up?*

'Absolutely, the best.'

When the train gets to Withernsea, Charlie can't get away fast enough. He slams open the door and leaps on to the platform. 'You pair of shits,' he laughs. 'You could have helped me out there.'

'Better get going,' says Bob, still chuckling. 'It's quite a way to Nettleton's field.'

Carrying the cases soon has them in a lather again. Then when they reach the site, Bob can't find where they're staying. All they can see are row upon row of caravans, all different shapes and sizes, each with the usual sentry-box toilet.

'Bloody hell,' says Joe. 'Where is the sodding thing?'

'Hang on a minute,' says Bob. 'There's a lot more on this bloody field since I last came. That's it. I've got it. Down this way, we're looking for a railway carriage.'

Eventually they find their goal, a light green railway carriage. 'No wonder I couldn't find it,' smiles Bob. 'It was blue last time I saw the beggar. What do you reckon?'

Charlie bursts out laughing. 'How much are we paying your uncle?'

'£9 15s 11d.'

'Any chance of a frigging rebate?'

'Bloody hell. What did you expect? The sodding Ritz?'

They go inside and have a good poke about. 'Look at these!' says Joe, retrieving a pair of knickers from the bedroom floor and waving them round his head. 'Who was here last? She must have been a big woman.'

Bob grabs hold of them. 'At least they're clean ... I think.' Peering more closely, he pulls a face and throws them away again. 'Told you it had all mod cons.'

'What?' laughs Charlie. 'A teapot and a bloody kettle.'

'We've got a frying pan,' says Bob, trawling through the cupboards. 'Who knows how to cook?'

'Anybody can use a frigging frying pan,' says Joe. 'I'll do it. Bacon and eggs for the next week, is it?'

'Good old Joe,' says Charlie. 'I knew we could rely on you.'

They have a small coal-fired stove for cooking and boiling the kettle, so they use a couple of firelighters to get a fire going and scout out some sugar and tea. 'Oh hell!' says Bob. 'No milk. We'll just have to drink it black for now.'

Over a cuppa they discuss where to go that evening. 'The Royal Oak's good,' says Bob. 'That's my old man's favourite. He's never away from the place.'

They finish their drinks, then go outside to see what's happening. Kids are kicking a ball about while their parents sun themselves, drinking from bottles of beer. The lads join in for a while but they soon tire of the game – the kids are much better than they are.

'How about trying the amusement arcades?' suggests Bob.

'Great idea,' says Joe.

There are plenty of pretty girls around in town. 'Looking good, lads,' says Charlie. 'Wait till we come back tonight. Do you think we ought to buy some you-know-whats?'

'What, potatoes?' chuckles Bob.

'No, you silly shit,' says Joe. 'Rubbers.'

'What, gloves?' says Bob, laughing even harder.

'Are you stupid or what? Durex, of course. Mind you, I hear it's like washing your feet with your socks on.'

Now they're all laughing – none of them has ever used a condom before. They head for the chemist and stop outside the door.

'Who's going in, then?' asks Charlie.

'Not me,' says Joe. 'There's a girl behind the counter. I'm not asking her for a packet of johnnies.'

'Me neither,' says Bob.

'Bloody cowards,' says Charlie, putting a brave face on it. 'Looks like it'll have to be me.'

He walks in and glances casually at the shelves while his friends watch through the window.

'Can I help you, sir?' asks the girl inside.

'Yes, I-I-I'd l-like. H-have you any con, anything for constipation?'

'Yes, of course.' She smiles fetchingly. 'Andrews Liver Salts are very popular, sir. Effective, too.'

'Thanks,' says Charlie. 'I'll have a tin, please.'

He goes to rejoin his pals. 'Did you get 'em?' asks Bob, snatching the tin from his hand. 'What the hell is this? Andrews bloody Liver Salts?'

'I know,' says Charlie ruefully. 'I tried asking for condoms but I couldn't get the word out. I ended up asking for something for constipation instead.'

'Chicken yourself,' says Bob. 'Give me the cash.' He goes inside and walks boldly up to the assistant. 'Durex please, Miss.'

'Just the one, sir?' she asks, glancing through the window at Joe and Charlie.

'No, three please,' says Bob.

She grins cheekily. 'Three packets, sir, or three condoms?'

'Packets, please,' says Bob. *I should be so lucky. Hope she thinks they're all for me*. He hands her the cash and she passes them over. 'Thanks, miss.'

He turns for the door.

'Have a nice night, sir,' she giggles. 'And I hope your friend feels better soon.'

Outside Bob gives his pals a packet each. 'She thought they were all for me,' he fibs. 'I'm sure she thinks I'm a sex maniac.'

'Well you are, aren't you?' laughs Joe.

'Not when it comes to older women,' says Bob. 'By the way, Charlie, she hopes the Liver Salts are a help.'

They buy a few groceries, then go for a bag of chips to

munch on the way home. There are two girls ahead of them in the queue – a blonde and a brunette – and Charlie goes straight into action.

'Where are you two lovely ladies staying?' he says with a smile.

'Nettleton's field,' says the brunette.

'That's a coincidence, so are we. Going anywhere special tonight?'

'Haven't decided yet,' says the blonde.

'We're off to the Royal Oak. Care to join us?'

'We'll think about it.'

As they approach the caravan, they see a tall shaven-headed figure waiting outside.

'Bloody hell,' says Bob. 'It's George!'

'How did you get here?' asks Charlie, slapping him on the back.

'By bus,' says George. 'I asked Bob's mam where you were. I thought I'd got the wrong caravan.'

'Love the haircut,' says Bob. 'How's army life, then?'

'Don't ask,' says George. 'I've finished basic training and I'm home on leave. It's great to be free for a while.'

'Was it that bad?'

'Twelve weeks of pain! I'll get my posting when I get back. I need some loving, lads. I've forgotten what a woman looks like. Well, not really. No way you could forget those Paragon girls.'

They stoke up the stove to boil enough water for a wash. There's a problem, though. With only three bedrooms, there's no bed for George.

'Can I muck in with you, Charlie?' he asks.

'Sod off,' says Charlie. 'I haven't missed you all that much. Bob's bagged the biggest bed. Bunk up with him.'

George smiles ingratiatingly.

'OK, mate,' says Bob grudgingly. 'But no letting off wind. And only if I've no woman in with me.'

In the evening they join the crowds heading into town. The two girls they met earlier now seem to have three friends with them, giving the lads five to choose from.

'Sweet, sweet, sweet,' says Charlie. 'Take your pick, lads. One left over. One of us could have two.'

'That's me,' says George, running his hands over his newly shaven skull. 'You know I've been starved of female company. I only have to look at a woman to get hard.'

'Nothing new there,' says Charlie, giving him a push. 'You've always been like that.'

The lads walk over and introduce themselves. Each girl links arms with one of them, apparently choosing her partner for the evening. George, of course, ends up with a girl on each arm. He's over the moon. *One isn't much to look at*, he thinks heartlessly. *Beggars can't be choosers, though. And there's nothing wrong with her friend.*

Charlie has paired off with the brunette he met at the chip shop. 'What did you say your name was again?' he asks her.

'Beryl.' *He's a bit of all right*, she thinks.

'Nice to meet you again, Beryl. I'm Charlie.'

'Good to meet you too, Charlie.'

The Royal Oak is smoky and busy but they manage to snag a table. 'Who's for a drink, then?' asks George.

'How about a kitty,' says Beryl.

'Good idea,' says Charlie, and they all drop some coins a glass.

'So you're a soldier then, Baldy,' says Sandra, the better looking of George's little harem.

'That's right, love. Commandos.'

'Bloody hell.' She snuggles up closer. 'You must be something special. Just imagine, a commando.'

'He's on an undercover mission,' says Bob. 'Top secret. Don't tell anyone, whatever you do.'

The girls are impressed. 'Undercover, really?' asks Beryl.

Charlie bursts out laughing. 'In bed at least,' he whispers to Joe.

They decide to stay put until closing time, but their evening is interrupted by three real thugs who come over and start arguing with the girls.

Emboldened by the beer, George jumps up. 'Why don't

you clear off? You're spoiling our night.'

'Sit down, lad,' says the biggest of the trio. 'Mind your own frigging business.'

'Don't tell me what to do, mate,' says George.

One of the girls pulls him back down again. 'Be careful,' she whispers. 'It's the Wise brothers. They've got a really bad reputation.'

George stands up again. 'The three Wise Men, eh.' He points to the door. 'Piss off, the lot of you.'

Immediately all hell breaks loose. The lads always look out for each other, so the other three wade in as soon as they see George in trouble. Drinks are spilled, glasses broken, and the girls soaked with beer. Charlie drags one brother off George, while Joe and Bob repel the other two.

Help arrives in the nick of time. A giant of a man grabs one their assailants and throws him out the door, while his mates make short work of the other two. 'Thanks, lads,' says George, as they all shake hands afterwards.

'That's OK. They're right troublemakers, them prats. They needed to be taught a lesson.'

'You're something else, George,' says Charlie. 'How the hell did we get out of that mess?

'They just didn't know who they were taking on,' says George smugly.

The small band strikes up again and the rest of the night passes in a whirl. At closing time they head back to Nettleton's field. George still has a girl on each arm – but Sandra is pulling him closer, away from her friend Jenny. They pile into the caravan, all very drunk, and Charlie and Bob take their partners straight to their respective rooms. Just before shutting the bedroom door, Bob turns to George. 'Have you got a you-know-what?'

'No,' says George. 'Have you?'

Bob slips him a Durex.

'Just the one?' says George. 'Bloody hell, I'm a commando. I need another at least.'

Charlie and Beryl are soon stripped and into action, but Charlie is fumbling with the condom he's left ready on the bedside table. 'Give it here,' says Beryl, snatching it away. 'Let me do it.'

That suits Charlie. All he has to do is lie back and enjoy the experience.

Meanwhile George has to make do with the living room floor. He puts on a condom and is soon in full swing, pumping away with Sandra beneath him. Jenny seemed to be oblivious, a little too worse for drink. Suddenly a hand snakes round his stomach and touches his private parts. *What's going on here?* he thinks. *Sandra's got both arms round my neck.* Bare breasts touch his back, then a body is moving in time with his as he makes love. He can't believe it. For all his boasting, he's never experienced anything quite like this before.

After a time the caravan falls quiet. George is exhausted, the two girls beside him sleeping soundly. *What a night*, he thinks. *Two in one go. Wait till I tell the lads.*

Joe wakes up in the early hours, desperate to go to the toilet. Looking down, he spots the rubber ring from his used condom. *What's this?* he thinks. *What happened to the rest of it? No sign of it round the bed.* He looks across at his sleeping partner. *It must be still inside her. Hope you find it, love.*

Inside the sentry-box toilet is a fixed wooden seat with a steel bin underneath, removable via a small door at the back. Everyone hates these toilets, partly due to the smell – they're only emptied once a week – and partly because you can see right into the bin. Even though it's dark, Joe tries not to look while he urinates as quickly as possible. He's already feeling sick and the smell is making it much worse.

Back in the caravan, George is still snoring away between his two naked girls.

Lucky sod, thinks Joe.

George is first up in the morning. 'Morning, my beauties,' he says, swigging from a bottle of lemonade. Not that they look quite that good just now.

Then Beryl appears in skirt and bra. 'Anything to drink? she asks. 'I could murder a cuppa?'

Charlie, Joe and Bob are all feeling grim. 'I'll light the

stove,' says Charlie.

'Never again,' says Bob, holding his head. 'I think I'm dying.'

'You're not the only one,' says Joe, slumping back in his chair.

'Don't be so wet!' laughs George. 'I'm fine. I could handle a nice fry up – eggs, some nice greasy bacon, beans, a few slices of toast.'

Bob beats the others to the horrible toilet, forcing Charlie and Joe to go round the back of the caravan. Meanwhile the girls tidy themselves up a bit, then head back to their own place, leaving the lads to sleep off their bad heads.

'Were your condoms OK?' Joe asks Charlie.

'Why?' asks Charlie, puzzled.

'Well, I ended up with a rubber ring round my you-know-what. I must have left the rest behind.'

'Behind what?' laughs George. 'The wardrobe?'

'She's probably hung on to it,' says Joe.

'Must have been a dud,' says Charlie. 'Mine was fine.'

'Same here,' says Bob.

'All mine were good,' says George, grinning. 'I certainly didn't see anything hanging around. What a night, though.'

'All?' laughs Bob. 'I only gave you two.'

'Just joking,' says George, rubbing his scalp, forgetting that his precious head of hair has disappeared completely.

They're good for nothing that day but a brief tour of the amusement arcades and an early night, but the following morning they're feeling much livelier. It's warm out and they decide to head to the beach. The sands are pretty busy, with children paddling and girls laid out enjoying a rare glimpse of the sun, so the lads put on their trunks, set out their towels and sit chatting and relaxing.

'Anyone fancy a swim?' says Charlie.

'Not me,' says George. 'I can't swim. I only go in up to my ankles.'

Joe and Bob aren't keen either. 'It looks pretty choppy out there,' says Joe. 'There's nobody else in the water.'

Lying disconsolately on his towel, Charlie spots a young

woman walking along the beach, tossing a stick into the water for her dog to fetch. Eventually she throws the stick too far out. The dog can't find it and the tide is carrying him out to sea.

'Rusty, Rusty,' she cries frantically, wading into the waves.

'Come on, lads,' shouts Charlie. 'She needs help.'

They run down to the sea and Charlie tries to pull her from the water. 'My dog,' she shouts, struggling free. 'My dog, he's going to drown.'

'Keep hold of her,' shouts Charlie, running into the water and striking out towards the hound.

'Come back,' bawls Joe anxiously. 'He's too far out.'

Charlie just ignores him. He's a good swimmer but the swell takes him by surprise and by the time he gets to the dog he's exhausted. He grabs it by the collar and turns back to the shore, but now the tide is against him and he can only use one arm. 'Come on, Charlie!' shout the lads. Hearing their voices seems to give him strength and he begins to make headway. At last he nears the beach and Joe swims out to meet him.

'Come on, mate,' he says. 'You can give me the dog now.'

Joe returns Rusty to his anxious owner while Charlie struggles the last few yards to the shore. He crawls part way across the sand, gets to his feet and staggers over to his friends. There he falls to his knees, coughing and fighting for breath. Shielding him from the gathering crowd, the lads help him to his feet.

'Shit, Charlie,' says George. 'You frightened us to death.'

Then the woman comes up to them, carrying the cause of all the trouble. 'I can't thank you enough,' she says. 'You risked your life to save my dog. Can I ask your name?'

Charlie catches his breath. 'Charlie,' he splutters. 'Charlie Robinson.'

'Well, you're a very brave man, Charlie Robinson. My name's Debra and I live up there in that row of houses facing the sea. Perhaps I could invite you for a drink? I'm sure my husband would like to thank you.'

'That's very kind,' says Charlie, 'but I really am fine now.'

'I'd still like to thank you properly. Perhaps you could

come round tomorrow. It's Number 29. Please come and meet my husband.'

'OK,' says Charlie.

'Around twelve?' says Debra.

'I'll try to be there.'

The crowd has disappeared now. The lads get changed and walk slowly back to the caravan. 'Daft sod,' says Bob. 'Fancy risking your life for a bloody dog.'

'I couldn't stand seeing her panic,' says Charlie. 'Thanks for the help, Joe.'

'No problem,' he says.

'I'd have swum out, too,' says George, 'but I got cold feet.'

'Yeah, yeah,' says Charlie. *That wasn't very bright*, he thinks, mulling it over later. *I could have drowned.*

After such a stressful day, the lads make plans to hit the town again that evening with the same five girls. They call to find them in various states of undress – and quite unabashed by their presence.

'Do you want us to shut our eyes?' asks Bob. 'We know how shy you all are.'

'Why?' says Beryl. 'Don't you like the view?'

'Love it,' says George, grinning. 'We could stay here all night, love. '

They set off on a pub crawl – a few drinks here, a few drinks there. The lads are determined not to overdo it – they don't want to end up with a bad head again – but the girls are ready for some heavy partying. George is the only one who can keep up with them.

Back at Nettleton's field they split up. Joe and Bob take their partners to the lads' caravan, while Charlie and George go with the girls.

'Enjoy yourself,' says Charlie, pulling Beryl into her room.

'I will,' shouts George. 'Night, Charlie.'

Early next morning they sort themselves out and return to their temporary homes. The lads swap stories about their nocturnal adventures, and George starts bragging about another eventful night, but eventually he has to stop and go to the toilet. He hates it, but there's no avoiding it. Fast on a nail inside are the neatly cut squares of newspaper they use as toilet paper. George is holding his nose as he sits reading the piece of paper grasped in his hand, when he hears a sudden commotion outside. *Must be the kids banging and clattering*, he thinks. Then the rear door opens and the bin disappears from beneath his seat.

'Bloody hell!' he shouts, clinging to the sides of the sentry box. 'What's going on? I'm trying to having a crap in here!'

'Sorry about that, mate,' says a gruff voice. 'Just emptying the bins. Hang on a minute while I slide it back.' He laughs. 'Never seen a paler arse, lad!' The bin slips back into place and the door closes. 'There you go. Finish your crap.'

It's no good: George can't complete what he started. He can't get out fast enough and rushes back to the caravan.

'You'll never believe what's just happened,' he says.

They all hoot with laughter.

'What about Debra, Charlie?' asks Joe. 'Are you going to see her?'

'I wasn't going to bother,' he replies, 'but I suppose I did half promise. All right then, won't be long.'

'You could be in there, you know,' says Bob.

'Don't be daft. She only wants to give her husband chance to thank me.'

'Just be careful, that's all I'm saying.'

'All right. But she doesn't look the type.'

Charlie walks along the row facing the sea, looking for Number 29 – a big, comfortable-looking house.

He climbs the steps and rings the bell. 'Hello, Charlie.' Debra answers the door with a smile. 'Do come in.'

He follows her into a lovely lounge with a beautiful sea view. A smartly dressed man sitting in one of the big, over-stuffed armchairs stands up as soon as Charlie enters the room. 'Hello,' he says. 'I'm Debra's husband, Nick. So you're the hero, are you?'

Sarky beggar. 'No, I'm Charlie. Pleased to meet you.'

'I know I should be thanking you but you were stupid to

risk your life for that dog. You might have drowned. I've warned Debra not to let him swim in the sea.'

'Could I get you a drink, Charlie?' says Debra, trying to cover her embarrassment. 'Tea or coffee?'

'Coffee would be fine, thank you.' *Ignorant prick*, thinks Charlie. He's upsetting her.

'I understand you're from Hull.'

'Yes. I'm here on holiday with friends.'

'Mmmm, we get a lot of Hull people in Withernsea.' Nick looks pointedly at his watch. 'Sorry, Charlie. I've got to be going. Business, you know.' Debra returns to the room with their drinks. 'See you later,' he says. 'I'll be home around six.'

'I'm sorry,' says Debra tearfully as she hands Charlie his coffee. 'I was hoping Nick would thank you properly. I really appreciate what you did.'

'Don't worry about it.'

'My husband isn't very sociable.'

You can say that again, thinks Charlie. *Perhaps it's time I was going.*

'Thanks for the coffee, Debra. I'm sorry about your husband.'

'He … well, let's say things haven't been right for a while.' She picks up the dog. 'Sorry, I shouldn't be telling you this. He can't stand Rusty, and Rusty is terrified of him.'

'Please don't cry,' says Charlie, laying his hand on her shoulder to comfort her. Debra puts the dog down and wipes her eyes, then moves closer. *What on earth?* thinks Charlie.

Cheeks wet with tears, she turns and embraces him, then she kisses him gently on the lips. 'I'm not sure I should have done that,' she whispers.

She strokes his cheek, then kisses him again, harder this time, opening her mouth and inviting him in. Charlie can't restrain himself. He feels an instinctive male need to respond to her advances. He pulls her close and kisses her, remembering his encounters with Pat.

'What if your husband comes home?' he asks.

'He won't,' pants Debra, scarcely pausing for breath. She thrusts her hand inside his trousers, 'Please, Charlie, please. I need this so badly.'

Before Charlie knows what's happening they're in bed together. He moves his head to her breasts, but Debra pushes it down further, moaning all the time. She's never made love like this before. She hasn't had sex for months, and Charlie knows just what she wants and how to provide it. She rolls on top of him, kissing him all over, desperate for love. She holds nothing back, wanting to touch him and enjoy the feel of a man. 'Oh yes, Charlie, yes!' She presses down harder. 'Please, more.'

She tenses, then gasps, crying out and digging her nails into his back as she submits to the pleasure of orgasm. Charlie squeezes her breast as he joins her. Afterwards they lie quietly together. *I won't forget that in a hurry*, he thinks. *What is it about me and older women? I can't believe how quickly she came on to me. She didn't look the type. What a beautiful woman, though. How can she stay with that Nick? She has no life at all.*

Eventually Charlie decides that it's time to go. 'We're fine,' Debra reassures him. 'Nick has his own business. He's never home before six.'

Still, Charlie pulls on his clothes and gets ready to leave.

'I must see you again,' she says, stroking his face and kissing him. 'I sometimes take Rusty down to the beach in the evening. Perhaps we could meet then.'

'Bye, Debra.' Charlie kisses her. 'I'll be in touch if I can. Can't promise anything, though.'

'Please try,' she says.

Charlie leaves the house and walks back along the promenade. *I'll be back in the fish house this time next week*, he thinks. *There must be more to life than this*. The sea is calm today and he stands a while, enjoying the breeze on his face and sniffing the salt air. He spots a ship way out on the horizon and for the first time senses the pull of the ocean.

'What took you so long?' asks Bob, when Charlie finally returns to the caravan.

'Just out and about,' he says. 'That husband of hers didn't have much to say. He turned out to be a right pillock.'

The week flies by, although the lads eventually start slowing down a bit – what with the night life and drinking more than they're used to. On their last evening – a Saturday – they dress up for the weekly dance at Withernsea Pavilion. It's a big do, with a lot of young ones coming out by special train from Hull. The Pavilion has a bar, so the lads can buy a beer or two, as well as a good live band. The music is blaring out and the dance floor is packed with youngsters jiving and bopping.

Some of the boys are throwing the girls around, and George can't wait to join the action. 'Be-bop-a-lula, lads. Let's get to it. All we need now are a few nice girls.'

Joe and Bob are happy to accompany him. Not so Charlie: he's been a bit down since the episode with Debra.

'Come on, Charlie lad,' says Bob. 'Buck up. Are you dancing or not?'

'I'm not in the mood. I'll just sit here for a while?'

'Feeling all right?' asks Joe.

'Fine. You go off and enjoy yourselves. I'm happy enough here.'

Charlie sits and watches the people around him: fishermen in their wide-bottomed trousers, double-breasted suit coat and essential white collar and silk tie; young lads dressed like teddy boys in drainpipe trousers, coat with a velvet-trimmed collar and thick crepe-soled shoes; girls in flared skirts that float up when the lads spin them round – the girls knowing the lads are enjoying the view.

George always attracts attention on the dance floor. *He's pretty good*, thinks Charlie. *The army's changed him. For the better, I reckon.* The seats around him are empty – most people are either dancing or drinking in the bar – and a girl comes and sits down nearby.

She looks a little lost and Charlie smiles across at her. 'Here on your own?' he asks after a while.

'No, my friends are in the bar. I don't drink, so I thought I'd just sit here for a bit. Why aren't you dancing? Don't you know how?'

'Of course, I do. Fred Astaire has nothing on me. Just joking, I don't feel like it, that's all. My mates are making up for me. I'm Charlie, by the way.'

'Pleased to meet you, Charlie. I'm Beth. So there's no Ginger Rogers, then?'

"Fraid not.'

Charlie moves closer and they sit chatting for a while. Beth has just moved to Hull from a village outside the city and lives quite close to him. They go for a coffee, then spend the rest of the night chatting together. *What a nice girl*, thinks Charlie. *Good to talk to as well.*

Beth and her friends have come by train, and at the end of the night Charlie agrees to walk her back to the station. The lads have been leaving him alone since they spotted him with a girl, so while she's fetching her coat, he goes to tell them that he'll see them back at the caravan.

'I've really enjoyed this evening,' says Beth, as they hurry for the train.

'Me, too,' says Charlie. 'Perhaps I could see you again sometime?'

'I'd like that a lot.'

'How about Wednesday night?'

'Fine.'

The crowd around them are all pretty tipsy, including Beth's friends. 'Are you sure you'll be OK?' asks Charlie solicitously when they get to the station.

'Of course.'

'Best be going then.' Charlie takes her hand. 'Really nice meeting you, Beth. See you next week.'

'OK, Charlie.'

She gives him a peck on the cheek, then turns and runs for her train. She looks back and waves when she gets to her carriage and blows him another kiss as she climbs aboard.

Smiling, Charlie blows her a kiss in return. Then the train pulls out and he walks back to the caravan, pondering all that's happened during the week.

Loud voices greet him as he nears the caravan, and he opens the door to find his three pals with several scantily glad girls – all dancing, singing and distinctly the worse for wear.

'Hi there, Charlie lad,' says Joe, slapping one girl on the bottom. 'Meet our new friends.'

Charlie says hello politely enough, but he soon sneaks off to his room. He wants to be on his own. As the night wears on, the noise is relentless. He hears a girl giggling. *No prizes for guessing what's going on there.*

Next morning everyone but Charlie wakes up with a very sore head. The girls are looking nothing like as good as they did the night before, and the lads soon kick them out and get on with their packing.

Joe has a few more days before he sails again, but Charlie and Bob will be back at work on Monday. George is the lucky one. He's still on leave for another two weeks before he moves to his permanent posting, Still, he's pulling a face. 'I've got to make one last visit to the thunder-box. Does anyone have a peg for my nose?'

They're all laughing as George goes outside.

'Thank God I've been constipated all week,' says Bob. 'At least I haven't had to go in that smelly shit-box.'

'Let's hope no one pulls the bin out from under him,' says Joe. 'I didn't see the girls from the site last night, by the way. They probably got off with some other guys. They sure liked a good time.'

'I'll get it in the neck if my uncle spots any damage,' says Bob, making one final check of the caravan.

At last he's satisfied and the lads set off for the station. George looks back fondly at the old railway carriage. 'Goodbye sex haven,' he calls sadly. 'Hope we'll meet again some day.'

They all laugh.

'Off home for a rest, lads?' shouts one of their neighbours. 'You must be knackered after the kind of week you've had.'

Arriving home in Hull, they feel as if they've never been away. 'I'm back,' calls Charlie as he walks in through the door.

Mary takes his bag and kisses him. 'I have missed you,' she says. 'Is that more dirty washing?'

'Yes, Mam.'

'An extra trip to the wash house for me, then. How was your holiday? Did you all behave? No one got arrested or anything? Just pulling your leg.'

'Nothing of the sort,' smiles Charlie. 'We all had a great time. We want to do it again next year.'

'I bet you haven't eaten properly for a week. What was it, fish and chips every day?'

'Pretty much. How are Dad and Eileen?'

'Dad's OK. Eileen's still upset about Howard, but she'll just have to accept it. She's beginning to show and the neighbours are starting to talk. You know how they gossip.'

'How's she going to manage, Mam?'

'She'll be fine. Looking after a baby will probably come naturally to her, like it does for most mothers.'

'I hope so.'

CHAPTER 8
HOSPITAL BLUES

Over the next few weeks, Charlie goes out with Beth a few times and even takes her home to meet his parents. He tries his luck repeatedly but he never makes much progress – a little kissing and cuddling is the most she will allow. *It's no good*, he thinks. *I don't think she has any feelings for me at all.*

Meanwhile Bob is keeping a low profile after the Lucy fiasco. He gets a dirty look every time he bumps into her at work but he doesn't care – the world is his oyster since he got back from holiday. His only worry is his sister Denise. She has a very persistent cough and is losing weight hand over fist.

One day he arrives home from work to bad news. 'Our Denise is in hospital,' says Jim. 'An ambulance came to collect her earlier this afternoon. Your mam's gone with her. They think it's TB. Now you're home I'll get off to Castle Hill, too.'

'I'll come with you,' says Bob. 'How bad is she?'

'She didn't look good at all, son. Sarah is very upset. You'd best stay and look after her.'

'OK, Dad. You get moving.'

When Jim and Barbara get home in the early hours of the morning, Bob is sleeping in a chair. He jumps up at once. 'What's happening? How is she?'

'It's definitely TB,' says Barbara. 'They're taking good care of her, but she'll be in hospital for a while. We have to get checked out too. It might be contagious.'

'Don't worry,' says Bob. 'I'll stay home until everything's sorted out.'

To their relief, the rest of the family are all pronounced clear. Denise is comfortable enough in hospital, but her spirits are low – the thought of months as an in-patient is making her very depressed.

Charlie is very upset by the news. Denise is a couple of years older than him and he feels like he's known her for ever. *She's always been there to look out for me*, he thinks, picturing her cheeky grin. *Time I did something for her for a change.*

'Can I come with you to visit one evening?' he asks Bob.

'Of course,' says Bob. 'I'm sure Denise would love it. You know how much she thinks of you. How about tomorrow?'

'Fine,' says Charlie.

The following evening they set off on the long, two-bus trip up to Castle Hill. When they get to the ward, Charlie peeps round the door. 'Hi there, beautiful!' he calls.

Denise looks miserable and wan, but her face lights up when she sees who it is. Charlie takes hold of her hand. 'Can I kiss your cheek?' he asks.

'Of course,' says Denise. *Just wish it was my lips.* 'What a lovely surprise. Thanks for coming to see me. '

'I had to,' says Charlie. 'I miss your smiling face.'

To his horror Denise bursts into tears. 'There, there,' he coaxes her. 'You'll soon be better and back home again.'

'Mam, Dad and Sarah all send their love,' says Bob, going to give her a hug. 'Now let's see that smile again.'

The lads do their best to cheer her up as they sit and chat. 'Are you still seeing June?' she asks Charlie.

'No,' he replies. 'Not for a while now. I've been a real hermit.'

'I'm sure,' laughs Denise.

Bob pulls a face at Charlie. *Whatever you do, don't mention Beth*!

Charlie takes the hint, but when visiting time is over Denise starts crying again. She clings to his hand as if she'd never let him go. 'I hate being stuck in here,' she says. 'I'd walk out if I could.'

'Don't be daft,' says Charlie. 'You've got stay until you're better.'

'Thanks,' says Bob, once he and Charlie are back on the bus.

108

'What for?'

'First, for coming with me; and second, for keeping quiet about Beth.'

'No problem, Bob.'

Charlie continues visiting regularly, even when Bob can't make it. Denise always quizzes him about his love life, but he manages to skirt round the subject. He knows what a crush she has on him and doesn't want to give her false hopes.

On Charlie's seventeenth birthday he goes out to celebrate with Bob and George. Joe is away, but George is home on leave before he goes to Germany. None of the lads have ever been out of the country and they're all excited about his posting.

'Are you flying or going by boat?' asks Bob.

They've never seen an aircraft close up, never mind travelled in one.

'By boat,' says George.

'Dad's told me about the war,' says Charlie. 'Hitler and all that. How Germany has built itself up from nothing since. West Germany, that is.'

'Aren't you the smart one?' says George. 'I don't know anything about the place. I just hope we can lay hands on some of the women, frauleins or something. One of our officers said there are some real lookers.'

'All I know is they like big sausages,' laughs Bobs. 'So that cuts you out, then.'

Then Eileen totters into the room, arching her back as though afraid of toppling over if she stands up straight. The baby looks to be due any minute, but she still has another month to go.

George didn't know she was pregnant. He looks at Bob and smiles but manages to hold his tongue.

They all say goodbye to the family and head off into town. 'Come on, George,' says Charlie. 'I bet you're dying to ask me who the father is.'

'What do you mean?' says George innocently.

'You could see Eileen's pregnant. You want to know who the father is, don't you?'

'Go on, then. Who?'

'You've seen him around. Howard – thin guy, big ears.'

'I know the bloke you mean. Is he going to marry her?'

'No, he's pissed off to Scotland or somewhere like that. If my old man lays hands on him, he'll rip his lugs off.'

'Sorry, mate,' says George, trying not to smile.

Charlie laughs. 'What for?'

In town they make for their usual haunts, less bothered about picking up girls than just having a good time. Typically, George suggests they go and have a laugh with the rough lot in the Paragon. They walk into the smoky room, sit down and order their drinks. A couple of old hags immediately train their eyes on them.

'Watch out,' says Charlie. 'Here comes trouble.'

'Looking for company, boys?' asks a thin, over-made-up peroxide blonde. Her painted eyebrows are closer to her hairline than her eyes. 'Fancy buying me a drink?'

'My, you're a stunner,' says George. 'I don't think I've ever met a more beautiful woman.'

Charlie and Bob splutter with laughter, spraying beer everywhere.

'I'm Maud,' she says. 'Fancy taking me home, love?' She smiles, showing her teeth – or those she has left. Her mouth is more gap than tooth.

'Love to, darling,' says George. 'We're all a bit strapped for cash, though.'

'It wouldn't cost that much.'

'We've only got our bus fares. Would that be enough?'

'Bus fares!' she shouts. 'You're taking the piss. Bloody tight-arses!'

Time to leave, they think, as a hail of abuse follows them to the door. They run up the road laughing, glancing back to see if she's following.

'Fancy waking up next to her,' chuckles Bob. 'What a nightmare.'

'You'd think you'd died and gone to hell,' laughs Charlie.

They find a quieter pub and spend the evening enjoying a drink or two before catching the bus home. As they sit down Charlie spots Beth.

She turns and sees him too. 'Hi, Charlie!'

'Hi, Beth,' he mumbles. It's been a while since they last went out. 'Had a good night?'

'I've been to the pictures with my friend.'

'We've been out celebrating my birthday.'

'He's been behaving himself,' says George. 'He's only had six pints.'

'Don't believe a word of it,' says Charlie. 'I wouldn't be able to stand up.'

They soon reach Beth's stop and she stands up to get off. 'Happy birthday, Charlie. I've got a present for you, you know. When can I give it to you?'

'Soon,' says Charlie vaguely. 'I'll be in touch.'

'Bad lad,' says Bob. 'I bet you've no intention of seeing her.'

'I might – just to get my present, though. Who knows, I might go back to Maud in the Paragon. Take her out instead.'

Joe gets back after a long hard trip to find his mother in tears.

'What's going on, Mam?' he asks. 'Why are you crying?'

'Vince has gone back to his place,' says Pat. 'We've been arguing. Everything was fine at first but he suddenly turned very possessive. It's all him and never me.'

'I've never known what you see in him.'

'I love him,' she says unhappily. 'At least I think I do. We were planning to get married. I'm sure it could still be OK. We just need to sit down and talk.'

'He'll be back.' Joe tries to comfort her. 'I'm sure you'll sort out your problems.'

'Thanks, love. I'm glad I've told you. I didn't want to worry you with my troubles. You've got to enjoy yourself while you're home. I often bump into Charlie and Bob, by the way. They're always asking after you. And wait till you see Eileen. Her baby must be due any minute. I can't believe she's going to be a mother.'

Joe has his tea, then heads round to Charlie's to catch up

with the news.

'George left last week,' says Charlie. 'We had a good night out for my birthday before he went. How's things with you?'

'Fine. We've a good trip in, so we should make a bob or two. I'm worried about Mam, though. She's been having a lot of trouble with Vince – jealous, you know. They've been arguing and he's walked out. She's really upset. I don't know whether to go and talk to him.'

Got to hide my true feelings, thinks Charlie. *The memories come flooding back every time I see her.* 'There's nothing you can do. Vince won't want you interfering. Leave it to them.'

'I suppose you're right, Charlie.'

'Did you know Denise Watson is in hospital? TB. She's pretty low. I'm trying to visit whenever I can.'

'I'm sorry to hear that. I'll come with you if you want.'

It's a weekday evening, so Charlie and Bob are too tired to go out with Joe. Instead a couple of his crewmates take him for a drink in town. They're quite a lot older than he is, but they swear he'll have a good time. They pick him up by taxi from home and take him to the Broadway to join some other crewmen and their wives.

The drinks are flowing and the company is terrific. The bachelors are eyeing up the girls and persuade a couple of them to come over to their table. The wives are chatting together, puffing away on their cigarettes, shouting to make themselves heard above the noise of the band. Their menfolk are drinking pints, never emptying one glass before they're back at the bar for a refill. Everyone is tipsy, and even Joe, who hasn't had that much to drink, is feeling rather unsteady on his feet.

When the pub shuts they decide to carry on partying at somebody's house. Taxis are ordered and everyone piles in, including the two girls they've acquired. Joe is in seventh heaven, wedged in the back seat with a girl on his knee, five or six people squashed in beside him, all smoking and dropping ash on their neighbours – arms, legs and bottoms everywhere.

They call at Pop's for a couple of cases of beer, and soon

the house is full – with the gang from the pub as well as a few neighbours. Records are placed on the radiogram and the music starts blaring out.

Some of the wives are taunting the younger lads, flashing their stocking-tops as they dance, while their husbands look on and laugh.

One woman thrusts her bottom against her young partner, urging him to put his hands on her hips and pull her closer. Suddenly, a man grabs hold of him. 'What the hell do you think you're doing with my wife, you little shit?'

A punch is thrown and a fight breaks out. The woman weighs in alongside her husband, others get involved, and the place quickly dissolves into chaos. Beer is spilled, glasses smashed and chairs pushed over. Joe and his girl both fall to the ground. She lands uppermost, laughing and pinning him to the floor. Suddenly she turns ominously pale. Joe pushes her off him and drags her outside – just in the nick of time. She retches and vomits on the pavement while people push past, ignoring her.

Joe has seen enough. 'Where are you off, Joe lad?' calls one of his mates. 'Come back!'

Not likely, thinks Joe. Up ahead, he can see the couple who caused all the ruckus, walking arm-in-arm and kissing as if nothing had happened. *Would you credit it*? He can still hear the commotion in the street behind him. *What a night*!

He gets home late, expecting his mum to be fast asleep.

Instead he can hear voices from the front room. 'Had a good night?' asks Vince, when Joe walks in.

'You could say that.'

'Vince has asked me to marry him,' says Pat in a rush.

After all you've said, thinks Joe. *I hope you're doing the right thing.* 'If you're sure this is what you want, then I'm pleased for you both,' he says at last. 'When are you going to tie the knot?'

'In a couple of months,' says Vince, smiling at Pat.

'Just family and friends?' asks Joe, looking at his mother.

'Yes,' says Vince. 'We want a quiet wedding, don't we, Pat?'

'Yes,' she replies. 'Just family and a few close friends.'

Up at Castle Hill, Denise can now walk around and chat with other patients. She's made friends with a girl called Eve, another TB sufferer around her age. Eve really struggles for breath, so Denise has to do most of the talking.

'Have–you–got–a–boy–friend?' asks Eve one day.

'Yes, well kind of,' says Denise, with a smile.

'What–do–you–mean "Kind–of"?'

'He's my brother's best friend. I've known him years. He's ever so nice and really good looking. We've got a lot closer since I've been ill, at least I think we have. I'm sure we'll end up being much more than friends – when, if, I get home. What about you?'

'My–boyfriend–came–a–couple–of–times,' sobs Eve. 'Not–any–more–though.'

'I'm sure there'll be someone for you when you get better.'

'I'm–afraid–I'm–not–going–to–get–better.'

'Come on,' says Denise, stroking Eve's hand to comfort her. 'We've got to try and keep cheerful.'

How uncertain life is, thinks Denise, lying in bed that evening. You never know what's around the corner. *All you can do is live your life to the full while you can.*

Next day Joe, Charlie and Bob all catch the bus up to the hospital.

'Mam and Vince have kissed and made up,' says Joe. 'They're getting married.' Charlie tries to hide his disappointment – he was hoping the split might be permanent. 'And you won't believe the ding-dong I got involved in last night.'

He tells the lads all about it. 'Nice quiet night, then?' grins Charlie.

'I'd quite a laugh too yesterday,' says Bob. 'I work with a woman called Molly. She's getting on a bit, not much to look at, and she seemed a bit down.

'"What's wrong?" I said.

'"Don't ask," she replied. "I don't want to discuss it."

'Anyway, I insisted. Turns out she'd only gone home early, walked into the house and found her husband wearing her new undies – stockings, suspenders and bra.'

'Get away,' laughs Charlie. 'What happened then?'

'"I lost my rag with him," she said.

'"Well, it must have been a shock," I told her.

'"Not really," she said. "I was just bloody mad. He looked better in them than I did."'

They hoot with laughter.

'Oh, Bob,' says Joe. 'Some story.'

Denise is thrilled to see them all. *Charlie really has filled out*, she thinks. *He looks more handsome than ever*. She can't take her eyes off him and directs all her questions towards him. Bob and Joe might as well have stayed at home. 'Come on,' says Bob. 'Let's go get a drink.'

As soon as they've left the ward, Denise leans across and runs her finger over Charlie's upper lip. 'Why Charlie, I do believe you're growing a moustache.'

'What do you think? Shall I shave it off?'

'No, I like it,' smiles Denise. 'It makes you look really sexy.'

'I don't need a moustache for that, do I?' he jokes.

'Not for me,' she says, running her fingers through his hair. 'I think you always look sexy.'

'I'm going to have to watch you, Denise Watson. You're trying to take advantage of me.'

'If only I had the chance, Charlie Robinson.'

'Do you think I could take you out on a date when you get out of hospital?'

'Can't wait,' she says, squeezing his hand.

Just then Bob and Joe return. 'What are you two lovebirds laughing about?' asks Bob, winking at Charlie.

'Nothing,' says Denise, blushing to the roots of her hair.

On the bus home the lads start talking about National Service. 'I suppose you two will be following George into the army,' says Joe. 'I'm glad I won't have to. I'm quite looking forward to the RNR.'

'I haven't really thought about it yet,' says Charlie. 'I'm not too keen after listening to George. I don't suppose there's much I can do, though.'

'Go on trawlers, then you can join the RNR like me. Otherwise it's got to be the army.'

'No way you'd ever get me on a bloody trawler' says Bob. 'I'd rather join the army.'

'Either way, you'll have to decide before you turn eighteen,' says Joe.

It's weeks since Charlie bumped into Beth and he still hasn't been round for his present. In the end she decides to take the initiative and call on him.

'Do you want to come round to our house?' she says. 'I've got the place to myself for a couple of hours this evening.'

'Fine,' says Charlie. He doesn't want to upset her.

'I thought I'd have heard from you by now.'

'Sorry,' says Charlie. 'Overtime, you know.'

Inside Beth's house a coal fire is burning in the grate. She puts some music on the radio, turns off the light and walks boldly towards him.

'Do you remember that I promised you a birthday present, Charlie.'

'I think you did mention something.'

She unbuttons her blouse and pulls it back to reveal her bra. Then she kneels between his knees, takes hold of his hand and places it on her bosom. 'Oh Charlie,' she says, kissing him and pulling him to the floor.

I don't think she'll say no this time, thinks Charlie. He unsnaps her bra and starts to fondle her naked breasts. No resistance at all. He slides his hand underneath her skirt and starts making love with all the passion he can muster. Bathed in the glow of the open fire, her eyes are closed. Their bodies are entwined; she moans at his every move, opening her mouth as if gasping for air.

'Charlie, Charlie!' she cries 'Yes! Oh yes! Please don't stop, I want you so much.'

But Charlie can no longer control his reactions. A feeling of warmth washes over him, then an explosion within. He tenses momentarily before collapsing in her arms.

'Happy birthday,' says Beth, rolling on top of him and

kissing him.

Charlie can't believe the change in her. They cling to each other, bathed in sweat, completely spent. But within minutes they're doing it all again, more slowly this time so Beth can enjoy every second.

Still, they can't ignore the clock. 'My parents will be home any minute,' says Beth, retrieving her bra and blouse. 'You'll have to go. When can I see you again?'

'I'm not sure, Beth.'

'What do you mean, you're not sure?'

'I don't mind seeing you now and then but I don't want to get serious. I'm too young to be tied down. I enjoy being out with my friends.'

'I knew I shouldn't have let you do it,' she wails. 'I thought it was the only way you'd want to see me again.'

'I'm sorry, Beth,' says Charlie firmly, kissing her on the cheek. 'There's nothing more to say. I don't want to make promises I can't keep.'

Beth follows him to the door, looking on reproachfully as he turns and walks away.

CHAPTER 9
A NEW BABY

With George in Germany and Joe at sea, life is quiet for a while. Charlie and Bob go out for the occasional drink but only when overtime and hospital visiting allow.

Eileen's baby is overdue. Mary is fussing around making preparations, and the local midwife is a regular visitor. Sister Wilson has worked round Hessle Road for years – wobbling down the streets and terraces on her bike, the tyres flattened by her weight – and she's on first-name terms with all the mums.

After a couple of false alarms, it finally looks like the real thing. Mary and Nora, a neighbour who helps the midwife, are trying to make Eileen as comfortable as they can.

'You'll be fine, love,' says Nora. 'Sister'll be here soon, won't she, Mary?'

Mary just smiles.

'Mam!' cries Eileen, grasping her hand. 'Oh, Mam!'

'Just relax, love,' says Mary anxiously. 'Sister's on her way. How are you doing?'

'Aaagh, shouts Eileen, clinging tight to her mother. 'It hurts.'

'I'm here,' calls Sister Wilson, perspiring and slightly breathless. She shakes her head as she takes off her coat. 'That bloody wind! I couldn't keep myself upright. Never mind. Right, love. Let's see how you're doing. Just relax, sweetheart. Get your legs up when I tell you. You're going to have to push down. I know it's hard. Just keep taking deeeeeep breaths, dear.'

Eileen is terrified but she tries to do as she's told. Mary and Nora wait patiently while Sister Wilson checks on progress. 'Deep breath, love,' she says, demonstrating again. 'Deep breath.' Finally she calls out, 'That's it, yes. Legs apart, dear, that's right.

No need for the splits. Just enough for us to get baby out. Here we go. Come on now, push. Attagirl.'

'I can't,' cries Eileen, covered in sweat. 'It hurts too much.'

Nora calmly wipes Eileen's brow, as she has for so many mothers down the years. Meanwhile Mary is running around frantically. She just doesn't know where to put herself.

'Push again, dear,' says Sister Wilson. 'Not long to go now. Come on, legs up. Keep them open, that's a girl.'

'No, no!' screams Eileen. 'It hurts!'

'Nearly there, dear. Here we go. This is it, I think. Yes, love. Push, push. Don't make it hard for me.'

Eileen is sweating even more profusely. 'God,' she shouts, face racked with pain.

'Here it comes. Yes, here's baby's head, sweetheart. Yes, that's it. Here we go again. That's it. Yes, yes. Lovely.'

Smiling, Sister Wilson helps the baby into the world.

'A lovely little boy,' she says, mopping her brow. She passes him to Nora, who hands him on to Eileen. The baby is crying now but Eileen gives him a big smile.

'Here, Gran,' she says proudly, offering him to Mary. 'Here's your grandson.'

Mary looks down at the baby and promptly bursts into tears.

Sister Wilson takes him back for a moment to do what has to be done, then finally returns him to Eileen. 'Has he got a name yet, love?' she asks.

'Maybe Michael Charles,' says Eileen, looking at her mother. 'What do you think, Mam?'

'Michael Charles Robinson,' says Mary, scrutinising every detail of the baby's face. 'Dad'll love that. Isn't he beautiful?'

'I can't believe he's mine,' says Eileen, giving him a kiss. 'Wait till Dad and Charlie get home.'

A short time later the front door opens and in walks Mike. Mary is waiting for him, beaming.

'What are you looking so cheerful about?' he asks.

She grabs his hand and leads him to the bedroom. 'Come and meet your grandson, Michael Charles Robinson.'

'You OK, love?' asks Mike, kissing Eileen on the

forehead.

'Yes, Dad.' Bursting with pride, she pulls the blanket back from the baby's face.

'Hello, little fella.' Mike gives him a kiss. 'He's beautiful, just like you, Eileen.'

Then they hear another voice. 'Where is everyone?' calls Charlie.

'In here, son.' Mike pops his head round the door. His expression – that, and a strong smell of Dettol – is enough for Charlie to guess what's happened.

Eileen offers him the baby. 'Here's your little nephew, Michael Charles.'

'Hello there, little one,' says Charlie. 'Welcome to the world.' He examines the baby more closely. 'Plenty of hair, hasn't he?' He glances at Mike. 'A lot more than his granddad, any road.'

Eventually Mike, Mary and Charlie drag themselves off for their tea, leaving Eileen and the baby to rest. Mike is smiling broadly to himself.

'What are you grinning at?' asks Charlie.

'Thank God the baby didn't inherit his dad's ears,' says Mike. 'Our poor Eileen might not have been able to push him out.'

The first visitors soon arrive and are followed by a constant stream of people throughout the evening. The crying baby keeps Charlie awake all night, but he'd better get used to it. It's going to be like this for a while.

Up at Castle Hill Denise is really concerned about Eve. 'I thought she was improving,' she tells Charlie, 'but they wouldn't let me see her yesterday.'

'Don't worry,' he says. 'I'm sure she'll be fine.'

But when Denise goes to visit her friend the following day she is confronted by an empty bed. 'Where's Eve?' she asks a nurse in panic.

'I'm so sorry, dear. Dreadful news, I'm afraid. Eve died peacefully in her sleep a couple of hours ago.'

Denise is numb with shock, haunted by Eve's lovely face, unable to believe her friend has passed away. To make matters worse, nobody comes to see her over the next few days. She's in a dreadful state, particularly when the nurses ask kindly, 'No visitor today, Denise?'

Next time Bob arrives on the ward, he finds Denise sobbing her heart out.

'What's up?' he asks anxiously. 'Come on, Denise, you can tell me.'

'It's Eve,' she wails. 'She died last week.'

'Oh, Denise. I'm so sorry.'

'Where is everyone? Where's Mam? Where's Dad? You've all forgotten about me. I just sit here on my own day after day. I've not seen Charlie either. I suppose he's found a new girlfriend.'

'It's not that at all,' says Bob. 'He sends his love. Of course he wants to visit. He's just too knackered. He's doing lots of overtime, and Eileen's new baby is keeping him awake all night.'

'That's just an excuse. He's not interested in me. I'm sure he's seeing someone else.'

'That's not true. It's just hard for us to to get up here. It's not because we don't love you.'

'I want to come home,' shouts Denise, tears streaming down her face.

'Don't be silly. You have to get better first.'

'I don't care. I'm coming home and no one is going to stop me!'

'Don't upset yourself.' Bob gives her a hug. 'I'm sure we can organise ourselves to visit more often.' He stays as long as he can, but he still can't get her to change her mind. Reluctantly he turns to leave. 'I'll be back tomorrow night. I'll bring Charlie with me, too.'

When he gets home Bob tells his parents what Denise is threatening. 'I know it's tough for a teenage girl,' says Jim, 'but she mustn't walk out. We go as often as we can. We'll just have to try even harder.'

'Her friend Eve has died and that's affected her. But she's mad with Charlie as well. He hasn't been up there recently. Overtime, you know, as well as the new baby.'

'Don't worry, son. Mam and I will go tomorrow night and talk some sense into her.'

Next day Barbara is alone in the house when in walks Denise.

'Denise love,' she says. 'What on earth are you doing here? You can't just walk out of hospital.'

'I can't stand it any more, Mam. Stuck there on my own every day.'

'Dad'll go mad. Please go back, sweetheart. Please.'

Nothing will persuade her. Sarah is first home. She runs to her sister and gives her a hug, then just sits holding her hand. Bob is next in. 'I knew it,' he says. 'It's no good, Denise. You've got to go back.'

Denise starts crying again, just as Jim walks through the door. 'What the hell?' he says. 'Get your coat on, Missy. I'm taking you back to hospital now.'

'No, Dad. No. I won't go back. I won't.'

'Shall I try fetching Charlie?' Bob whispers to Jim. 'Perhaps he can persuade her.'

He dashes round to the Robinsons and raps on the door. 'Is Charlie in, Mrs Robinson?'

'Certainly, Bob. Come in.' Mary calls through to the kitchen. 'Charlie, Bob's here.'

'Hi, mate,' says Charlie. 'What's up?'

'It's our Denise. She's walked out of Castle Hill. She's back home and won't listen to a thing we say.'

'Poor lass,' says Mary.

'She refuses point blank to go back,' continues Bob. 'Do you think there's anything you could do to help?'

'I can try,' says Charlie. 'I just want to see her well again.'

'Do your best to persuade her,' says Bob, as they walk back to the house.

'I will, Bob. But you know how strong willed she is. Do you think she'll really listen to me?'

When Denise claps eyes on Charlie she buries her head in her hands. She really doesn't want him to see her like this.

At Bob's prompting, Charlie takes her by the hand

and leads her into the front room. 'Denise, you know you're improving,' he says as soon as he gets her alone. 'You'll be home for good in a month or so. Please go back to Castle Hill.'

'I miss you,' sobs Denise. 'I miss my family. I miss my friends. Everyone is out and about enjoying themselves while I'm stuck there in the freezing cold. The windows are open all the time, whatever the weather. It's too much. I can't bear it any more.'

Charlie put his arms around her, plants a kiss on her forehead and wipes away her tears.

She looks up at him, yearning in her eyes. 'I've always had feelings for you, Charlie. You know that, don't you?'

'I do. I've got feelings for you as well. I'm only just beginning to realise it.'

'Are you seeing anyone?'

'Fat chance,' he smiles. 'I'm jiggered. I'm working overtime most nights, and little Michael Charles is keeping me awake with his crying. In fact, I've thought moving up to Castle Hill with you for a bit of peace and quiet.'

'I wish you would,' says Denise, smiling at last. 'How is Eileen? Is she doing OK?'

'Yes, she's coping fine. With Mam's help, of course. Please go back to Castle Hill, Denise. You'll only end up spending longer in there if you don't. We might never get together.'

'I will,' says Denise, 'if you promise to come and see me more often?'

'Of course. Can we tell everyone you'll go back tonight?'

She grips his arm. 'OK.'

Just then Barbara walks through the door. Denise seems to have quietened down, she thinks.

'I think Denise has something to tell you, Mrs. Watson,' says Charlie, glancing encouragingly at her.

'I've decided to go back, Mam.'

'Oh, sweetheart,' says Barbara, giving her a hug. 'I'm so pleased. It's for the best, you know. I'll go tell Dad.' Thanks, she mouths to Charlie.

Later on Bob sees Charlie to the door. 'Thanks for your help, mate.'

'No problem,' says Charlie, putting an arm around Bob's shoulder. 'I'll go up whenever I can. I think such a lot of her, you know.'

'Sorry if Denise caused you any trouble,' mumbles Jim apologetically when he returns his daughter to the ward.

'Don't worry,' says the nurse briskly. 'It's not the first time it's happened and I'm sure it won't be the last. We'll just get her settled back into bed and she'll be fine.'

'Remember, someone will come to visit you every day,' Jim reminds his daughter before he leaves.

But Denise isn't listening. She has only one thing on her mind: *Charlie does have feelings for me after all.*

Back home little Michael Charles is playing up again. Mary is trying to settle him, rocking him gently and tapping him on the back.

'What an evening,' says Charlie, settling down to tell her the story.

'Thank God she's getting better,' says Mary, shaking her head. 'That TB can be a killer. A friend of mine had it, and she died.'

Charlie shudders. 'Don't even think about it. I'm off to bed. Night, Mam.'

One of the lads in the fish house is off to do his National Service. He's none too bright and some of the girls are really winding him up, saying he'll be sent to some horrible imaginary country.

Charlie can't help laughing, but he doesn't like them teasing the poor lad.

'Just ignore them,' he says, 'especially that Maggie. They're just pulling your leg. My friend George has gone to Germany, you know.'

'Are you sure it's safe there?' asks the lad anxiously. 'With the Germans and everything?'

'Course it is,' smiles Charlie. 'We're all friends now. Don't worry, mate. You'll be fine.'

I'll have to make up my mind soon, thinks Charlie. *Fish house and the army or sign on a trawler and join the Royal Naval Reserve. God, it's cold and miserable here. Can I really stand it for the rest of my life?*

Walking home, Mike climbs off his bike and falls in beside him. 'All right, Charl? You've been very quiet today.'

'I'm fine, Dad. Just wondering what to do about National Service.'

'Everyone has to do his two years in the army, lad. There's nothing else for it.'

'I was thinking of the RNR,' says Charlie hesitantly.

'But you have to be a seaman for that.'

'I know, Dad. I'm thinking about going on trawlers.'

'Oh no, son. Not them bloody things. Far too dangerous. Do your time in the army.'

'I haven't decided yet. I need more time to think. I know you hate the idea of trawlers but I want a chance to better myself.'

'I know,' says Mike, with a smile. 'I'm only telling you what I think. You're sensible enough to make up your own mind. Here, push my bike for me, would you?'

Everyone fusses over the baby. Even Charlie picks him up now and again – if he can beat his parents to it. Mary has bought a pram from a neighbour whose child has outgrown it and Eileen loves pushing it down the street.

Pinny-clad, headscarves covering their big curlers, Mrs Booth and Mrs Brown are standing gossiping outside their front doors as usual.

'Just look at her, Else,' whispers Mrs Booth, digging her friend in the ribs. 'No shame.'

'How's the bairn?' she shouts to Eileen.

'Fine thanks.'

'Heard 'owt about the father, Else?' whispers Mrs Booth.

'Nothing. These young'uns don't care nowadays. Not like when I was a girl.'

'Bloody hell, that was a long time ago.'

'Don't be so ruddy cheeky. You're no spring chicken either.'

Mrs Booth readjusts her substantial bosom. 'Do you and your Jack … still have sex?' she asks, her voice fading away conspiratorially.

Mrs Brown looks right, then left, then right again. 'When we were younger, Jack and me could put the kettle on before we started making love and he'd be done before it bloody boiled. Not now, though. He likes a bit more foreplay.'

That gets Mrs Booth's attention. 'How long does … you know ... the whatdyacallit ... the foreplay, last before you, you know, you … actually, you know, do it?'

She moves closer, not wanting to miss a word of the reply.

'Well,' whispers Mrs Brown. 'If we started in June, he might be ready by December. Even that'd be pushing it, mind.' She slaps her knees, roaring with laughter. Eventually she recovers enough to speak. 'Do you and your Len still, you know, do it?'

Mrs Booth shivers theatrically. 'The other Friday night I went in to fetch something from the back kitchen while he was getting his bath. He jumped out of the water, grabbed hold of me and tore off all my clothes.'

'He never did,' says Mrs Brown. Now for the juicy bit. 'Did he do it, then?'

'Did he hell. "I've finished with the water," he said. "Get in while it's hot." Then he went upstairs to get dressed.'

They start laughing again, both enjoying the banter.

'Now that lass's brother Charlie,' says Mrs Booth. 'He's a nice lad. Bloody good looking, too.'

'You're right there.'

'No point giving him the glad eye, love. You've no chance there. Even the coalman would turn you down. You'll have to keep paying for your nutty slack. Not like Mrs North. She gets two free bags a week. No wonder her sheets are black as hell when she takes them down the wash house.'

'You know,' says Mrs Brown. 'Every night before we go to sleep, my Jack tells me how beautiful I am.'

'Really?' says Mrs Booth sceptically. 'Did he ever get those new specs?'

Mrs Brown ignores her, checking again for eavesdroppers. 'You know him down our terrace, died recently. Mrs Spencer's husband. Did you know I laid him out?'

'Is that so?' asks Mrs Booth, eager for a bit of gossip to trade.

'Well, you know he went unexpectedly at home. But what I bet you didn't know is that … he died … on the job. Apparently he liked it every Saturday night. According to Mrs Spencer, he climbed on top as usual. After a bit she thought this isn't like him, he's taking an age. Well, he'd only gone and bloody died.'

'Get away,' laughs Mrs Booth. 'Was he, y'know, still inside her?'

'Yes. She says he hadn't been that hard in years.' They can hardly speak for laughing. 'That's not all, though. He never got chance to tell her whether he wanted to be buried or cremated.'

'What did she do?' asks Mrs Booth.

'She had him cremated,' says Mrs Brown.

'But what if he wanted to be buried?'

'She'd thought of that. She brought the ashes home and buried 'em.'

Still giggling, they turn and go inside.

Joe returns from his latest trip to find that Vince has moved in with his mother. She seems happy enough on the surface, but Joe can sense something isn't right.

He tackles her about it the following morning after Vince has left for work. 'Everything OK, Mam?'

Pat forces a tired smile. 'Yes, Joe. Everything's fine.'

'Wedding still on then?'

'Of course, next time you're home.'

Pat turns away, but Joe doesn't believe her. He walks over and turns her to face him. 'Is there something you're not telling me, Mam?'

'Everyone has their up and downs, Joe.'

'What are the downs?'

'We just argue sometimes, that's all. I do love him, though.'

'Are you sure that's everything?' says Joe, beginning to

lose his temper. 'Come on, Mam. You can tell me.'

Pat says nothing, just puts her coat on. 'Don't worry, Joe,' she says eventually. 'Everything will be fine.' She gives him a kiss. 'See you later. Hope you make good money from the catch.'

With that, she marches out the door, leaving Joe to wonder what's really going on.

Joe spends the day with some of the crew and eventually – rather the worse for drink – he decides to call on Charlie.

'Hi, mate,' says Charlie. 'Looks like you've had a good time.' He thrusts little Michael Charles towards his friend. 'Meet the new addition to our family.'

'What a smasher,' says Joe. 'Congratulations, Eileen … all of you'.

'Let's go through to the front room for a chat.'

They get themselves settled in the armchairs. 'Mam and Vince are getting married next time I'm home,' says Joe. 'I'm bothered about her, though.'

'Why? I thought you said everything was good between them.'

'I did. Something's wrong, though, Charlie. I just know it.'

'Maybe you're imagining things.'

'I don't think so,' says Joe. 'We'll just have to wait and see, I suppose. What's your news?' Charlie tells him about Denise. 'Is it on with you two, then?'

'Depends what you mean. I think a lot about her. Well, more than that really. But we've plenty of time. We're too young to get serious.'

'Remember Denise is two years older than you. She probably thinks a bit differently.'

'Perhaps. By the way, I've some other news. I'm thinking about going on trawlers.'

'Wow, that's a surprise. You'd need to start with a couple of trips in the galley, then sign on as a deck learner. I'm hoping to move up to spare hand now I've more experience. That's the next step on the ladder, although lots of fishermen never get further than that. Just a few make it to bosun, mate or skipper. You have to go to Nautical College and pass your certificates, and even that doesn't guarantee promotion. You need luck and knowledge of the fishing grounds. Once the skipper leaves dock it's up to him to return with a good catch. But if you do make it, it means a big difference in your income and standing.'

'That's all I need to hear. I want a job with prospects. I've made up my mind.'

'You'll definitely find it hard at first, but you'll soon get used to it. The crew will help you out, even if they do take the piss now and again.'

'I can stand that. I'll give the fish house another month or so, then I'll pack it in and try to sign on a trawler.'

'I might be able to help you there. I'll introduce you to the Lord Line runner, a chap called Jack. Now, how about a night out?'

'Fine, but nothing too heavy, with work and everything.'

'Don't worry, Charlie. I'll contact Bob. Leave it all to me.'

Back at the house the atmosphere is bristling with tension. Emboldened by drink, Joe marches straight up to Vince. 'What's going on?' he asks.

'No business of yours, son,' barks Vince.

'Don't call me "son",' snaps Joe. 'Do you and Mam have some kind of problem? She looks scared stiff.'

'Scared? What the hell are you on about?'

'Just look at her.'

'She says you've been asking questions about us. It's nothing to do with you.'

'She's my mother and this is my home. You're not part of our family yet. '

What Vince lacks in height he makes up for in breadth, and he puts himself right in Joe's face. 'Butt out, you nosey little arsehole.'

Pat tries to pull them apart but Vince swats her aside. *That does it*, thinks Joe. He aims a punch at Vince but Pat tries to step between them. Vince pushes her harder this time and she falls to the floor. Joe catches him on the nose, drawing blood, but Vince responds with a right to the eye, following it up with a succession of blows, deflecting all Joe's attempts to retaliate.

Pat picks herself up, then runs across the terrace screaming for help. She hammers on the Robinsons' door. Mike and Charlie have heard the commotion and rush to follow her. By now Vince is completely out of control, raining punches on the defenceless Joe. 'What in hell's name do you think you're doing?' roars Mike, grabbing hold of Joe's assailant.

Vince swings vainly, while Mike lands a couple of punches in his own right, then hauls him to the door.

Pat has clearly been struck in the face. Meanwhile Joe has a black eye and a cut lip. 'You OK? asks Charlie. 'Just wait here. I'm off to help Dad.'

The powerfully built Mike has Vince in a headlock – no longer struggling but cursing like a trooper. Between them he and Charlie half drag, half frogmarch the miscreant to the end of the terrace. Joe arrives carrying a heap of clothes and tosses them over. 'Get your arse out of here, you woman beater. Piss off and don't come back.'

'Just leave,' says Mike, pointing Vince up the street. 'We don't want any more trouble.'

Pat's erstwhile fiancé slinks away, glancing back nervously to make sure he isn't being followed.

'Thanks, Mr Robinson,' says Joe, sticking out his hand. 'I really appreciate your help.'

'No problem,' says Mike. 'Time to get you cleaned up, I think.'

Pat and Charlie are watching from the doorway. 'Oh, Joe!' says Pat. 'Just look at your face. Let me get some warm water and a flannel.'

'Thanks, Mam. Had he hit you before?'

She won't say anything while I'm around, thinks Charlie. *Time I was off.* 'Night, both.'

Then the floodgates open.

'Vince is a real Jekyll and Hyde,' Pat tells Joe. 'He was just jealous at first, then he started putting his fist in my face, losing his rag over nothing. He always apologised afterwards. Always said it would never happen again. He promised he'd change after we were married.'

'Well, it's definitely not going to happen again,' says Joe, putting his arm around Pat's shoulder. 'The bastard's gone for good.'

That puts an end to the lads' night out, but the following day Bob and Charlie walk Joe down the dock to sail on the evening tide.

'Hi, Joe,' shouts one of his crewmates as they climb aboard. 'Bloody hell, you're in a state. What happened to you?'

'Walked into a door,' laughs Joe, and it goes no further. Black eyes and thick lips are no novelty among fishermen. They often get into fights during their short time ashore, usually under the influence of drink.

Joe takes Charlie and Bob to the fo'c's'le, then down the stairs to the accommodation. There are bunks all round the cabin – some level with the seating and some above – all in a very tight space. In the middle is a fireplace with a metal surround and a grid in front of it to hold back the coals when the ship is rolling around in heavy weather.

I could soon be living somewhere like this, thinks Charlie, showing more interest than before.

'This is a big improvement on the *Lord Middleton*,' says Bob.

'Definitely,' agrees Joe. 'The only problem is running aft to go on watch or eat when it's really blowing hard. That can be a real pain in the backside. You get soaked if you time it wrong and a wave catches you. You can end up sliding along the deck on your arse.'

'Sounds bloody dangerous to me,' says Charlie.

'No one bothers. It's just part of a fisherman's life.'

By now most of the crew are gathered in the fo'c's'le, chatting over bottles of beer. It's fun to listen to them pulling Joe's leg and talking about their exploits ashore.

'Me and my Maud had a real good time in the Paragon,' says one of the older blokes.

'Maud?' Bob whispers. 'Isn't that George's little beauty?'

'Reckon so,' sniggers Charlie.

'We're letting go, lads,' comes a call from the upper deck.

131

'Better scarper unless you want to sail with us.'

'No chance,' says Bob. 'Let's do as he says.'

Back on deck they all shake hands, then Charlie and Bob climb down from the trawler. 'Don't worry,' shouts Charlie from the quayside. 'Dad and I will look out for your mam. We'll make sure she has no trouble from you-know-who.'

'Thanks, mate,' calls Joe. 'Appreciate it. If he does turn up, tell your old man to give him the same again.'

They all laugh. Charlie and Bob give Joe one final wave, then saunter off the dock.

Back home, Mike is sitting listening to the wireless.

'Joe's asked if we'd look out for his mam,' says Charlie. 'Otherwise there's only his Uncle John. He visits occasionally but he doesn't know anything about the situation.'

'No problem, son. Tell Pat to get in touch right away if she sees that shit again. We'll kick his arse.'

Charlie walks across the terrace and knocks nervously at the door. He still has strong feelings for Pat.

'Hello, Charlie,' she says. 'This is a surprise. Come on in.'

He follows her inside. *No doubt about it*, s*he really is gorgeous*.

'Please thank Mike for his help,' she says. 'You too, Charlie. I don't know what would have happened without you. I really do appreciate it.'

'Joe has asked me and Dad to keep an eye on you, just to make sure there's no more trouble.'

'I haven't seen hide or hair of him since. I made a big mistake, Charlie. He seemed such a nice bloke at first. Obviously not, though. And Charlie, I've got to apologise for what happened between us.'

'No need,' says Charlie insincerely. 'No harm done.'

He still has only one thing on his mind, and he's pretty sure Pat feels the same way.

'Joe's been telling me about Denise,' says Pat hastily.

'Yes, she's back in hospital now.' *I wonder if Joe's said anything about her and me*? 'She's doing fine.'

'Better go, I suppose. Let us know if you see Vince again.'

'I will.'

As Pat reaches across Charlie to open the front door, she comes so close he can smell her perfume. That's it. He can't resist any longer and leans forward to kiss her. She closes her eyes and seems about to respond, then abruptly she pulls away.

'No, we shouldn't. It's not right.'

'Of course it's right if we care for each other.' Charlie tries again to pull her to him but she drags herself free.

'I'm sorry, Charlie. It's over. Please don't make it hard for me. Our relationship has no future. You know that yourself deep down. Joe would be heartbroken if he found out. You're his best friend. He'd feel we'd betrayed him.'

Disconsolately, Charlie apologises and walks way. He stops for a moment, turns, but then nods and carries on home. *She's right*, he thinks. *I'd hate it if Joe found out*.

Pat watches him go, then closes the door and leans against it for a moment. She shuts her eyes and sighs. Only she knows how near she came to relenting.

CHAPTER 10
GYPSY ROSE

On Friday 11 October Charlie and Bob are having a quiet drink near home. It's the week of Hull Fair, with visitors arriving from all over Yorkshire, and they decide to go for a laugh.

'It's not that late,' says Bob. 'How about taking our Sarah with us? She'd love it.'

'Fine, Bob. Let's go and see what your mam and dad say.'

Barbara and Jim agree at once. They can't afford to send Sarah to the fair more than once a year, they know Charlie and Bob will look after her – and she jumps at the chance for a second visit.

The two boys put Sarah between them and slide their arms through hers. Constantly looking up and smiling at Charlie, she feels a real grown-up. She knows why Denise can't leave him alone.

As they get nearer the rides in the main part of the fairground, they can hear music and the buzz of conversation. Stalls are selling hamburgers, candy floss or toys, with a few offering the chance to win a cuddly toy or some other small prize.

'I'll treat you both to a hamburger,' says Charlie. He grabs a kiss-me-quick hat from one of the stalls, laughing as he plants it on Sarah's head. She turns blood red when he and Bob both kiss her on the cheek, but she's loving every minute.

At a sort of coconut shy, they try and knock some tins from a shelf for a couple of pennies a go. Eventually Charlie manages to clear the lot. His prize is a small teddy bear and he offers it to Sarah.

'He's lovely, Charlie,' she says, kissing him on the cheek. 'I think I'll call him Chuck.'

They all laugh. 'Chuck,' says Bob, slapping Charlie on

the back. 'That's a good one.'

As they reach the rides the waltzers are just coming to a halt. 'Come on,' shouts Bob, and they all get in, laughing as the car begins to move. A showman comes over and gives them a big spin, making the car go even faster and leaving Sarah crying with laughter.

They try several rides, then roam around for a while. 'That's it for me,' says Bob eventually, looking rather pale. 'I'll be sick if I go on anything else.'

'What about the big wheel?' asks Sarah.

'Don't worry,' says Charlie. 'I'll take you.'

They climb aboard and slowly the wheel starts to turn. As they climb higher, the sounds grow fainter until, at the very top, they can hardly hear the music. The wheel stops briefly, allowing them to see the fairground below and the bright lights of the city beyond. Sarah starts pointing out different streets and buildings, clinging tightly to Charlie when the wheel begins to move again. He smiles, then looks up into the sky, admiring the lovely clear night.

After two more circuits they climb down and rejoin Bob. 'Are we done, then?' asks Charlie. 'Time to go?'

'I think I've had enough,' says Bob. 'I'm still feeling a bit queasy.'

'Oh, Bob,' says Sarah, hugging her teddy bear. 'Don't be such a baby.'

Charlie puts his arms around them both. 'I think we've all had enough for tonight. Come on, it's getting late. Let's head home.'

Their way out takes them past a beautifully decorated caravan, the board outside showing photographs of famous people with one 'Gypsy Rose Lee, Fortune Teller to the Stars'. Sitting in the doorway is a wrinkled old woman in typical gypsy dress, her skin dark and her eyes even darker. 'Come on in, lads,' she shouts. 'I'll tell you your fortune. Two bob a time.'

'Come on, Charl,' says Bob, pushing him forward. 'What do you say, for a laugh?'

Charlie and Sarah both agree, and in they go.

'Sit down,' says Gypsy Rose. 'Which of you two young

men would like to go first?'

Charlie and Bob exchange glances, and Bob volunteers.

Gypsy Rose takes him to the far end of the caravan and sits him at a table bearing a pack of strange cards and a crystal ball. She draws a curtain across, plunging them into semi-darkness. Gazing at him, she holds his hands for a few seconds, then closes her eyes. Eventually she opens them again, expression grave.

'I see you'll have a good life, young man. You will experience the occasional setback, but you'll always find a way to cope with any problems.' She pauses. 'I also see sadness in your life, but this will only make you stronger. You will know when you find the right woman. I see a happy family. Do you have a very close friend connected to the sea?'

Bob went in thinking this was all a bit of a game but now he realises the woman is serious. She isn't just stringing him along.

'I suppose so,' he says, thinking of Joe.

Gypsy Rose falls silent for while, then ends with a few trivialities. She squeezes Bob's hand as he gives her the money and finally draws back the curtain. 'Your turn now, sonny.'

Bob winks at Charlie as they pass.

Again Gypsy Rose sits Charlie down and shuts the curtain, then she smiles at him and takes his hand. She stares at it for a while, then looks up at him again.

'I see a strong young man in his element in wide open spaces. They make you feel free. Do you have any connection with the stars?'

'Maybe,' he says, mystified.

She bends even closer over his hand, then suddenly releases it. 'I'm sorry. I can't concentrate. Perhaps you could come back some other time?'

Why the hell has she stopped? thinks Charlie. Still, he starts withdrawing some change from his pocket.

'No, sonny. No charge. Sorry, I'm not feeling too well.'

'Thanks anyway,' says Charlie, pulling back the curtain and going to rejoin his friends.

'What did you think?' says Bob, outside the caravan. 'Is it all just bullshit?'

'Don't use rude words,' says Sarah, tugging at his arm.

'She didn't tell me a thing,' says Charlie. 'She just said she wasn't feeling too well.'

'Did you pay her, Charl?'

'No. She wouldn't take any money. What a strange carry-on.'

Laughing, they make their way home, taking it in turns to try on Sarah's hat.

'Thanks for taking me to the fair,' says Sarah to Charlie. 'And for the teddy bear. Wait till Denise finds out. She'll be so jealous.'

They're still laughing as they say goodnight, but as Charlie walks home he can't stop thinking about Gypsy Rose and her strange question.

Charlie is still worried that Joe might find out about his short-lived relationship with Pat. Although he tries to smile and say hello, he's always embarrassed when he sees her. It's so hard to forget the very intimate times they spent together.

Bob and Charlie are chatting on the doorstep one day when Pat comes walking down the terrace. She knows Charlie isn't happy with her, and things are even more awkward now Vince is out of the picture.

'Hi, lads,' she says.

'Hi, Mrs Harrison,' says Bob brightly.

'Hi, Mrs Harrison,' mumbles Charlie, blushing and trying his hardest to avoid eye contact.

Better not prolong the conversation, thinks Pat. 'Joe'll be home soon,' she says, heading for the door.

'Great,' says Bob. 'We were just organising a night out.'

'Joe will like that. See you both.'

Something's not quite right here, thinks Bob. He looks at Charlie. 'What is it, mate? You never said a word to Mrs Harrison and you've turned crimson. Have you two had an argument?'

Charlie shakes his head. 'Of course not. Why would I fall out with Mrs Harrison?'

'Charlie, we've been friends for years. I know there's something up.'

Charlie hates telling lies and uncharacteristically starts to stutter. ' I–I can't tell you.'

'Come on, Charlie. What's been going on?' Bob knows Charlie has a crush on Pat Harrison but he's never really thought any more about it.

'You have to promise you'll never tell anyone.'

'Tell them what? I'd never pass on anything you told me in confidence'

'Pa … Mrs Harrison. Oh shit, Bob, I don't know how to tell you. I, we, we've been having ...'

'Oh Charlie,' Bob interrupts him. 'Don't tell me you and her. Is that what you're trying to say. She's Joe's mother. You're the last person I'd expect to do something like that. '

'I know.' Charlie can't look Bob in the eye. 'I'm so ashamed of myself. It's all over now. Has been for a while.'

'How the hell did this happen, Charlie? It's not like you at all.'

'I don't know, Bob. I'd change it if I could. Whatever happens now, she has her life and I have mine. Please don't say anything to Joe, or anyone else. It's just between you and me.

'I'm amazed. It's not for me to judge, though. I'll never say a word. You know that. If you say it's over, that's it as far as I'm concerned.'

'Thanks, Bob. I had such strong feelings for her, even though she broke things off. Still do, I can't explain it. I never wanted to hurt Joe, though.'

'He'll never find out from me. I know what you're like. I just don't know why these bloody women keep throwing themselves at you.' Bob bursts out laughing. 'I wouldn't mind some of it too.'

'It's quite different with me and Denise, Bob. You do know that, don't you? I'd never hurt her.'

'I do, Charlie. I've forgotten what you said already.'

'Come on,' says Charlie, smiling. 'I'll walk with you to the end of terrace.'

Slouching along, hands in pockets, Bob looks across at his friend. 'You haven't been feeling around anywhere else, have you?'

'Don't be daft. Who are you thinking of?'

'Only your pal Mrs Booth.'

That makes them both chortle.

Bloody hell, thinks Bob, walking home. *Who'd have thought it?* Mrs Harrison and Charlie.'

For the next few weeks Charlie, Joe and Bob have no chance to go out. Between work and hospital visits, Charlie and Bob have hardly any time to themselves, and when Joe is home between trips he's out and about with his crewmates and their wives. He invited Pat along one time and she hit it off straight away with the only bachelor among them, a guy called David. He's a good-looking fella, around her age. Apparently, he'd lived with a girl for a while, but she was messing around behind his back while he was away at sea. Although Pat always says she'd never marry another trawlermen, David has really impressed her, and they've been seeing quite a bit of each other.

Charlie has finally handed in his notice. Mike pleaded with him to change his mind but he refused to budge. 'I don't want to go in the army,' he insisted. 'And I want a job with prospects.'

On his final day at the fish house all the girls are sorry to see him go. 'Are you sure you won't marry me?' asks Big Maggie, giving him a kiss.

'Only if you promise to lose some weight first, or if you come into money.'

'You're a little devil,' she laughs, grabbing hold of him and squeezing tight. 'I love you, though.'

Irish Rose comes over and gives him a long hug. Then she stands back and looks at him. 'You take care now, mi love.'

'I will, Rose,' he says, with a smile.

'Make sure you leave some for us,' shout their pals.

Charlie is a good worker and no one has a bad word to say about him. 'Best of luck,' says one of the bosses, shaking him by the hand. 'We're really sorry to see you go. I'm sure your dad here will let us know how you get on. And remember, you'll always be welcome back if things don't work out.'

'Thanks,' says Charlie. 'I appreciate that. I've enjoyed my time here.'

Father and son leave together, with the girls shouting their farewells, blowing kisses and coming to give Charlie one last hug. Walking home, Mike puts an arm around his shoulder. 'I'm proud of you, lad. You can change your mind any time, you know. No one will think any less of you'

'I know, Dad. But I've made up my mind. I want to go on trawlers.'

Mike smiles. 'Stubborn, just like your mother. But I love her and I love you too. You have my blessing, son.'

Joe is home, and next morning he and Charlie go down the dock as planned.

'Well, Charlie. This is Jack's office. Let's go inside.'

I know I'll only be the galley lad, thinks Charlie apprehensively. *But I don't mind that as long as I get a start.*

'Hello, Jack! Meet my mate, Charlie Robinson. He wants to go to sea. Anything for him?'

'How old are you, son?' asks the ship's runner.

'Seventeen and a half,' says Charlie, standing tall to make a good impression.

'Ever been to sea at all, pleasuring or anything?'

'No,' says Charlie. He knows lads who went 'pleasuring' on trawlers during the school holidays with their father or brothers. Some decided to make a career of trawling but others were put off for life.

'OK, son. We might have a spot for a galley lad in a few days time. Come and see me next Friday morning, ten o'clock sharp.'

'Thanks a lot,' grins Charlie. 'I'll be here.'

'And, Joe. You're sailing Monday.'

'Fine, Jack. Early morning tide?'

'That's right,' says the runner, beckoning a waiting fisherman to come inside and sign on.

Charlie and Joe say goodbye, then stand looking at the trawlers in the dock. 'This'll be you soon,' says Joe.

'Suppose so,' says Charlie. He can't believe what he's just done. He'll soon be a fisherman.

'Don't worry,' says Joe, slapping him on the back. 'You'll

be fine.'

They make their way home, Joe telling Charlie exactly what to expect, and get back to a surprise. George is waiting outside Charlie's door. He looks great. He seems even taller and his hair is now longer than ever.

He greets them with a hug. 'What have you two been doing, then? No more nights out with them Paragon girls, I hope? You won't believe what I've been up to in Germany. Talk about frauleins! I've experienced all shapes and sizes. I've even learned to speak a bit of German.'

'Like what?' says Charlie. 'Frankfurter?'

'Good to have you back, George,' laughs Joe. 'Still your usual self, I see.'

'I know,' says George. 'Let's go round and surprise Bob.'

'Come in, lads,' says Barbara, when they get to the house. 'Bob won't be long. Good news, Charlie love. Denise might be out of hospital in a few days. She's so excited! She told me to keep quiet because she wanted to tell you herself, but I just couldn't wait.'

'That's great news, Mrs. Watson. I'll go and see her tomorrow. I won't let on that you spilled the beans.'

'Thanks, she'd kill me if she knew.'

Joe and George both wink at Charlie, then Bob walks through the door, cheerful as ever.

'Well, well. Just look what the wind's blown in.' He gives George a hug. 'Nice to see you, mate. How's Germany?'

'He's going to tell us later,' laughs Joe. 'He's been very busy. Undercover operations, if you know what I mean.'

Bob nips upstairs to get changed, then they head to Joe's so he can do the same. When they walk in, Pat and David are sitting holding hands.

'Hello, Dave,' says Joe. 'Say hello to my mates, Charlie, Bob and George. Charlie's off on his first trip soon.'

'Nice to meet you,' says Dave, offering his hand.

'George is in the army. He's just back from Germany on leave.'

George rakes his fingers through his hair, then reaches

out to shake hands. 'Hi, mate,' he says. 'What were you two doing? Making out?'

'Making out?' splutters Pat.

'What? Did I say the wrong thing?'

'Trust George,' grins Joe. 'He never changes.'

'And last but not least, here's Bob. He's just been sprucing himself up for the girls.'

Charlie is glad when they finally get away. No matter how he tries, he can't bear the thought of Pat with another man. It was bad enough with Vince and this is no better.

'Cheer up, Charlie lad,' says Joe as they climb aboard the bus. 'Come and enjoy yourself. You'll be rolling round on a bloody trawler soon enough.'

The Loco is packed with young ones, all drinking and having a good time. The lads find themselves a table next to five or six girls, and once the barmaid has delivered their drinks they soon get chatting. As usual live music is blaring out from a band on the small stage, and some of the drinkers are getting up and singing.

Suddenly George jumps up. 'I think I'll join them and give you a tune.'

'You?' says Joe. 'You must be joking! You can't sing! You're never going up on stage?'

'Yeah, I am. Just watch me.' George runs a hand through his hair, smiling at the girls who are cheering him on.

'This'll be a laugh,' Charlie whispers to Bob.

All eyes are on George. He speaks to the pianist, turns to face the crowd, takes hold of the mike, then gives a slight nod. The band begins to play, George runs both hands through his hair, looks directly at the girls and starts to sing. The room falls silent for a moment, but the sound of his voice brings an immediate burst of applause.

'Bloody hell,' says Charlie. 'He's good. Just look at him. He's a frigging professional.'

The audience all join in and by the end everyone is whistling, clapping and shouting for more. George just loves all the attention. He gives the pianist another title and sings a couple more songs before returning to the table.

'You were wonderful,' sigh the girls next to them.

'That was great,' says Charlie. 'How long have you been singing?'

'We went to a bar in Germany and just started singing along. A few people were doing solos. There was a chap who spoke good English sitting nearby and he suggested I have a go. I did and I really enjoyed it. It gets me a lot of attention from the frauleins.'

'What are the women like there?' asks Bob.

'Well,' says George. 'This is just one of my many experiences.'

They all settle down to listen – even the girls.

'When we first arrived, some of our mates told us about certain areas, if you know what I mean, where a certain type of woman hangs out. So off we went one night, just for a jolly. Anyway, this woman came up to me and asked if I wanted to take her home. Of course I said yes. She was very nice. We went to her flat, one thing led to another and we finished up in bed.'

The girls are giggling, listening intently.

'Anyway, in the early hours I got up and got dressed. "Hey you, Englishman!" she shouted as I opened the door. "How about ze marks."

'"Eight out of ten," I said, and scarpered.'

They're all in stitches. 'Bloody hell,' says Charlie. 'We thought you were being serious.'

'But I was,' says George, baffled, making them laugh even more.

As usual George spends the evening playing the field, while Joe and Bob are making good progress with two of the girls at the next table. Only Charlie is hanging back.

'Look,' says Bob. 'You're helping Denise through a rough patch just now, and once she gets out of hospital you can decide whether or not to take things further. That shouldn't stop you tonight, though. I wouldn't let on.'

'Thanks, Bob. I didn't want you getting the wrong idea.'

Charlie starts pursuing a quiet little blonde, so at the end of the night they each have a girl to take home. Charlie and his conquest walk home chatting. When they get to her house she backs up against the wall and he moves to give her a kiss.

She puts her arms round him. 'You're so nice, Charlie. Not like them noisy friends of yours.'

He kisses her again, but when he tries to touch her breasts she brushes his hand away. Undaunted, he gives it another go, with exactly the same result. *I'm not getting anywhere here*, he thinks.

'Stop it, Charlie. I'm not that sort of girl. I want to find someone who really loves me before I start any of that.' They stay outside for quite a while. 'I have to go in now,' she says eventually. 'Thanks for walking me home.' She smiles. 'Sorry to disappoint you, I hope you understand. Perhaps we'll see each other again sometime.'

Unlikely, thinks Charlie. 'I'm off on trawlers, so I won't be around for a while.' I'm sure she'll meet Mr Right one day, but it won't be me.

Joe has sailed again, Bob is back at work, and George is preoccupied with the girl from the Loco. One day Charlie receives a message telling him to come round to Bob's as soon as he can. Denise opens the door, hazel eyes sparkling. She's made a real effort to impress and looks quite beautiful. 'Hello, Charlie Robinson,' she smiles, kissing him on the cheek. 'Come on in.'

'Denise, you're home. I'm so glad. You look gorgeous.'

'I couldn't wait to get out of hospital,' says Denise, hugging him. 'It seems like a lifetime since I went in there.'

'Well, you're back now, fit and well.'

'I'm OK. I can't go out yet. I have to convalesce for a week or so, then I might get the all clear.'

'That's great. I've a surprise for you, too. I've handed in my notice. I'm signing up as galley boy on a trawler. I should be sailing Friday.'

'Oh, Charlie!' cries Denise. 'You can't do that. I'll miss you terribly.'

He takes her hand and leads her into the front room. 'It's no good. I've made up my mind. We've got a couple of days before I go away. We can spend them however you like.'

144

Barbara is out shopping, Jim and Bob are at work, and Sarah is at school, so the house is empty. Denise reaches for him and they kiss. Suddenly her feelings overwhelm her. Her body craves his touch. She strokes his hair, caresses his face. 'I want you, Charlie.' She looks deep into his eyes, pulling him closer. 'I've waited so long for this moment.'

'I want you too, but we can't. Your mam might come back.'

'She'll be a while yet. Please, Charlie. Please.'

In her excitement, Denise is perspiring heavily, her body stiffening at his touch. It's her first time and she moans with pleasure as he explores her intimate places. Tentatively she touches him, gasping at his hardness and pulling him closer still.

Suddenly they hear the front door open. They jump apart, Denise trying desperately to straighten her clothes. A few seconds later in walks Barbara. 'Oh hello, Charlie!' she smiles. 'Doesn't she look well?'

'She looks great,' he mumbles.

'Could Charlie stay for tea?' asks Denise, peeved at the interruption.

'Of course, if he wants to,' says Barbara. She realises she's embarrassed them and turns to leave the room.

'Thanks, but no,' says Charlie. 'I've got to get back.'

'You'll be coming round later, won't you?' says Denise.

'Of course.' He gives her a wink. 'About seven, if that's OK with you.'

Charlie has a lot on his mind as he makes his way home. *One more day and I'm off down the dock.* It's no good, he's still worried about going to sea. He's also confused by his feelings for Denise. He thinks a lot about her, true enough, but he still doesn't feel the quite same spark he experienced with Pat. *We got a bit carried away there*, he admits to himself. *I wonder what'll happen tonight.*

Back home, little Michael Charles is acting up and getting all the attention as usual. Eileen is turning out to be a natural mother and has won over most of the neighbours, although some of the women are still a bit sniffy. Charlie sits quietly, watching his mum and sister fussing over the baby.

'All right, son,' says Mike. 'No second thoughts?'

'No, Dad,' says Charlie. 'I'm OK.'

'I miss you at the factory. The girls are always asking about you.'

'I miss them too,' says Charlie wistfully. He stands up. 'I'm just off to see Denise. I promised I'd go round.'

'Give her my best wishes,' says Mike. 'The girl's had a tough time of it recently.'

Denise meets Charlie at the front door. He goes to says hello to Bob and the family, then she takes him through into the front room. She puts on some music and they sit and chat for a while.

'Do you really want us to be together?' she asks eventually. 'I sometimes worry that you just feel sorry for me.'

'Of course I do. I wouldn't be here otherwise.'

She walks over, sits on his knee and kisses him long and hard.

'Watch it,' says Charlie. 'Someone might walk in.'

'Don't worry.' Denise smiles knowingly. 'I told them not to disturb us.'

As she kisses him, his hands are everywhere and his excitement is growing. Through her silky dress he can feel her bottom, her stockings and suspenders. She positions herself so she can feel him hard beneath her, then moves her buttocks slowly to arouse him even more. His hand slides beneath her dress, tracking slowly up her thigh, fondling her stocking-tops and then her yielding flesh.

'Oh, Charlie,' she sighs, biting his neck.

He kisses her, fingers constantly exploring. She kisses him again, watching him intently, then raises herself slightly and lifts her dress to her waist. Once she's in position, he enters her, breathing harder still. She lowers her dress, hiding everything that's happening beneath. He can hardly bear the slow rotation of her hips. He clasps her waist and moves with her. She's moaning now, unable to restrain herself. He's ready to let everything go but wants to hold on and prolong his enjoyment. He unfastens her bra, fondles her breasts, squeezes her nipples. She can't stand it any more. Taking a deep breath, she pushes down as hard as possible, stifling a cry, trying not to let her parents hear. Pushing deeper still, Charlie senses a flow from his body. They're both completely spent, his face buried in the nape of her neck, while she slumps forward exhausted.

They sit motionless for a while, then Denise stands and straightens her dress. She sits down beside him again and smothers him with kisses. 'I love you so much, Charlie. You're my first, you know. I've never done this before.'

Looking deep into her eyes, he can see it is true.

No one bothers them. They're locked in an embrace, reluctant to move or talk. Eventually they hear Barbara shouting. 'It's getting late, dear. Time to go home, Charlie.'

They steal one last kiss.

'Goodnight, Mrs Watson,' calls Charlie. 'I'm leaving now.'

'I'd never do that with anyone but you,' whispers Denise. 'You know that, don't you?'

'Of course I do. I'll come and see you again before I sail.'

She releases his hand and follows him to the door, eyes locked on him as she watches him walk away.

Meanwhile Charlie is remembering his dad's advice: 'Remember to get something on it'. *I never used any protection*, he thinks guiltily. *I hope Denise will be OK.*

On Friday morning Charlie leaves the house early and heads down the dock, wanting to show how keen he is. Arriving around half nine, he finds plenty of fishermen standing outside the tiny office, hoping to replace a crewman who's been sacked or forced to sign off for some reason. The runner, or ship's husband, can see them all through the window and occasionally summons one of the chosen few.

Charlie feels rather lost among the crowd. Behind him in the dock the trawlers are being prepared to sail. Then a man walks out of the office and waves him inside.

'Now then, young'un,' says Jack, looking him up and down. 'You can sign on the *Lord Leopold*. Full name, age and address, please.'

He notes all the details in the log book, then asks Charlie to sign.

'You've just signed on your first trawler as galley lad. You'll be sailing Monday morning at two a.m. Don't be late. You can buy any clothes you need from the fisherman's stores. They're open all tides. Once you've joined a crew proper, items can be charged to you and paid for when you settle.'

Charlie is finding it hard to take it all in.

Jack hands him a slip of paper with his sailing time. 'And remember, don't be late.'

Charlie walks out in a bit of a daze. 'Just signed on, lad?' asks one of the men waiting outside.

He nods.

'First trip?'

'Yes.'

'Don't worry,' he smiles. You'll be fine.'

Then Jack calls out a name. 'That's me, must go.'

Charlie wanders slowly away. Elsewhere on the dock fishermen are standing outside the other company offices, settling or looking for work. More men are moving from trawler to trawler, doing repairs. He enjoys watching all the different tradesmen working away, laughing and chatting or calling out to their mates.

Back home Mary greets him anxiously. 'What happened, love?'

'I signed on the *Lord Leopold*. We sail early Monday.'

'Oh, Charlie,' she says, coming to give him a hug. 'We'll miss you so much. I wish you'd stay at the factory with Dad.'

'Don't worry, Mam. I'll be OK.'

'What will you need? We'll have to get you the right clothes and everything. Toiletries, of course. Anything else?'

'I'll sort all that out later. I'm off out for a drink with George this afternoon. He's going back to Germany soon and I want to see him before I sail.'

'You're a lot braver than I am,' says George in the pub. 'The army's not too bad. The time soon passes. Two years is easy. Joe seems to like it on trawlers, and you might too, but you wouldn't get me on the bloody things in a million years. How's your love life, by the way? Denise is older than you, isn't she? Lucky sod. You always seem to pull the good ones.'

'Only by two years. It's nothing. Are you still seeing that girl from the Loco?'

'Am I? I'm in love! The only problem is her name.'

'Why, what's she called?'

'I asked as I walked her home. "Dilly", she said.

'"And your surname?" I said.

'"Pratt," she replied.'

Charlie bursts out laughing. 'Dilly Pratt! I don't believe it.'

'Short for Dolores, apparently. Dilly's a nice girl, though. And boy is she hot.'

They down a couple of pints and by the time they leave the pub they're both pretty tipsy. 'How's your old man doing with Miss Whiplash?' asks Charlie. 'You haven't been round there again, have you?'

'Dad told me he stopped by her house the other day and there was a fruit cart outside. He went to the back door just as this chap was coming out, big smile on his face. He winked at my old man. "First time I've delivered here," he whispered. "Wow, what an experience, but by hell my arse is sore.""

Charlie and George are both laughing.

'You're kidding me, aren't you, George?'

'Course I am, Charl.'

Charlie shoves George so hard he almost knocks him over. 'You prat.'

'Don't tell Bob.'

'Not a word.'

'Take care, Charlie mate.' George burps loudly. 'See you next time I'm home. Don't do anything I wouldn't do.'

Charlie embraces his friend before they part. 'See you, mate. Give my love to Dilly Pratt.'

'Charlie! Don't make me laugh.'

Mike and Eileen are both home when Charlie walks in. 'I still can't believe you're going on trawlers,' says Eileen, coming to give him a kiss.

'Never mind that now,' says Mike briskly. 'Let's make sure you've everything you need for the trip.'

'Thanks, Dad. Appreciate it.'

Charlie manages a short kip to sober up a little before going round to see Bob and Denise. The Watsons' house is like a second home to him. Jim and Barbara always love to see him and Denise is fussing around as normal. He makes them laugh with the story of Dilly Pratt, then he tells them he's sailing Monday morning.

Denise can hardly hold back the tears.

'Three weeks isn't that long,' pleads Charlie.

'Just a day is long enough on one of them things,' says Bob.

Silence descends.

The Watsons have decided to give Denise and Charlie a bit of time alone. 'Mam and I are taking Sarah out for a couple of hours,' says Jim eventually.

'I'm off too,' says Bob. 'I'm going out with her from the Loco.'

Denise takes Charlie back into the front room. 'I'll miss you so much,' she says, tears streaming down her face.

Charlie puts his arms around her and gives her a kiss. 'I'll miss you too.'

Just then Sarah opens the door. 'We're off now, Charlie. See you soon.'

'Bye, Sarah.'

Then Bob appears. 'Behave yourselves, you two. ' He looks Charlie in the eye. 'Bye now, mate.'

Charlie gives him the thumbs up. 'See you, pal.'

Finally Charlie and Denise are left alone. She's so slender and pretty, just looking at her is enough to get him aroused. He takes her hand and kisses her.

'I don't want you to leave,' she says, flinging her arms around him.

Kissing her hard, he runs his hands to her hips and slides them beneath her dress. She stands motionless, gazing at him intently. As his hands begin moving upwards, she throws back her head and moans. He grips her buttocks and brings her gently towards him. She unbuttons his shirt, then runs her hands across his chest and down his back, digging her nails into him.

They both tear off their clothes. *What a beautiful body, what a lovely face*, he thinks, gazing down as he lays her gently on the floor, kissing her breasts and feeling the silky smooth skin between her thighs.

'Please don't stop,' says Denise. 'I've never felt anything like this before.'

Nor has Charlie. He's in ecstasy. *I'm sure it wasn't as good as this with Pat and Debra.*

Denise is so demanding. Her body is on fire. She wants him to kiss her and touch her in places she's never dreamed of. She reaches for Charlie's manhood, moving slowly, holding him, caressing him, kissing him. She doesn't want to rush things. She wants to give her feelings space to linger and flow, letting her body enjoy his every touch. She lays on top of him, then gently places his hardness between her legs and then inside her at last. She kisses his chest, digging her nails into his back as he cries out. The pain is part of the pleasure. Sensing this, she moves as though floating on air, looking down on him, enjoying his blissful expression.

He moves with her and she leans in closer. 'Yes, Charlie. Yes. Please don't stop.'

He grabs hold of her, pulling her towards him, then pushing up and into her as deeply as he can. She screams and he can't hold back any more. His whole body is rigid with excitement. Just before he surrenders, she can feel him inside her. She shudders and moans.

Afterwards they lie kissing and cuddling for a while. 'I love you, Charlie,' she tells him.

'I love you too, Denise.' He's never said that to anyone before.

Still greedy for each other, they start all over again, whispering their desires and learning how to please each other. Charlie can see how much Denise yearns to satisfy him.

Eventually, however, they remember that they could soon be disturbed. 'Better get dressed and tidy ourselves up,' says

Denise.

Then they sit holding hands and talking about the future, wondering if this might be the start of a life together.

CHAPTER 11
GALLEY LAD

Early Monday morning Charlie is staring apprehensively at the clock, desperate to leave and anxious to stay all at the same time. Everything he needs is in his kit bag, and Mike and Mary are waiting up to say goodbye.

He checks the time again. 'Best be off, then.'

'Take care, son,' says Mike. 'We'll miss you.'

Mary comes over and kisses him, trying not to cry. 'Bye, son. Love you.'

Charlie picks up his bag and they follow him to the door. 'Bye, Charlie,' calls Eileen from upstairs.

'Bye, sis,' he shouts back.

He walks up the terrace, watched every inch of the way by his parents. He turns and waves one last time, then disappears round the corner. Two bobbers are also heading for the fish dock, their clogs ringing off the cobbles.

Despite the early hour the dock is crowded. 'Where's the *Lord Leopold*?' he asks one bloke, then makes his way over to the vessel and climbs on board, walking aft side to the accommodation.

The two men talking by the entrance give him a hard stare. 'You the galley lad?' asks one.

'That's right,' says Charlie.

They direct him to his bunk, all very familiar from Joe's first trip. Charlie sets down his bag and makes his way back on deck. A very tall, bright-eyed man is walking toward him, bottle of beer in hand.

'Hello!' he says. 'Are you the galley lad?'

'Yes, I'm Charlie.'

'I'm Bert, the cook. This your first trip, then?'

'Yes.'

'Don't worry, Charlie. You'll be fine.' Bert takes a sip of beer. 'You'll soon get used to it. Follow me, I'll show you round. I'll point out where everything is and introduce you to the crew.'

Charlie does his best, but there's a lot to take in.

'We start work at six preparing breakfast,' says Bert. 'Try to get a couple of hours' shut-eye as soon as we let go.'

They soon move out into the river Humber. While the ship looks clean enough, the smell of diesel hangs over everything, and another strange aroma is making Charlie feel a bit sick. The breeze is fresh and he watches the lights onshore. *Won't be seeing them for a bit.* The noise of the engines thrums through the accommodation as he heads for the mess room. Most of the crew are busy securing the deck, but a couple are sat drinking beer. One offers Charlie a bottle.

'Want one, young'un?'

'No thanks.'

Charlie is feeling pretty seasick and all he wants to do is lie down. He takes to his bunk and flops down, fully clothed. As soon as the trawler leaves the shelter of the Humber it starts rolling around straight away. He sleeps fitfully, disturbed by all the banging and clattering, glancing now and then at the clock on the cabin wall.

Next thing he knows Bert is shaking him awake. 'Come on, Charlie. Time for work.'

Still feeling ill, Charlie gets up and heads for the bathroom, where he promptly throws up in the sink. The toilet is outside, accessible only by leaving the accommodation. He swills everything away, splashes his face with cold water and goes to the galley. Bert shows him how to set the tables and get everything ready, then starts cooking breakfast. But the smell of bacon and kippers is too much for Charlie, who keeps having to interrupt his work to go out on deck and be sick.

The weather is rough for the next three days and Charlie is ill most of the time. Still, he has three meals a day to serve, at seven in the morning, twelve noon, and six in the evening – two sittings apiece. He also has to look after the crew's mess, the officers' mess, the chief engineer's berth and the mate's berth, as well as clean the deckhands' accommodation in the fo'c's'le. He never seems to stop.

The crew are good to him, joking about his plight, and the young deck learner Eric is particularly kind. He tries to help whenever he can and Charlie always enjoys talking to him.

Eventually the weather fines away and the sea flattens out, allowing the crew to get on with their work on deck. Charlie watches when he gets the chance. He's starting to learn a few names and relax a little. The skipper doesn't talk much, though. Charlie never gets thanked when he takes a mug of tea up to the bridge – the skipper simply points to the mug rack and carries on sitting and staring out the window. The crewman at the helm, behind the big wooden wheel, always gives Charlie a wink, as much as to say, *Don't worry about him.*

According to Eric, the skipper only talks to the mate and the chief engineer. 'Wait until we start fishing. Bill the Bastard will be screaming at us from the bridge then.'

'Bill the Bastard? Why do they call him that?'

'Pretty obvious,' laughs Eric. 'He can be an absolute b****r, that's why. He shouts all the time, telling us we're useless bastards. He's a good skipper, though. Always manages to land good trips. The weather has to be pretty bad to stop him fishing. Most skippers are bastards when it comes down to it. I want to be one too. I wouldn't care what they called me if I was on a skipper's money.'

They both laugh, and Eric goes back on deck chuckling to himself.

Charlie has scarcely eaten a thing since they left dock, but eventually he starts to recover his appetite. It turns out he hasn't been missing much. 'Where the hell did you learn to cook?' one of the deckhands asks Bert. 'In prison? I bet all the crooks went straight just to escape your shitty food.'

Their complaints are like water off a duck's back. 'This bunch of bastards wouldn't know good food if they saw it,' says Bert. 'I could cook for royalty.'

If they're slimming! thinks Charlie. *Or perhaps if they've no taste buds.*

By the time they get to the Icelandic fishing grounds, it's getting pretty chilly. In their flat caps and mufflers, big rubber thigh boots protecting their trousers from a soaking when the occasional sea comes on board, the men on deck don't seem to care. They never shave – and they're not that bothered about bathing either. Charlie tries to take a bath but soon gives up the idea. It takes forever to fill the steel bath with a handpump, and the water is never that hot, so it's just the occasional wash from now on.

The toilets are another problem. You have to leave the accommodation, dash to the port quarter and open a steel door – a tricky manoeuvre in poor weather. If the ship is head to wind the water comes on deck and runs into the aft toilet. The door is in two halves, but the waves can hit up the front of the casing side with such force that they penetrate the gap between them. One stormy day, Charlie just has to go and ends up with water to his waist, the contents of the bowl swirling around him.

He makes a speedy exit back to the accommodation. 'Fly a pigeon when the weather's bad, Charlie lad,' says one of the crew.

'Fly a pigeon? What do you mean?'

'Shit in a bucket and chuck it over the side. If you can get outside, that is. If the weather's too bad, just throw it out the door. The water on deck will wash it away.'

Soaked through, trousers round his ankles, Charlie can't help but laugh.

At last the skipper calls all hands on deck to start fishing. He stops the engines until the gear is down. 'Get that f***ing gear over the side!' he shouts. 'What are you b*****ing around at?'

Everyone jumps to it. 'Off we go again,' a deckhand mutters to his mate.

Charlie admires how skilfully the crew handle the heavy fishing gear. The mate is shouting instructions all the time, punctuated with volleys of abuse from the skipper on the bridge. The gear is soon over the side, and the skipper manoeuvres the ship to start lowering it to the sea bed. The mate and third hand are behind the winch, paying the warps away, calling out each new length to the skipper.

He tells them when to stop, and as soon as the gear hits the bottom the engines are set to tow. The ship is steady now – much to Charlie's relief. Some of the men come down to the galley for a gulp of tea before going back out on deck. They have other jobs waiting before they start to haul.

'Well, son,' says one. 'What do you think so far? Watching your first haul is great, but it starts to get a bit monotonous when you've seen as many as these old farts.'

Charlie laughs. He loves listening to all the banter.

'Come on then, you bloody lot,' shouts the mate. 'Before Bill the Bastard starts calling for your blood.'

They make their way back out on deck, leaving Charlie to his chores. He can't wait to see his first haul.

When he finishes work for the day, the weather seems to be freshening. The telegraph sounds in the engine room to stand by the engines: it's time to haul the gear. The men start donning their protective sou'westers and rubber frocks, and Charlie heads to the upper casing to watch.

'Stay off the deck, young'un,' shouts one hand. 'The weather's not too clever.'

Just then a sea comes on board, completely engulfing the crew. Charlie is worried, but the water drains away through the scuppers and they carry on regardless.

Now the gear begins to appear. Eric is scurrying around the deck doing his job. The wind is howling now, and the mate has to bawl to make himself heard. Charlie moves behind the entrance hoodway to protect himself from the bitter air. The nets are streaming out on the starboard side. He can see fish inside and more – apparently escaping – floating on the water. The men are hauling on the nets with their bare hands.

'Heave,' shouts the mate, ensuring they all pull together.

An occasional sea drops on board but it doesn't stop them working. Soon the nets are on board, followed by the cod end. The mate lets the net go and the fish flow out on deck, knocking him off his feet, but he bobs up again and starts making it ready for the next haul.

The men run straight through the mass of squirming,

wriggling fish and put the nets back over the side. Charlie decides it's time to go back inside and get warm. Bert, too, is heading for his bunk. 'Get off to bed, Charlie boy. They won't let you help in this weather – on deck or in the fish room.'

'OK, Bert.'

Just then another group of hands arrive for a slurp of hot tea. They're all wet through, their faces red with cold, each rolling a bit of tobacco in a cigarette paper and lighting up before going back on deck to gut the catch.

Last to arrive is Eric. He only has time for a quick drink. 'See you in the morning, Charlie. Wish I could go to bloody bed.'

Eighteen hours on deck in this shitty weather, thinks Charlie as he climbs into his bunk. *Am I really sure this is what I want to do?*

Opposite him Bert is snoring and grunting. Meanwhile the bosun, on his watch below, is climbing from his bunk, cursing roundly because he has to get up and go to the toilet – just a pee outside the door to the accommodation. Bert jumps up after a particularly loud snore, looks around dopily, then settles down again. The bosun returns, still swearing loudly, dressed in nothing but a pair of filthy old longjohns.

'You're keeping me awake, you noisy bastard,' he grumbles.

He lifts his leg and stretches to reach his bunk, revealing the holes in the crotch of his pants, and really lets rip with a ripe one.

Bert looks up. 'Holy shit, what a performance. It's enough to turn a queer straight. If this trip's a good 'un, treat yourself to a new pair of drawers.'

What a couple, thinks Charlie, stifling a laugh. Then his thoughts turn to home – and his lovely Denise. He misses her dreadfully. His family, too. He knows his parents don't want him to sail, but he's determined to go through with it. He falls asleep at once, knowing he has to be up early again the next morning.

Despite a couple of good hauls during the night, Charlie sleeps like a log. He doesn't hear a thing until Bert gives him his wake-up call. The skipper comes down for breakfast and takes his usual seat. Charlie lays the food out in front of him and leaves him to help himself. 'Thanks,' says Bob the Bastard, much to Charlie's astonishment. It's the first word the skipper has spoken to him.

In the crew's mess Eric seems to be out on his feet – until breakfast arrives, that is. He sits up straight, piles the food on his plate and dives in.

'Greedy little sod,' says a deckhand. 'Are you sure you can't get anything else on there?'

'I need it all to keep me going,' laughs Eric. 'I'm a growing lad.'

'Bert'll have a heart attack if he sees you with that lot. He'll think he's going to run out of food.'

The next few days crawl by. Other trawlers are fishing around them, sometimes passing so close they can see the crew on deck waving. Charlie is growing used to the daily routine, and when the weather allows he spends his evenings helping the crew – in the fish room chopping ice, or on deck filling braiding needles while Eric is on his watch below. The weather has been really changeable, sometimes freshening up within the hour – and very, very cold. Charlie can't burrow under the blankets fast enough when he gets off deck, usually around eleven at night.

Eventually they have a nice catch on board and a rumour begins to circulate that they'll be going home soon. Charlie is surprised how little the skipper sleeps. Bob the Bastard never misses a trick, watching the crew like a hawk, ever ready to launch a torrent of abuse when he thinks they're not up to scratch. He definitely knows how to catch fish.

'Get the gear on board and clew up,' he shouts now to the mate, as Charlie watches them haul for the final time.

Everyone has a smile on his face. They can't get everything on board and stowed fast enough. Soon the word reaches the engineers, the cook and the watch below. Charlie is thrilled at the thought of seeing Denise and his family again. *What will little Michael Charles will be like*? he wonders. *I bet he's grown.*

The following day the crew are clean shaven and dressed in fresh clothes. Only the old bosun is still wearing the same manky underwear.

'Do you think he's planning to go home in them longjohns,' asks Charlie.

Eric laughs. 'Can you imagine his wife getting all dolled up? Then he appears in those grotty old things. They'd put you off sex for life.'

They laugh even more.

'What's your bird called, Charlie?'

'Bird? You mean my girlfriend?'

'Of course I do.'

'Her name's Denise. She's my best friend's sister and she's very good looking. I can't wait to see her.'

'Are you getting your leg across then?'

'God, you are a nosy bastard. Mind your own business.'

'I don't have a regular girlfriend yet. I'm still feeling around, if you know what I mean. We'll have to have a night on the tiles, Charlie.'

'Perhaps, Eric. We'll see.'

The crew spend the next three days preparing the nets for the next trip and cleaning the ship from top to bottom. No matter how long they've been away, they're always excited just before they dock, anxious to see their families, wives and girlfriends again. As they sail into the Humber in late afternoon, Charlie and Eric on deck together.

'Here we are,' says Eric eagerly. 'Good to be home.'

Soon they're making their way alongside the jetty, where Mike and Bob are waiting and waving. As the ship touches and the ropes come ashore, Charlie jumps down and gives his dad a hug.

'How did it go?' asks Mike, putting an arm around his son.

'Fine, Dad. How's things at home?'

'Good, son. Eileen and the bairn are both fine. Mam's OK, too.'

Charlie turns to Bob. 'And how's Denise?'

'Need I say, Charlie? She's been getting ready for days.'

The three of them walk off the dock and head for home,

Mike and Bob bringing Charlie up to date with all the news.

'See you later, Bob,' says Charlie, when they get to his terrace. 'Tell Denise I'll be round after I've said hello to the family.'

He opens the front door. 'Anyone home?'

'Well, look at you!' says Mary, rushing to give him a hug. 'You've changed so much.'

'I've only been away three weeks, Mam. Feels more like years, though.'

Eileen comes through, carrying Michael Charles.

'Look how he's grown,' says Charlie, reaching for his nephew. 'Come here, big boy.'

It feels strange to be back on dry land, but Charlie soon gets settled. Mary fusses round him, while Mike looks on proudly. Charlie remembers how the time seemed to drag while he was at sea. Now an hour flies by. 'Just off round to the Bob's,' he says. 'Back later.'

'How did you like it on trawlers?' neighbours call out to him on the way.

'It's great,' he shouts back.

Denise must have been waiting behind the door because she answers his knock within seconds. She stands there gawping at him. 'Aren't you going to ask me in, then?' he laughs.

She flings her arms around him and clutches him to her, cheeks damp with tears. 'Oh, Charlie. I've missed you so much.'

She kisses him over and over again.

'I've missed you too,' he says.

'I've some news for you. I've got a job now. I'm working at Woolies.'

'That's great. Do you like it?'

'I love it. You'll be able to pop in and see me during the day.'

Denise takes his hand and pulls him into the back room, where the rest of the family are waiting. She can't wipe the grin from her face.

'How was the trip?' asks Jim. 'Good weather?'

'Did you like it?' adds Sarah. 'Are you going back?'

'Too many questions,' says Barbara. 'Stop harassing the

poor lad.'

'I've got some news for you,' says Bob. 'I've got a new girlfriend.'

'Who is it?' asks Charlie.

'I'll tell you later when these nosy parkers aren't around.' Everyone laughs.

'Oh come on, Bob,' says Sarah. 'Who is she?'

'Mind your own business,' says Bob. 'Have you got a boyfriend yet?' Sarah turns crimson. 'Look, Mam, she's blushing,' he chuckles. 'She must have a boyfriend.'

Denise takes hold of Charlie's hand. Her eyes have never left him for a moment. 'Can I take Charlie in the front room, Mam?'

'Of course you can, love.'

Jim and Bob exchange knowing smiles.

'See you later, mate,' says Bob.

As soon as Charlie gets Denise alone, he pulls her close. He looks deep into her lovely eyes, stroking her face then kissing it all over. He kisses her lips, his tongue sliding into her mouth as he explores every inch of her body. She's like putty in his hands. He squeezes her buttocks and she arches her back, pressing herself into him, saying his name over and over again. His tongue flicks slowly in and out of her mouth, then she does the same for him.

Denise leans back on the settee and pulls him down on top of her. Charlie can hardly restrain himself. He's been imagining this moment every night for the past three weeks.

'Please, please,' she mutters. Feeling how much he's aroused, she takes of hold of him, squeezing gently then letting go. They're both in ecstasy, wanting to prolong these moments for ever. Charlie lifts her dress, moving his hand slowly up her leg, to her thighs and finally her most intimate parts. She's panting now, pulling him closer, wanting to feel him inside her. As he enters her, she digs her nails into his back and kisses him, tongue against tongue. He starts to move slowly in, then out, teasing her again and again. Denise can't bear it any more. Her body is beaded with sweat and she shudders as she reaches orgasm. Charlie too can't hold back any longer and quickly follows her into the pleasure dome. In a few short minutes they've been transported to a realm where their feelings are as one.

They lie entwined, kissing and cuddling. Lazily she puts her hand inside his shirt, then kisses his chest. Charlie kisses her breasts.

'I've been thinking about you every night,' says Denise. 'Dreaming that we'd be together, doing just this. Please don't leave me again.'

'I won't ever leave you. You'll always be at my side even when I'm away. Now I know how much I want to be with you.'

Charlie starts making love to her again, more slowly this time. They let themselves go, fulfilling all their desires, oblivious to everything – protection included.

When Charlie leaves, everyone else has gone to bed. 'See you tomorrow night,' he tells Denise. 'Be ready at seven. I'll take you out for a drink.'

A quick hug and a kiss and then he's off. Denise watches him go and blows him a kiss, then quietly closes the door.

Next morning Mary is fussing around, making Charlie a big fry-up.

'What about me?' asks Mike plaintively.

'Just finish your toast and get to work,' she laughs.

'Bloody hell, looks like going to sea is the only way to get a fry-up round here. I don't care. I don't like 'em anyway.' He taps Charlie on the back. 'Good luck, son. Hope you do well today. See you later.'

'Say hello to my mates at the fish house,' says Charlie.

Eileen and baby Michael are also at the table. 'You got in late last night, Charlie,' says Eileen with a smile. 'I imagine you went round to see Denise.'

Mary puts his breakfast down in front of him.

'God, Mam. There's enough here to feed an army.'

'Get it down you, son.'

'You've met Pat's new boyfriend, haven't you?' says Eileen. 'I've heard he's moved in with her. He's at sea now, though. He and Joe sailed a couple of days ago.'

163

After breakfast Charlie is anxious to get down the dock before the crew arrive to settle. As he leaves the terrace, Mrs Booth and Mrs Brown are on guard as usual.

'Fisherman now, y'know,' says Mrs Booth in a stage whisper, arms folded beneath her substantial bosom. Charlie walks past them, smiling. 'You OK, Charlie?'

'Fine, thanks.'

'Wish I was eighteen again,' she whispers to her friend.

'Me too. By hell, he's a good-looking bugger. Looks more of a man these days.'

'You're looking lovelier than ever, Mrs Booth,' calls Charlie.

She beams, readjusts the turban covering her rollers, then hoists up her breasts with both hands. 'Such a nice lad,' she says.

Mrs Brown chortles. 'He's pulling your leg, you silly cow.'

'You're only jealous, skinny.'

Down on the dock, the usual crowd is gathered outside the runner's office looking for work. Charlie finds a spot close to the door and waits for the crew to turn up.

'Hi, Charlie,' shouts Eric cheerfully. 'Seems like we made a good trip. You should be fine.'

Eric disappears inside, then the crew begin to arrive, acknowledging Charlie on their way in. One by one, they saunter out again, stopping to talk with friends before handing him his money. He feels rather embarrassed at first, but he soon begins to relax. *I've worked hard for them*, he thinks. *I deserve my reward.*

Bert hands Charlie a ten bob note. 'Skipper's given me the sack,' he fumes, cursing his way back to the taxi.

Then the skipper comes out and beckons to Charlie. He gives him two quid, then heads for his nice new car. His wife is waiting in the passenger seat – dressed to kill and looking a million dollars.

After seeing all the crew, Charlie goes into the office to get the official sailing time for his next trip. 'You're sailing Tuesday, midnight,' says Jack. 'Keep up the good work, son. And don't be late.'

Eric is waiting for him outside so they can go to the pub together. 'Bob the Bastard's not that bad,' says Charlie. 'He gave me two quid.'

'Bloody hell, that's generous. He must have got his leg across last night. That wife of his is a stunner.'

'I know. I saw her in the car just now. Wow!'

'That could be you when you're earning as much as he does. I'm definitely going to be a skipper someday.'

A couple of men are still outside the office. 'That bloke's the new cook,' says Eric, pointing. 'He looks a lot younger than Bert.'

'Fancy Bert getting the sack. He always said his cooking was good enough for royalty.'

'Are you kidding? It's shit.'

'You're wrong, you know. He's going to work for the Princess Royal.'

'You must be joking!'

'No, I'm not. He's got a job in the kitchens at the Princess Royal Hospital!'

'You prat, I thought you were being serious for a minute.'

Laughing, the two lads walk off the dock and into the nearest pub for a pint or two. Charlie dare not count his money. He knows he's done well, though.

'Best make hay while the sun shines,' says Eric. 'We'll soon be off again.'

'I'll get the drinks in. Pint of mild, is it?'

'That's right.'

Charlie returns with their drinks. 'I don't want to overdo it,' he says. 'I'm taking Denise out tonight. I'm hoping Bob can join us and bring his new girlfriend.'

'What if I bring a girl? Can I come too?'

'If you want.'

'Where are you going?'

'Andrew's Club, I think.'

'It's a date. If I can find a girl, that is.'

Then two of the crew come over to say hello, downing pints like there's no tomorrow. Charlie makes his excuses after a couple of drinks, but Eric stays on, promising to see him later.

When Charlie walks in the door, Mary and Eileen both look up expectantly.

'What's wrong?'

They both start laughing. 'We've been wondering how you got on,' says Mary. 'Did you do OK? We were worried you might have worked three weeks for nothing.'

'I did a lot better than I expected,' grins Charlie. 'The crew were great. They all gave me a treat, the skipper included.'

Mary looks relieved, then her face clouds over. 'Are you going back then, Charlie? Don't do it if you've any doubts at all.'

'I want to go back. I'm hoping to sign on as deck learner next time I'm home.'

'Don't worry, Charlie,' says Eileen. 'You do whatever you want. We just want what's best for you, don't we, Mam. I'm starting work again soon, you know. Mam's going to look after Michael Charles for me.'

'Are you sure it won't be too much for you, Mam?'

'Don't be daft,' laughs Mary. 'I brought you two up, didn't I?'

Charlie puts his feet up for an hour, then sets off to meet Bob from work. Walking down the street he sees the same old faces. Mrs Rust is on her hands and knees as usual, muttering to herself, backside swinging from side to side as she scrubs her front step. She looks up at Charlie as he passes.

'Those bloody kids won't keep off my bloody step. I'll kill 'em if I catch 'em.'

Charlie remembers knocking on her door and running away when he was younger. She'd come outside, threatening all kinds of retribution if she got hold of him. A couple of young lads are following a horse and cart, shovelling the dung into a bucket to take home for the rhubarb on their dad's allotment. *Kids have been doing that for years*, he thinks. *We certainly did.*

'Hey, Charlie!' shouts one. 'Mi dad says putting horse shit on your rhubarb makes it grow like hell. Will it do the same if you put in your shoes?'

'Depends how much you can get in there,' Charlie calls back, smiling to himself. 'And we like custard with our rhubarb, not horse shit.'

Charlie spots Bob among the crowd coming out of the shoe factory. 'Hi, Bob!' he shouts.

'Hi, Charlie! Great to see you. What are you doing here?'

'We never got a chance to talk last night. I'm taking Denise out for a drink tonight. I was hoping you could come with us. Andrew's Club around seven thirty.'

Bob glances at the woman beside him. 'Fancy a night out, Shirley?'

'Fine with me,' she says, smiling.

I wonder who she is, thinks Charlie.

'Charlie, meet Shirley,' says Bob proudly. 'Shirley, this is my best mate, Charlie.'

'Nice to meet you,' says Shirley.

'Likewise, I'm sure,' says Charlie.

'Best be off,' she says. 'I'll meet you there, shall I?'

'Is that the mystery girlfriend?' asks Charlie as she walks away. 'She seems a bit older than you.'

'She is, Charlie. She's lovely. She's ten years older than me to be exact. But we get on really well together.'

'Age doesn't always come into it,' Charlie reassures him, thinking of Pat.

'We just got talking at work one day and I asked her out. She's just split up with her husband.'

'He doesn't work at the shoe factory, does he?'

'No, he's a lorry driver, but he delivers there. She has two kids – two and four.'

'Might be a few problems if you get serious. Don't tell me she lives with her mother.'

'Bloody hell, Charlie. I'm not that daft. She lives with her dad.' They both laugh. 'Just joking. It's only the kids.'

'Have you heard from George at all?'

'No. The big news is that David's moved in with Pat. They're planning to get married.'

'That's quick,' says Charlie. 'Particularly after her problems with that other prick.'

'It's their business, Charlie. They must know what they're doing.'

'Everyone at work sends their regards,' says Mike. 'Some of the girls send their love as well. I never realised you were so popular.'

'Must be what they saw when they put that hosepipe down my pants,' grins Charlie. 'I miss them, though. They were always good for a laugh.'

Leaving the house again, Charlie bumps into Pat. He still thinks she's gorgeous, but Denise really is something special.

'Hi, Charlie,' says Pat. 'How are you?'

'Fine thanks.' He smiles uncomfortably. 'Just back from my first trip.'

'Joe was sorry to miss you.'

'Hope we'll soon be home together. Got to go now, though. I'm meeting someone. Good to see you.'

'Hope she's nice,' smiles Pat. 'Bye, Charlie.'

Denise comes in while Charlie is chatting with her parents. Black hair shining, she kisses Charlie on the cheek. 'Young love,' beams Barbara indulgently. 'Oh, to be eighteen again.'

Bob gets up impatiently from his chair. 'Are we off then?'

As soon as they get outside Denise links arms with Charlie. 'You just can't leave him alone,' jokes Bob.

'Of course not,' says Denise. 'So I'm going to meet the mystery woman, am I?'

'You are,' says Bob, winking at Charlie. 'Hope you like her, sis.'

Shirley is waiting rather apprehensively outside the club. Bob gives her a reassuring kiss. 'Shirley, this is my beautiful sister Denise. And Denise, this is Shirley.'

The two women smile tentatively and start making polite conversation, but Bob makes sure they sit next to each other and soon they're chatting away like old friends.

'I've got to report for National Service after Xmas,' Bob says to Charlie.

'No surprise. How do you feel about that?'

'It has to be done, I suppose. George has no complaints. He seems to have settled down all right. I'd rather go in the army than on trawlers like you.'

'I'll have to register for the RNR soon, but I'm looking forward to it.'

'At least the navy has a better uniform. The army's looks likes shit.'

'If you and Shirley get married, they'll give you a bloody medal for taking on two kids,' whispers Charlie.

They both start laughing.

'What's so funny?' asks Denise suspiciously.

Charlie can only shake his head in reply. The band starts up and suddenly he hears a voice behind him. 'I'm here, Charlie boy.'

It's Eric.

'So this is your beautiful girlfriend,' he says, ogling Denise. 'I'm always available, darling, if you ever think of packing him in.'

'Sorry,' she says curtly. 'You're not my type.'

Eric has brought a girl as promised. She's much taller than he is, with a big nose and a prominent forehead. Everything seems hilarious to them. Neither is exactly sober, slurring their words more and more with every drink. 'What do you think of my bird?' he asks. 'Isn't she gorgeous?'

'I bet she has to fight them off,' says Charlie. He can only smile at the way she smokes – taking a big draw on her cigarette, closing her mouth, tilting back her head, pouting her lips and blowing the smoke into the air. She and Eric seem to have their own personal cloud above their heads.

'I think my lovely girlfriend and I are going to dance,' says Eric.

They stagger on to the dance floor, hardly able to stand. She locks her arms around his neck, he puts his arms around her waist, and they stay in one spot, propping each other up, simply swaying in time to the music – much to the amusement of those sitting nearby.

Shirley and Bob are sitting as close as they possibly can, obviously happy in each other's company. Meanwhile Denise is never too far away from Charlie. She squeezes his hand. 'Is Eric like this all the time?'

'Yes, even when he's sober. He can be really funny, though. He'll think it's a hoot when I tell him about it later. '

The four of them eventually pour Eric and his girlfriend into a taxi, then walk home. Bob is taking Shirley back to her house, so he drops Charlie and Denise at the end of their road.

'See you tomorrow, Charlie. Bye, sis.'

'Nice meeting you both,' says Shirley. 'I hope we can go out again soon.'

Denise and Charlie walk down the street, stopping for the occasional kiss. She's had a couple of drinks and is feeling a little tipsy.

'I'd better not stay too late,' says Charlie.

'Looks like Mam and Dad are still up. Never mind, we can go in the front room.'

'Is that you, Denise?' shouts Jim.

'Mmmm, yes,' she calls while Charlie nuzzles her neck. 'Oh Charlie,' she giggles as he runs his hands all over her body.

They make themselves comfortable on the sofa. 'Will I see you again before you sail tomorrow?' she asks.

'I've got to be down the dock an hour or so before sailing,' says Charlie. 'I'll probably just have time to pop in and say goodbye.'

Denise kisses him, unfastens her dress and guides his hands to her breasts. She just can't get enough of him. 'I don't want you to go. I miss you so much.'

Charlie needs no second invitation. His hands climb her legs, enjoying the yielding smoothness of her skin. Denise caresses his bare chest, then runs her hands over his shoulders. She digs her long nails into his back. 'Take me, Charlie. Make love to me. I've never wanted anything more than I want you.'

She opens her legs wide. She's on fire down there and she wants him to know it. Now her breasts are in his face and he's biting her nipples, kissing them, teasing her, making her squeal with delight. She slides her hand into his trousers. She's desperate to take hold of him. They want to make this a night to remember, a night without end.

She moves to admit him and he moans as they move together. He's never experienced such intense desire before. Denise is the spark in his life, with her beautiful body and the way she makes love. His feelings for her have grown stronger and stronger.

'I love you so much,' he says.

'I love you too, Charlie. There'll never be anyone else for me.'

Together they reach the peak of excitement and their bodies go rigid. Then they collapse into each other's arms, clutching each other tightly.

When they hear Bob come in and go upstairs, they both hurry to get dressed.

'I'd better go now,' says Charlie.

'Stay a bit longer,' says Denise.

'No, I must,' says Charlie firmly. They walk slowly to the door, kiss and say goodnight. 'I'll try to see you tomorrow, probably just after tea.'

CHAPTER 12

ON THE UP

Next day Charlie is putting his feet up at home. His bag is packed, Michael Charles is sitting quietly on Eileen's lap, and Mary is busy washing and ironing. Suddenly the peace is disturbed by a knock at the door.

'Who on earth could that be?' says Eileen.

Mary goes to answer it. Outside is Howard, smartly dressed in an RAF uniform. 'Hello, Mrs Robinson,' he says apprehensively. 'Could I see Eileen, please?'

Mary scowls. For two pins she'd shut the door in his face. 'Please,' he says again.

Charlie jumps up when Howard walks into the room. 'What the hell do you want?'

Eileen just bursts into tears.

Howard is gazing wistfully at Michael Charles. 'I'm so sorry, Eileen. Please forgive me. Could I give our baby a hug?' He holds out his hands expectantly.

Eileen stands up and passes him the baby. 'We've called him Michael Charles.'

The little lad immediately starts tugging at his father's ears. Charlie can't help but laugh. He remembers joking with his dad that Howard was like Dumbo.

'I joined the RAF when I left,' Howard is saying to Eileen. 'But I've never forgotten you or the baby. I really wanted to get in touch but I was too frightened of your dad.' He turns to Mary. 'Would you mind if Eileen and I talked in private, Mrs. Robinson?'

Eileen is clearly keen and Charlie also nods his agreement. 'OK,' says Mary. 'I'll take Michael Charles while you two go and talk.'

'I'm so sorry I left you,' says Howard, taking hold of Eileen's hand. 'I made a big mistake. I miss you dreadfully and I want to take care of you both. Would you do me the honour of marrying me?'

Eileen is speechless. She can't say 'yes' fast enough.

Howard kisses her. 'What do you think your father will say?' he asks anxiously.

'He'll come round ... I think. I'm sure he'll be happy for us.'

'At least Howard is back and willing to contribute,' Charlie is saying to Mary. 'I still think Dad will kill him, though.'

Just then Eileen and Howard come back into the room, grinning from ear to ear.

'Howard's asked me to marry him,' says Eileen.

Lucky girl, thinks Charlie. *She's put on even more weight recently.*

'Where are you stationed?' he asks his brother-in-law to be.

'Leconfield, not too far away.'

'That's handy. Don't tell me you're training to be a pilot?'

'No, I'm what you'd call ground staff.'

Eileen and Howard disappear with Michael Charles to go and visit Howard's mother.

Mary is thrilled at the turn of events. At last the baby will be with his mum and dad. 'You won't believe what we've got to tell you,' she says as soon as Mike walks through the door.

'Believe what, love?'

Mary turns to Charlie for help. 'Howard turned up this afternoon,' says Charlie. Mike's expression darkens at once. 'He wanted to see Eileen and the baby, Dad. He wants to take care of them. He's even asked Eileen to marry him.'

'I'll give him marriage,' says Mike. 'I'll break his bloody neck, the little shit.'

'I think he's genuine,' says Mary. 'Charlie and I believe him, anyway. The three of them have gone round to see his mam.'

'Why now?' asks Mike, calming down a little. 'What's taken him so long?'

'He was scared of you, Dad,' says Charlie. 'Would you believe he's joined the RAF?'

'Don't tell me he's a pilot,' says Mike.

He and Charlie both burst out laughing.

'No, Dad. Ground crew.'

'Why join the bloody Air Force if you never leave the ground?'

'Someone has to look after the planes, Dad. Make sure they're fit to fly and everything.'

'I wouldn't fly on any plane that little shit is involved with,' harrumphs Mike. Charlie reckons he's warming to the idea. 'How long are they going to be?'

'An hour or so, I reckon.'

Charlie would rather be out of the way before then, so he makes his excuses and goes round to see Denise before he sails.

'I can't stop,' says Charlie. 'I'll miss you, darling.'

Denise clings to him, sobbing. She looks up and kisses him. 'I love you so much, Charlie. You'll never know how much I miss you.'

She falls silent, too upset to speak. He strokes her hair to comfort her. 'I have to go now, darling. Bye.'

As he walks away, he turns and blows her a kiss. 'Love you,' he mimes.

She waves and blows him a kiss in return. Then she turns to go into the house, powerless to stem the tears.

Back home, Charlie finds his parents talking quietly to Eileen and Howard. *That's a surprise*, he thinks. *I was expecting to hear shouting and screaming.* 'Hi, everybody!' he calls.

They all turn and smile.

'Eileen and Howard are planning to postpone the wedding for a few weeks,' says Mike. 'They want you to be home, son.'

'Thanks,' says Charlie. 'I'm glad you've got everything settled.'

'We're going to live with Howard's mam for a while,' says Eileen eagerly. 'Then we'll get a place of our own.'

'That's great,' says Charlie. 'We'll miss the little one, though.' He turns to his mum. 'I think I'll try and get an hour's kip before I go down the dock.'

'Okay, Charlie. I'll give you a call.'

Hardly has he shut his eyes before Mary seems to be calling him again. He has a hot drink, then picks up his bag and throws it over his shoulder like an old fisherman. Mike walks over and hugs him. 'Take care, son.'

'I will, Dad.'

Mary just gives him a kiss.

'Bye, Mam,' says Charlie. 'Bye, Dad.'

Charlie walks through the dark streets alongside a handful of bobbers clomping their way to work. He soon reaches the *Lord Leopold*, climbs on board and heads for the galley. The new cook is there already, chatting with another member of the crew.

'Hi!' he says. 'Are you the cook's assistant?'

I prefer that to galley boy. 'Yes. I'm Charlie.'

'I'm the new cook, John. Nice to meet you, Charlie. You know the ropes. Just carry on the good work. Sam here says you're an excellent worker.'

Charlie is thrilled at such praise from the crew. He stows his bag, then goes up on deck, meeting Eric en route.

'How's my old pal Charlie, then? Don't say a word about that beauty I brought with me last night.'

'It made my eyes ache just looking at her,' jokes Charlie.

Eric slaps him on the back. 'What about me waking up beside her? I thought I'd end up in Casualty.'

'What are you two laughing about?' asks one of the deckhands.

'Just some lass I picked up last night,' says Eric.

They leave the dock and once clear of the Humber the crew set about their regular tasks. Charlie stands on deck looking out to sea, feeling the magical pull of the ocean. No one likes going away, but with the wind in his face and a peace impossible to find on land, the sea gives him a feeling of deep satisfaction.

Bob the Bastard hasn't changed, though. He's never happy unless the men are working and the mate is driving them

175

on. All the gear has to be made ready to start fishing, and a sudden spell of bad weather can always disrupt things badly.

Charlie and John are soon getting on well together. John is a much better cook than Bert, and a lot cleaner into the bargain.

'Good news, Charlie!' says Eric one morning. 'The mate's giving me a start as deckhand next trip. One chap is finishing this time.'

'That's great, Eric.'

'Why not ask if you can sign on as deck learner in my place?'

'Great idea. I'm not sure he'll say yes, but I'll ask him anyway. Nothing to lose.'

'Go for it, Charlie. Got to go now. See you later.'

They start fishing in fine weather, so Charlie has the opportunity to impress, helping down in the fish room for a couple of hours every night. One evening he catches Ted the mate alone in the mess room.

'I understand Eric's coming back as deckhand next trip,' he says. 'If you don't mind me asking, is there any chance I could sign on as deck learner?'

Charlie waits anxiously for the reply.

'Not sure,' smiles Ted. 'We can't afford to lose a good cook's assistant.' Charlie's face falls. 'Only joking! I'll tell the runner when we dock. If you keep up the good work – and I know you will – the job's yours.'

'Thanks, Ted,' says Charlie. *The first step on the ladder.* 'I won't let you down.'

'I know you won't, Charlie. You're a good lad.'

The weather holds for the next six days, and they're catching plenty of fish, but Eric has been working with a poisoned hand – probably caused by a fish bone. The hand has been swollen for a while now and looks to be turning septic.

Ted reports the problem, and the skipper calls Eric to the bridge just as he's about to go on watch below. He walks up there slowly. He knows what will happen next.

'Show me that hand, lad,' says Bob the Bastard. He examines it carefully. 'OK, son. We've got to do something about this before the poison spreads any further.' He calls for Charlie, who races to the bridge. 'Go to the medicine chest and get me the pouch with the scalpel and scissors. Then bring me some hot water from the galley.' He takes Eric to his bathroom and runs some water into the sink. 'You okay, lad?'

'Yes, skipper.'

Charlie returns with the hot water.

'This is going to hurt,' says Bob. He stretches Eric's fingers and finds a yellowish patch where the bone entered the hand. He locks the hand under his arm and over the sink, then turns to Charlie, 'Pass me the scalpel.' The skipper lances the infected tissue and a stream of yellow pus gushes from the hand. Eric yelps in pain. He looks about to faint.

Glad this isn't me, thinks Charlie.

Still, the skipper carries on pressing all round the poisoned area until the pus stops flowing. He cleans the whole thing with hot water, then asks Charlie for gauze and a bandage. Deftly, he wraps Eric's hand. 'There you are, son. Go on, get to your bunk for your watch below.'

'Thanks,' says Eric gratefully, scooting off to bed. Amazingly, the pain has gone. The skipper's doctoring has done the trick.

'Clean this up, lad,' says Bob to Charlie. 'Then get yourself back to the galley.'

Charlie is very impressed by the skipper's actions. Bob the Bastard never shows much emotion, but Charlie reckons he's a good man at heart.

The fishing is excellent on this trip and the skipper has been exceptionally lucky with the weather. Although it's been touch and go at times, they've never needed to stop working – unusual for this time of year. The crew hate working in severe conditions but they have to carry on regardless. Now, though, it's freshened up so quickly they're having problems just getting the gear back on board. Once that's done the skipper calls them all off deck. But it's starting to freeze, with ice forming on the wires and anything else exposed to the weather. They'll have to go out again to chop it away before it overloads the vessel.

Down in the mess, the entire crew – including the watch

below – are waiting anxiously for news. Then Ted walks in: 'Right, lads. The skipper's going to put the bow into the wind. Grab anything you can to chop the ice away. Be very careful. Make sure you keep clear of the radar scanner on top of the bridge and remember to watch out for anyone working close to you.'

Everyone is concerned, but they're familiar with this kind of weather, so they just go out and get on with it.

Outside the wind is howling, with a huge swell and the occasional large sea coming aboard. Of course there are other trawlers in the area, all experiencing the same problems. The skippers are conferring by radio and decide to try and ride it out. Normally they would look for a harbour on the Icelandic coast or try to get under the lee of the land until the weather moderates, but now it's too dangerous for them to run before the wind and the sea.

The mate is everywhere, making sure everyone is OK, and the crew are too busy chopping ice to feel the cold. Their clothes are saturated, their thigh boots full of salt water, and every now and then a man is washed off his feet.

Charlie has no time to feel seasick. Back in the galley he and John are trying to fasten things down. Every time the ship rolls, the pots and pans clatter together. Sometimes they fall on the floor. 'Bloody hell,' says John. 'It's not good out there, Charlie. How in God's name can we cook with the ship rolling around like this? Let's make a lovely big pan of shackles for the lads. That'll warm 'em up a bit. It's easiest to manage, too. Better one big pot in these conditions than a load of pans all over the stove.'

After what seems like hours some of the crew come down for a hot drink. 'The ice is forming again as fast as we can chop the bastard stuff off,' says one man, face red, nose running, hands swollen with the cold. 'Better get back out there, I suppose. Let the others have their turn.'

The first group don their gloves and sou'westers and go out to relieve the men on deck. Then the second group appears, Eric among them. He takes off his gloves and peers at the bandage now dangling uselessly from his hand. He tries to undo the knot to retie it, but his fingers are too cold.

'Come here,' says Charlie. 'Give me your hand.' He unfastens the knot and removes the bandage. The wound has got very dirty and the hand beneath is a bit of a mess. He cleans everything up and rebandages it properly. 'There you are, mate. Should be okay now.'

'Thanks,' says Eric shivering.

'Take this, mate.' Charlie hands him a mug of hot tea. 'Drink it while you've chance.'

'Thanks, Charlie. Bit cold out there. Can't feel my bloody toes.'

'Yeah, you take care out there.'

Soon everyone is back on deck, where Ted has kept working throughout. Bob the Bastard asks for a drink and Charlie carries it up to him through the engine room and the skipper's accommodation. The skipper is sitting exhausted in his chair. He looks across and smiles as Charlie sets the drink in the mug rack. 'Thanks, son.'

Charlie just nods and returns to the galley, clinging to whatever is to hand as the vessel rolls from side to side. The pan of shackles is ready for the crew as soon as they can get down to eat it. Then as fast as it arrived, the bad weather moderates again. It's still freezing, but the swell is subsiding and conditions are improving all the time.

The crew enter the mess, everyone knackered. Nobody has slept for an age, and some are struggling to keep their eyes open, nodding off over their plates.

'Get your stew down you,' says Ted. 'Then we'll start fishing again.'

Is this really for me? thinks Charlie. *No wonder fishermen drink when you see the conditions they have to endure. I don't care how much folk at home call them for it.*

Eventually the weather fines away and most of the trawlers in the area start fishing again. The next haul is excellent, and Charlie watches as the cod end bursts out of the water, then the net – full of fish – lays out on the surface. *More hard work for the crew*, he thinks. *It just never ends*. He has to show willing and, after finishing in the galley, he goes down the fish room to help.

After another three days they have a very good trip on board and everyone is delighted to hear the skipper call 'Clew up'. All the anxieties and miseries of the previous week are forgotten. They're expecting a good market and a very nice pay-off for three weeks away.

Charlie's mind turns to his lovely Denise, dreaming of the good times they've spent together. He knows she's the girl for him. He lies in his bunk, imagining her standing in front of him – her beautiful body, shiny black hair and wonderful hazel eyes. She wants him to touch and caress her, and he drifts off to sleep relaxed and happy.

After a speedy trip home, they clean the trawler from top to bottom and stow all the fishing gear in preparation for docking at 1500 hours. All the crew are wearing suits, bathed and clean shaven. No one can say that fishermen aren't smart. Charlie is on deck as they come alongside. He spots Joe waving to him from the jetty, and as soon as they touch the quayside he's off like a bullet from a gun.

'Nice to see you, Joe. How's things? Everyone OK?'

'Fine, Charlie. Everyone's fine. We got in yesterday. You've a nice trip on board, I hear. Should be good money.' They set off on foot for home. 'Lots to tell you,' continues Joe. 'I've seen Bob. He's still in love with that Shirley. George is home on leave soon but I don't know when. And Mam and David have set a date for the wedding.'

'What about you?' asks Charlie. 'Are you going out with anyone?'

'I am.' Joe smiles.

'Who's the lucky girl?'

'She's called Beth.'

'Is that the Beth I'm thinking of?'

'It is, Charlie. I like her a lot.'

'I'm glad, Joe. She's a nice girl. You don't have a birthday coming up, do you?'

'Why?' says Joe suspiciously.

'Only joking,' laughs Charlie. *Just watch out if she wants to give you a present, that's all*. He changes the subject rapidly. 'I'm glad everyone's OK. It's good to be home again.'

They turn into their terrace and Charlie bursts out laughing, 'Three weeks away and Mrs Rust still has her arse stuck out that doorway. If she spends much longer scrubbing the step, there'll be nothing left.' They laugh. 'Mind you, I'd rather look at her arse than her face.'

That makes them laugh even more.

'I suppose you'll be going round to see Denise later,' says Joe.

'That's right. I can't wait.'

'See you tomorrow then, mate.'

When Charlie walks in the door, his mum grabs hold of him and won't let go. 'Come on, love,' says Mike. 'Let his old man give him a hug.'

'How's things?' asks Charlie.

'Eileen's still with Howard's mother,' says Mike. 'She seems happy enough there and she's been bringing the baby round to see us. How was your trip?'

'Fine,' says Charlie, not mentioning the storm. He doesn't want to worry his family. Fishermen never tell their loved ones about the conditions they're forced to endure. Even when tragedy intervenes, they keep silent. 'I'm signing on deck learner next trip.'

'You seem to be settling down,' says Mike. 'I'll never understand why, but I'm happy for you. What about deck clothes? We'd best get you sorted.'

'Don't worry, Dad. I can get everything from the fisherman's stores. They'll take the money from my settlings next time we land. I'll be on a share as deck learner – not as much as a spare hand, but still a share.'

A knock at the door interrupts the conversation. It's Denise.

'Come in,' says Mary, with a smile. 'You look lovely, Denise. Charlie will be so pleased to see you.'

She blushes shyly. 'Thanks, Mrs Robinson.'

Charlie goes to kiss her on the cheek. 'Hi, gorgeous,' he whispers, making her blush even more.

They all sit and talk for a while, Denise and Charlie

constantly stealing glances. 'Why don't you two go in the other room?' says Mary. 'I'm sure you'd like to be alone.'

The two lovebirds leave the room hand in hand, while and Mike and Mary smile fondly at each other. 'Do you still feel that way about me?' he asks.

'Get away, you silly old fool,' she replies, kissing him nonetheless.

"Cos I do.'

Mary puts her arms around him and kisses him again.

Charlie takes Denise in his arms. 'I've missed you so much,' he says, kissing her hard.

Denise kisses him back. 'I couldn't wait to get you on your own.'

'Nothing we can do now,' he says. 'Mam or Dad might disturb us.' They sit chatting and kissing until Mary calls them through for a bite to eat.

'Do you want to come back to my house afterwards?' asks Denise.

'Fine,' says Charlie.

On the way out they spot Joe shutting his door. 'Do you fancy coming round here tomorrow night?' he calls. 'We're having a bit of a 'do', an engagement party for Mam and David. I'm hoping Bob can come, too. What do you think?'

'Sounds great,' says Charlie. 'Shall we ask Bob?'

'Please,' says Joe. 'See you tomorrow.'

'There's a party tomorrow night at Joe's,' Charlie tells Bob. 'You and Shirley are both invited. Can you come?'

'Of course, mate. It will be great to get together again.'

Denise keeps looking at the clock, hoping her parents will take the hint. 'Just look at the time,' she says, glancing meaningfully at Barbara. 'Nine o'clock already.'

'We've been monopolising Charlie far too long,' says Jim. 'Let the young'uns go in the front room. They don't want be listening to us all night.'

Denise and Charlie jump from their seats, Bob winks at his friend, and Sarah just giggles.

Denise shuts the front-room door firmly and sits on the sofa, motioning Charlie to her side. 'You're insatiable,' he laughs, as she flings herself at him.

'Darling Charlie, I've thought about nothing but you since the day you sailed.'

'I've been thinking about you, too,' he says, pulling her into a passionate embrace.

Her hands scrabble to undo his shirt and pull it from his shoulders. She kisses his chest, his shoulders, his neck. She pants with desire as he caresses her beautiful body, skin smooth as silk. She runs her hands through his hair, then grabs it, pulling him to her lips. Her body boils as he touches her between the thighs. She reaches for him and soon they're in a world of their own, a realm of pure pleasure.

The fire raging inside him is all engulfing. Any more and he'll lose control. 'Yes, Charlie, yes,' cries Denise. 'Please don't stop.' Then as fast as they arrived, these feelings recede and the two lovers lie entwined, contented and relaxed, glowing with the intensity of the experience.

Denise laughs when she hears her parents going to bed. 'Don't disturb them,' Barbara is telling Jim.

Eventually Charlie has to drag himself away. 'I don't know what your parents would say if they found me here in the morning,' he insists. 'See you tomorrow night.'

Early next morning he's up bright and early, ready to go down the dock in hope of some good backhanders. I'll be on a share next trip, he thinks. It'll be good not having to rely on the crew any more.

Joe is going for his sailing orders, so the lads leave home together, watched by those two local busybodies, Mrs Booth and Mrs Brown. 'Morning, Mrs Booth,' says Charlie, giving Joe a nudge. 'Lovelier than ever, I see. '

Mrs Booth takes a deep breath to make her breasts look even bigger, then stoops to address her friend. 'I'm thinking of bleaching my hair, y'know, Else.'

'It'd make no difference if you bleached your head,' says Mrs Brown. 'They're taking the mickey again.'

'Have you looked in the mirror yourself lately? Second thoughts, better not. You'd probably crack it.'

'Bloody hell,' laughs Joe. 'You had her going.'

'They never change round here. You know Mrs Brady over the road. She has the odd visitor when her old man's off in his lorry, working away. I've seen a chap sneaking into the house. She always seems a quiet sort of woman, keeps herself to herself, but no – she likes to share it around. You'd think she'd have enough on her plate with six kids.'

Down at the dock, Joe leaves to go check his sailing time, while Charlie waits for the crew. They each give him a good backhander, and John has a treat for him too. 'I wish you were staying in the galley,' says the cook.

'Appreciate it,' says Charlie. 'But I really do want to get a start on deck.'

He goes inside to sign on as deck learner and returns to find Eric waiting for him outside. 'Where's it to be then, Charlie boy? In town or somewhere local?'

'Let's wait for my mate Joe, then we can all go together. I think it'll have to be local. Joe's having a bit of a 'do' tonight, so we don't want to cane it this afternoon. Here he comes now.'

'Bloody hell, Charlie,' says Joe. 'You made a good trip. Much better than ours.'

Charlie introduces his two friends. 'Just don't let Eric sort you out a blind date, Joe. If she's anything like his last conquest, you'd be better off with Mrs Booth.'

'Don't believe a word of it,' says Eric. 'My last girl was a stunner, quite out of this world.'

'Yeah, an alien from bloody Mars,' laughs Charlie.

'Do you want to come to the party?' Joe asks Eric. 'It's an engagement do for my mam.'

'Maybe. I promised I'd get together with some of the crew.'

'He'll probably be stoned by teatime,' says Charlie. 'Or devoured by some loose woman or other.'

'I don't get stoned,' protests Eric, laughing. 'I just get pissed.'

Eric calls a taxi to take them to the pub, but after a couple of pints Charlie nudges Joe – time for them to leave. More crew members have arrived and things are getting a little too lively for their taste. David has given Joe some money for booze, so they make their excuses and go round to Pop's to buy the drink for the evening.

'I'm pleased for Mam,' says Joe. 'She needs a man and I think David's right for her. She's too young to spend the rest of her life alone.'

'You're right,' says Charlie. 'She needs to be with someone. She's a good-looking woman.'

'Don't tell me you've a crush on her?' smiles Joe.

Charlie can feel himself flushing. *Hope I've not given the game away*. 'Come on, Joe. Where did that come from? Although you do have a lovely mother.'

'I know, Charlie. I was only joking. I'm looking forward to tonight. Beth's coming round about seven.'

'I'll make sure we arrive at the same time. I wish George was home. It would be good if we could all celebrate together.'

The girls from the shoe factory are sitting outside on their tea break and whistle at them as they walk by. 'Hello there, Charlie! Doing anything tonight? What about you, Joe? Fancy a good time?'

'Bob gets that all day,' laughs Charlie. 'No wonder he likes the place.'

They go into Pop's beer-off. 'A couple of cases of beer and dozen bottles of Babycham, please,' says Joe. 'Oh yes, and a half-bottle of whisky.'

'Bloody hell,' says Charlie. 'We should have brought a barrow.'

'I'll lend you one,' says Pop. 'But bring the bloody thing straight back.'

As they push it down the terrace, Mrs Booth is still outside gossiping. 'Looks like you're having a party, lads. Can anyone come?'

'I'd take you myself if I didn't have my girlfriend with me,' says Charlie.

'Lovely lad,' smiles Mrs Booth, giving her bra a good push up.

They drop off the booze at Joe's house, then Charlie heads home to get ready for the evening. Mary is fussing around as usual. 'It's only an engagement party for Pat and her boyfriend,' says Charlie.

'Well, don't drink too much. You know you'll only suffer if you do. Denise won't like it, either.'

'I won't, Mam. I know when to stop.'

On his way round to Bob's, Charlie hears his name being called. 'Hey there, Charlie boy!'

He turns. George is walking towards him.

'I don't believe it!' says Charlie. 'Joe and I were only talking about you this afternoon.'

'My bloody ears were burning, Charlie. I knew you were missing me. I've just got home. Couldn't get round here quickly enough.'

'Great to see you, mate. I'm going to collect Bob and Denise, then we're off back to Joe's. He's having a 'do' for his mam and her boyfriend. You've got to come with us.'

'No other plans, Charlie. Of course I'll come.'

'Come on. We'll go and surprise Bob.'

'Do you think there'll be any spare women?' laughs George.

'Don't know. I could always fix you up with Mrs Booth. She did ask.'

'Bloody hell, Charlie, thanks but no thanks. I don't mind a mature woman but that's going a bit too far.'

Round at Bob's, it's Denise who answers the door. 'Why are you going to the party with this miserable fart?' asks George. 'Surely you'd rather go with me. Say you will, Denise. Please.'

'Sorry,' she says. 'Charlie has a special something you could only dream of.'

'What?' laughs George.

'Himself, of course.'

'Guess you don't fancy me, then?' says George, wiping away mock tears.

'You guess right,' says Denise. 'Come on through.'

'Hello George,' says Bob. 'I didn't realise you were home.'

They swap news for a while, then set off to meet Shirley. Denise is hanging back. She has some big news for Charlie – she thinks she might be pregnant. She can't wait to tell him but she doesn't want to spoil the night.

'Who's this Shirley, then?' asks George. 'Nice, is she?'

'She works at the shoe factory,' replies Bob, not mentioning her age.

Eventually Shirley appears, looking great. 'Say hello to our mate George,' says Bob. 'George, meet Shirley.'

They both shake hands, then they all walk round to Joe's.

A couple of David's friends have already arrived, and music is playing from a borrowed record player. The neighbours have loaned a few chairs so everyone can sit down, and Pat has made a few sandwiches. The lads all help themselves to a beer, while the girls settle in for a good natter.

George takes Bob to one side. 'Shirley's certainly a looker, mate. But isn't she a bit old for you? I've heard a whisper that she has two kids.'

'I like her a lot,' snaps Bob. 'There's nothing I can do about the children. I just want to be with her.'

George puts his arm round him. 'I understand, mate. I'm not criticising, honest. Just asking as a friend.'

Bob smiles. 'That's OK, George.'

Charlie and Joe are swapping tales of really bad weather at sea. 'Probably see plenty more in years to come,' says Joe. 'It comes with the job.'

'We've been friends a long time,' says Charlie, 'so I hope you don't mind me asking. But I remember your dad. He used to play football with us in the street. It must have been really hard for you when he was lost, knowing you'd never see him again.'

'Actually, I see him every day,' says Joe. 'He picks up his bag, kisses Mam and gives me a hug. Then he walks out the door and never comes back. I hated seeing other kids with their dads, I was so envious of them. Mam became a bit of a recluse afterwards. Yes, it was difficult.'

'He was a such nice man,' says Charlie. 'We weren't that old, but I remember when the trawler was lost. We all sang "For Those in Peril on the Sea" at school assembly that morning. And the headmaster talked about fishermen and the dangers they faced. Sorry, Joe. I shouldn't have mentioned it.'

Joe smiles sadly. 'That's OK, Charlie, I understand. Will it bother you, being away for Xmas and New Year?'

'I suppose so. I've always spent Xmas with my family. But we can't worry about it.'

'You're right, Charlie. Let's just go and enjoy ourselves.'

The night rolls on. Some people are dancing, others are singing along – all having a good time. As usual George is the life and soul of the party, getting up now and then to give them a song. Everyone thinks he's great. The girls seem to be getting on all right, although to Charlie's embarrassment Denise keeps glancing across at him … as does Beth.

Squeezing through the crowd of people dancing and talking, Charlie goes outside to the toilet. He stands for a while in the back yard, looking up at the sky. It's a beautiful clear night and he stays there for some time stargazing, just as he did on the deck of the *Leopold*.

Back in the kitchen, Pat is arranging some sandwiches on a plate. She's spent most of the evening arm in arm with David, talking to their other guests. 'OK there, Charlie?' She looks across at him and smiles. 'We haven't spoken all night.'

'Sorry, Pat. By the way, congratulations. I hope you and David will be very happy together.'

'Thanks, Charlie. You and Denise are another lucky couple. She's a lovely girl, and very pretty too.'

Seeing him blush, Pat walks over and strokes his hair. Then she kisses two of her fingers and places them gently to his lips. For a moment he can see him and Pat in bed together. Then David walks in. 'Come on, love, everyone's starving. You OK there, Charlie?'

'Fine thanks, Dave.'

They go through to join the others. Denise is sitting by the fireside, and Charlie goes up and puts his arm around her, looking down at her fondly.

'Charlie,' she says, grabbing his hand and squeezing it. 'I want to tell you something.'

'Tell me what?' he says, distracted for a moment by

George.

Denise goes quiet. 'Nothing. It's not important.'

'Sorry,' he says, laughing with the lads. 'What did you say?'

'Nothing, darling. It's OK. I'll tell you later.'

Joe whispers something in Charlie's ear. 'Tell Charlie what you just told me about that German bird,' he says to George.

Shirley is fitting in nicely and has even managed to persuade Bob to dance. He picks her up, swings her round his waist and on over his back. 'Go on, Bobby lad,' shouts Charlie. 'Show 'em what you're made of.'

'Put me down, Bobby Watson, or I'll smack your bottom,' says Shirley.

'That a promise, sweetheart?' laughs Bob, getting a clip round the ear for his trouble.

Meanwhile Beth is looking on rather disconsolately. Joe eventually gets her to dance but she rejects all his advances and asks to leave the party early.

Joe offers to walk her home and they set off down the street in silence. 'Did you have a good time?' he asks, putting his arm around her.

'Very nice, thanks,' says Beth.

'I'm sailing tomorrow, so I'll be away for Xmas and New Year. Do you think I could have my present now?'

'Sorry, Joe. If you mean what I think you mean, the answer's no.'

When they reach her house, she turns to Joe and kisses him. 'I'd better go in, it's getting late.'

'Come on, Beth,' says Joe. 'Just a few minutes.'

'Stop it, Joe,' she says weakly. Joe takes no notice. He's too busy trying to catch a feel of what he can, while he can. 'Stop it, Joe, please. I don't want to.' She pushes him away half-heartedly.

'Come on, Beth.'

He moves her into a doorway and lifts her dress. Again she tries to stop him – but not too hard. 'My dad'll play pop if he catches us,' she says. When Joe touches her, she closes her eyes and bites her lip, pressing herself into him and opening her legs.

Joe has got exactly the present he wanted. Beth clings to him, moaning, half wrapping a leg around him. 'Don't do it in me,' she says softly. Minutes later Joe is walking home with a broad smile on his face.

Meanwhile George has also found himself a girl. 'I'm in here,' he whispers to Charlie.

'Bloody hell,' laughs Charlie. 'She's nothing to write home about.'

'Any port in a storm, mate.' George leans in closer. 'I'm taking her home.'

'Bloody hell, surely you're not that desperate?'

'I am, Charlie. I am. Tonight anyway, might do better tomorrow.'

'Anyone would think you were testing a bike.'

'Perhaps I am, Charlie. After all, it's all about getting a good ride!' The girl is waiting for him, smiling happily. 'Just look at her,' says George. 'She knows it's her lucky day.' And with that he says goodbye, turning to wave as he breezes out the door.

Shirley has to get back for her babysitter, so she and Bob also leave early. They think the world of each other, but she's still concerned about the age difference and the kids. 'None of that matters,' says Bob. 'It doesn't affect my feelings for you at all.'

When they walk in the door, Shirley's husband is sitting on the sofa, very drunk. He glares at Bob. 'What are you doing here?' Then he points at Shirley. 'And where have you been? Leaving my kids with some young lass while you go out boozing with your fancy man.'

'Don't talk to her like that, mate,' says Bob. 'She hasn't been out in ages.'

'Piss off and mind your own business. And don't call me "mate". It's my wife you're messing around with.'

Bob takes a step towards him, but Shirley intervenes. 'I'm not your wife any more,' she shouts. 'Get back to your girlfriend and leave us alone. The children are fine. Funny you taking an interest now. You've never bothered before. You haven't seen the kids in months.'

Mad as hell, he lunges at her. Bob grabs him and, swapping blows, they fight their way into the hall. They both fall over and Bob pins him to the floor, still throwing punches.

'Stop,' cries Shirley. 'Bob, please. Enough, both of you. Stop it now.'

Bob holds him down a few seconds more, then drags him up by the collar and shoves him out the door. 'Get your arse out of here now!'

Wiping the blood from his nose, the man turns and points at Bob. 'I'm off. You haven't seen the last of me, though.'

'I'm scared stiff,' sneers Bob. 'Get lost, mate.'

All the commotion has woken the children and they're upstairs crying their eyes out. Shirley goes to reassure them and stays until they drop off, then she returns to the living room. Bob is sitting on the sofa, head in his hands.

'I'm sorry, love,' says Shirley I didn't want to get you involved in all this.'

He gets up and gives her a kiss. 'But I want to be involved. I wouldn't be here otherwise.'

She puts her arms around his neck and kisses him back. 'Stay with me tonight,' she says, taking his hand and leading him upstairs.

Denise has spent the evening worrying whether or not to tell Charlie about the baby. She's had a bit too much to drink and is feeling rather tipsy. Walking home, they're all over each other. Charlie kisses her neck and nuzzles her breasts. 'Better get inside before we're arrested,' she says eventually.

The house is in darkness and they tiptoe into the front room. 'Shut the door quietly,' whispers Denise. 'We don't want to wake anyone up.'

She waits for him to sit down, then comes and stands in front of him. Slowly and sexily, she starts to remove her blouse. Spellbound, he watches her unzip her skirt and let it drop to the floor. He reaches out to her but she gently pushes him away. She's enjoying the tease as much as he is.

She unfastens her bra and peels it back, revealing her beautiful breasts. She slips off her stockings one after another, then, last of all, she calmly removes her panties, letting them slide down her legs before flicking them clear with her toes. Now she's completely naked. She edges closer, desire oozing from every pore. She moves closer still, she wants to touch him, feel his excitement. She sits on his knee and kisses him, then helps him take off his clothes.

Once he's stripped, they lie down on the floor together. 'My darling Charlie.' She looks up at him and smiles. His movements are precise. He knows exactly where to touch her to arouse her more. Soon their bodies are united as they make love slowly, lost in their own private world. Eventually they can hold on no longer, clinging to each other as they abandon themselves to the orgasm of their lives.

An hour later Charlie has to leave. 'Do you love me?' asks Denise. 'I mean really, really love me?'

'Of course I do,' says Charlie, wiping away her tears. 'Why do you ask? You must know that by now.'

Now's the time to tell him, but she can't find the right words. All of a sudden she's afraid that he won't stand by her. 'Don't go, Charlie. Stay here with me. I so wanted us to spend Xmas together.'

'I can't, Denise. I've decided to be a fisherman. If I want to be a skipper one day I'll have to spend most of my time away. This is my opportunity and I have to take it.'

Denise kisses him again. 'You're part of me and always will be,' she says. 'Not a day will pass without me thinking of you, longing for the moment when we're together again.'

One last kiss, and Charlie turns to go.

Denise watches as he walks away, tears streaming down her cheeks. *I should have told him*, she reproaches herself. *I should have told him.*

CHAPTER 13
DECK LEARNER

The following day Joe and Charlie are leaving on the same tide. 'Hi, Charlie,' says Joe, when he pops round for an hour before they sail. 'Enjoy yourself after the party last night?'

'Quiet, you know.'

'I bet. I took Beth home. I like her but she can be a strange girl sometimes.'

'In what way?' asks Charlie.

'I shouldn't be telling you this but she's a real tease. I don't think we've much of a future. First she wants it, then she doesn't. Then once we get going, she can't get enough. '

'Isn't it always the way?' says Charlie. 'Did you know George is planning to come down the dock with us. If he can prise himself away from his new girlfriend, that is.'

'If he gave her one last night, he must have put a bag over her head first.'

Just then Eileen arrives with baby Michael. 'Here's your Uncle Charlie,' she says, pointing. 'I've brought him round to see you before you go.'

'Come here, little fellow,' says Charlie. 'Just look how you've grown.'

'How's Howard?' asks Joe. 'Is he away?'

'At the moment, yes, but he gets plenty of time at home. You're both sailing today, aren't you?'

'Yes, different ships, of course.'

'Then take care both of you.'

'Don't worry, Eileen. We can look after ourselves. We'll be fine.'

'Was that a knock at the door?' says Charlie.

'I'll go answer it,' says Eileen.

'Eileen!' says George. 'You're looking lovely today. Is

Charlie in?'

'Yes, he's with Joe. Come on in.'

She walks into the room, big bottom swinging from side to side. *Sorry I said that*, thinks George, following her. *She might have taken me seriously.*

'What a night, lads,' he tells them. 'She just wouldn't leave me alone.'

'No wonder,' says Joe. 'Have you no pride? I bet no one's ever asked to walk the poor lass home before. Did you promise to see her again?'

'I did.'

'You never! Are you serious?'

'Through a window, maybe,' laughs George, pretending to squint. 'I'm sure my eyes aren't quite as sharp as they were.'

'Too right,' says Charlie.

Charlie said goodbye to Mike when his dad left for work. Now Mary comes in, asking if there's anything else he needs.

'I'm fine, Mam,' he says. 'We'd better be going soon.'

'I'll just slip home to fetch my bag,' says Joe.

Mary comes over and gives Charlie a hug. 'Take care of yourself, son.' She clings to him, trying hard not to cry.

'Come on, Mam,' says Charlie, giving her a peck on the forehead. 'Don't upset yourself.'

'OK, Charlie. I won't. We'll miss you, son. We'll be thinking of you at Xmas.'

'Don't forget me,' says Eileen. 'I've a hug for you, too. See you, broth.'

When Charlie and George meet Joe outside, David and Pat are there to wave them off.

'I thought you and David were on the same trawler,' George says to Joe.

'He is, but he's taking a couple of trips off before the wedding.'

Suddenly Charlie hears the sound of his name. He turns. Denise is running towards them. 'What's the matter?' asks Charlie. 'Why aren't you at work?'

'I had to see you before you left.'

'George and I will carry on,' says Joe. 'Give you two a chance to talk.'

'Charlie,' says Denise. 'I've something important to tell you. I can't let you go without saying anything. I hope you're not mad at me.'

'Mad at you? Why should I be mad at you? What is it?'

'I'm … I'm.' She starts to cry. 'Oh Charlie, I'm pregnant.'

'Are you sure?' He can't think what else to say. He doesn't want to upset her even more.

'I'm certain. What are we going to do?'

Charlie forces her to meet his gaze. 'There's nothing we can do right now, sweetheart, but we'll sort things out when I get home. I'll take care of you both whatever happens. You know that, don't you?'

'I do, Charlie.'

'It's our baby. We're responsible for it and we'll look after it. Don't worry, Denise. I'll always be here for you. Have you told anyone else?'

'No, darling, only you. I'm sorry I didn't speak up earlier. I really did try. I was afraid you might reject me.'

Charlie wraps her in his arms and gives her a kiss. 'We'll keep it to ourselves till I get home, sweetheart. I must go now. Don't worry.'

'I won't say anything, I promise. I'll miss you. I'll be thinking of you every day.' He picks up his bag and kisses her again. 'Oh, Charlie. Here's a letter for you, darling. Open it on Xmas Day.'

He puts the envelope in his pocket and kisses her one last time. 'Remember I'll always be here for you,' he whispers, turning to rejoin the lads.

She watches him as he looks back and waves. Tearfully, she raises her hand and waves back.

'Is there a problem?' Joe asks Charlie. 'You two haven't broken up, have you?'

'No, we're fine. There's nothing to worry about.'

Must be more to it than that, thinks Joe. *Mustn't press him, though. He'll tell us in his own good time.*

They arrive first at the *Lord Stanhope*. 'Hope we're home

together next trip,' says Joe. 'We can have a night on the town.'

'Look forward to it,' says Charlie. 'See you, mate. Merry Xmas and a Happy New Year.'

They shake hands, then Charlie and George carry on to the *Leopold*. 'All aboard, Charlie boy,' says George. 'Rather you than me, mate. You'll never catch me on a bloody trawler. I'd be sea sick.'

Charlie forces a smile. 'George–I–no, it doesn't matter.'

'Come on, Charlie. Joe and I both know that something's up.'

Charlie puts down his bag and stares at his friend. 'This goes no further than us, George.'

'Whatever you say, Charlie.'

'I've just found out Denise is pregnant. I never thought I'd end up in the same shoes as our Eileen. Mam and Dad will be upset but I really do love Denise. It's hard to leave but I've no choice.'

'Your parents know you're nothing like Eileen and Howard. Is Denise planning to keep the baby, or shouldn't I ask?'

'I want her to keep it. I haven't really had time for it to sink in yet. I love her so much and I know she loves me. Am I old enough to get married, though? I'll have plenty to think about over the next three weeks. It's going to be tough.'

'Charlie, you're the most sensible of the lot of us. I'm sure you'll make the right decision. I know I joke around but I understand how you feel. No one will hear about the baby from me, I promise.'

'Thanks, George. You're a good mate.'

Some of the crew are already climbing aboard, calling to Charlie and kidding him about his first trip as deck learner.

'Got to go now, George,' he says miserably. 'Hope you're still home when I get back.'

'You take care,' says George. Don't worry, I'm sure everything will work out fine.'

Fancy having to sail with that news, he thinks. *Still I'm sure they'll cope. They both have good families to support them.*

Charlie and Eric are together on deck as the *Leopold* sails down the Humber and into the North Sea, working to make everything secure.

'Sorry, I didn't get to the party,' says Eric. 'Heavy day, you know.'

Their tasks completed, they head to the mess room for a drink. There Charlie meets the new cook's assistant, a lad who's been on trawlers before.

'Hello,' says Charlie. 'I'm Charlie, the deck learner. I was galley lad on here last trip.'

'Nice to meet you, Charlie. I'm Les.'

'It's my first trip on deck. Just let me know if I can help you with anything.'

'Thanks, Charlie. The cook seems OK. Was he all right with you?'

'No problem there. Just do your job and he'll be happy enough.'

'The last cook I sailed with was a right prat. I had to sign off in the end. Lucky I managed to sign on here.'

They sit and chat until Les is called away to the galley. Charlie takes Denise's letter out of his pocket and contemplates it for a while. *Can't believe I'm going to be a father*, he thinks. He's tempted to open it, but she did say to wait for Xmas Day.

'Penny for 'em,' says Eric. 'Why so bloody miserable, mate? Not having second thoughts, are you?'

'No,' smiles Charlie. 'Nothing like that.'

'What's the problem then?'

'I'd rather not discuss it at the moment.'

'That's fine. Talk to me any time, Charlie. Don't let your problems stay in your head though, pal. It can drive you crazy being away from home and not able to sort things out.'

'Thanks, Eric. You're a good mate. It'll have to wait until we're back, that's all. Now tell me more about your dirty deeds.'

'My pleasure. Listen to this!'

Other crewmen come and join them and Charlie forgets his worries for a while as they they all sit around laughing and telling tales.

The weather is particularly good for December. Charlie enjoys

197

all the banter on deck, and he and the crew manage to prepare the gear without any problems.

Bob the Bastard watches from on high, snapping out orders whenever he spots a problem. Charlie is starting to like the skipper. *His bark is definitely worse than his bite*, he thinks. True, the skipper does sometimes fish on in bad weather when others might bring up their gear, laying and dodging while they wait for conditions to ease. But the crew all have in faith him and his handling of the ship.

Late one afternoon Eric and Charlie are standing on deck. 'Now then, you old sea dog,' says Eric. 'How are you enjoying it so far?'

'I love it. Look at the weather, flat calm. What more could you want?'

'How about a big blonde?'

'I don't give a shit what colour her hair is as long as she's big,' calls a spare hand. 'I like big women, me.'

'Big tits definitely,' laughs Eric. 'Yes, I like big tits.'

'Dinner-o!' comes a call from aft, and the first group head down to the mess while the men about to go off watch wait for the second sitting.

All evening the sea remains like glass – not a ripple on the water. 'Nice, isn't it, lad?' says Sam, one of the older hands.

Charlie smiles. 'Best weather I've seen since I came to sea.'

Old Sam puts his hand to his chin and looks at the sky. 'Listen to me, lad. The sea can be cruel. It's like a panther, creeping up and catching you unawares. Before you know, it's changed in a flash. When you've been at sea as long as I have, you develop a sixth sense for these things. I'm getting that feeling right now.'

He must be kidding, thinks Charlie.

Sam draws deeply on his cigarette. 'See you, son. I'm off to my bunk.' Then he ambles away, tutting to himself.

He can't be right, thinks Charlie. *No one can sense what the weather's going to do.*

It's dark now, the sky crystal clear, the stars glittering like diamonds. Except for the surreal quietness, the scent of the ocean and the vast emptiness around him, it's just like the night in Pat's yard. He stands for a time simply absorbing the beauty of it all. He wishes Denise was here to share it with him, experiencing something completely unknown to landlubbers.

The weather remains fine approaching the fishing grounds off north-west Iceland, and the crew are waiting for the skipper's call. When the telegraph rings stand by, Charlie and his pals don their oilskins and make their way on deck.

The mate soon joins them. 'Come on, lads. Let's get that gear over the side.'

Charlie listens excitedly to the bosun's instructions. 'Watch carefully, Charlie. You'll have to do this every time we shoot the gear or haul it.'

'Yes, bosun. No problem.'

The mate and skipper are calling out orders, and everyone is rushing round. Anything not done in double quick time brings a volley of abuse. Now the gear is over the side. 'Pay away the warps,' shouts the skipper to the mate. Charlie stands beside him at the winch, eager to learn as much as possible. Eventually the gear hits the bottom and the engines are set to tow. Then the skipper turns his attention to the echo sounder, checking for fish marks on the sea bed as well as the current depth of water.

Back in Hull Denise is going to work as usual, but her friends are getting worried about her.

'What's up with you, Denise?' asks Andrea one morning. 'You've been very quiet the past few days.'

'Nothing. I'm not feeling too well, that's all.'

'Is everything all right with Charlie?'

'I can't tell you. I promised. Sorry, I've got to go to the bathroom.'

But Andrea is not so easily deterred. She follows Denise and finds her throwing up in the toilets. 'Oh, Denise. You should go home, love.'

'I can't go home,' says Denise. 'They'll ask why I'm sick and if I have to go to the doctor they'll find out I'm …' She stops. She knows she's said too much.

'You're pregnant, aren't you?'

Denise stands up, pale and woozy. 'Yes, please don't tell anyone.'

'Does Charlie know?'

'Yes, I told him just before he sailed,'

'How did he take it?'

'He was fine. We're going to keep the baby but we wanted to wait till he gets home before we tell our parents. I can't stop thinking about him. I love him so much. I don't want to lose him.'

'Don't worry,' says Andrea, giving her a hug. 'Everything'll be OK. Just tell them you're ill and go home. You can't stay at work feeling like this. '

The manager is very understanding. He sends Denise home straight away. 'And don't come back until you're feeling better,' he adds sternly.

I've already broken my promise, thinks Denise miserably as she waits for her bus. *I don't know what Mam and Dad will say if I have to tell them. I'm sure they'll stand by me, though.*

Barbara is busy ironing when Denise walks in. 'Hello, darling,' she says. 'What are you doing home so early?'

'I'm not feeling too good, Mam. I've been sick.'

'Lie down on the sofa, sweetheart. I'll get you a drink. You'd best see the doctor. We'll go when Dad gets home. We need to make sure it's not TB again.'

The doctor, thinks Denise. *That's the last thing I need.*

'Don't worry, Mam. I'll be OK tomorrow. I must have eaten something that disagreed with me.'

Barbara puts a pillow under Denise's head and makes sure she's comfortable. 'You do look pale, love. Try to get some sleep.'

Bob is first home, followed by his dad. 'Denise isn't feeling too well,' says Barbara. 'They've sent her home from work.'

'She'd better see the doctor straight away,' says Jim anxiously. 'We don't want to take any risks. We don't want her ending up back in hospital.'

'It's probably just a tummy upset. She was sick at work. She's asleep now but she says she'll be fine in the morning.'

'All right, but if she's no better tomorrow she's going and that's that.' Next day Denise is sick again. 'That's it,' says Jim. 'Off to the doctor with you, young lady.'

Later that morning Denise and Barbara take a seat in the doctor's waiting room. Denise is panicking but she knows there's no escape. The doctor calls her name and takes her through into the surgery. He asks the usual questions, but after her recent bout of TB he also takes blood and urine samples.

When these have been checked he calls them back in. 'How long have you been feeling nauseous?' he asks Denise.

'A week or so,' she mumbles.

The doctor glances at mother and daughter. 'Well, first the good news. It's not TB.'

'Thank God for that,' says Barbara, tapping Denise encouragingly on the knee.

'The problem is, my dear, you're pregnant. You're suffering from morning sickness. I can give you something to help with that and I'll also make arrangements for your regular check-ups.'

Barbara looks at Denise in shock, but she knows her daughter needs love and understanding – not a telling-off. She doesn't say a word until they get outside. 'Who's the father, Denise? Is it Charlie?'

'Of course it is, Mam. I've never been with anyone else.'

'Have you told him yet?' asks Barbara.

'Yes, just before he sailed. We planned to break the news to you when he's gets back. I'm so sorry, Mam. I know I should've said something sooner.'

Barbara gives her a hug. 'Don't worry. It'll only make you feel worse. I'll tell Dad when we get home. What will be, will be. We all know Charlie, love. He's a good lad. I'm sure he'll be a wonderful father.'

'He wants us to keep the baby. I'm just sorry we weren't more careful.'

Jim isn't best pleased but Bob and Sarah are both thrilled at the news. 'I'm going to be an auntie,' beams Sarah, turning to her parents. 'And you two will be a gran and granddad.' Then she sees their faces. *Better shut up now*, she thinks.

'It's a shock, love,' says Jim. 'I can't say anything different. But we'll face it together as a family. We'll always be here for you.'

'While we're all together I've got some news,' says Bob.

'Don't tell me you've got your girlfriend pregnant, too,' says Jim, shaking his head.

'No, Dad. But I am moving in with her.'

'I hope you know what you're doing, son. You're a bit young to take on two kids.'

'Don't worry, Dad. I do.'

'What a night,' says Jim. 'I could do with a nice cup of tea. What about everyone else? Do you have anything to add, Sarah?'

'Only that I could do with a new pair of shoes.'

That makes them all laugh.

In bed that night, Denise lies there in the dark, touching her stomach and thinking of Charlie. *Goodnight, my darling, wherever you are. I love you, sweetheart.*

The weather stays fair for several days and the fishing is excellent. The deck crew are getting very tired after the usual timetable of eighteen hours on and six off, but Charlie is coping well enough – even if his thoughts do wander from time to time.

But now the wind is strengthening and the *Leopold* is starting to roll around. Soon it's howling about the ship and Charlie can see the swell building rapidly.

'It's freshening all the time,' moans Eric, wiping his nose with his sleeve. He scrapes the snow from his face. 'And it's getting bloody cold.'

'What a bastard of a place,' calls one of the crew. 'Only to be expected this time of year, I suppose. At least we've done well so far. It's Xmas Day tomorrow. I'm looking forward to opening my presents.'

'Silly old sod,' comes another voice. 'Don't tell me you're expecting Father Xmas?'

'I don't think that f***er will come out here, mate. Not the way this weather's shaping up.'

Everyone laughs.

Then comes a call from the skipper. 'Make everything secure down there. Bad weather on the way.'

They exchange glances. 'Shit,' says Eric. 'I knew it couldn't last.'

The crew are still trying to gut the last haul and get it in the fish room before the nets go down again. Old Sam leans towards Charlie. 'I told you we'd pay for that good spell, son. Remember, I can smell it. Mark my words, this is going to be a bad one.' He sniffs, shakes his head and looks again at the sky. 'Definitely a bad one …'

The wind is howling like a banshee – so strong it's creating a layer of white foam on top of the sea. Charlie has never seen anything like it. Meanwhile the swell is building fast, the occasional sea is coming over the rails, and the *Leopold* is starting to roll around more heavily.

With the deck finally clear of fish, the men stagger down to the galley to snatch a drink before they start hauling the gear again. Charlie manages to reach his bunk forward and grabs hold of Denise's letter. No time to look at it now. He stuffs it in his pocket to read later, when and if he gets the chance. Then he runs aft to the galley.

'I bet it's bloody cold out there,' says Les.

Charlie forces a grin. 'Yeah, it's freezing like a bastard.'

They haul the gear with great difficulty, scrambling to get it on board. The haul is a good one, making the job harder still. Time and again the deckhands are washed off their feet, but they carry on as usual, soaking wet and frozen to the bone. Once the gear and fish are on board, Ted looks expectantly to the bridge. Surely the skipper will tell him to secure everything. Surely he'll make ready to look for a lee and some protection from this appalling weather.

Bob the Bastard leans out the window and hesitates briefly. 'What are you f***ing waiting for?' he shouts. 'Get the gear over the f***ing side.'

Hope he knows what he's f***ing doing, thinks Ted. 'Get it over, lads,' he shouts.

The crew are incredulous. No one thought the skipper would put the gear down again. By the time they start trawling again, the conditions are truly terrifying. The white-topped seas are pounding on board relentlessly, repeatedly washing the men off their feet and making it almost impossible to work. Fish are swilling around the deck and Charlie is chasing around, trying to stop them going through the scuppers. Ice is also forming quickly on the wires and the superstructure. Hardened as they are, the men are exhausted. Everyone has his head down: no chatter or banter now. All they want is to gut the catch and grab a few minutes off deck before the next haul.

Where are all the other trawlers? thinks Charlie. He tries to shout above the wind. 'What's happened to everyone else? Have they disappeared?'

'They've pissed off for a lee, son,' shouts old Sam. 'Gone under the land before the weather and icing gets really bad. That's why you can't see anyone. Wise, that's what they are, wise.'

'Bloody hell, Charl,' says Eric. 'Your nose has an icicle on it.' He tries to wipe his own nose, leaving a trail of fish blood from his gloves.

'My bloody dick has an icicle on it,' says Charlie, trying to make Eric laugh. He rubs his hands together in a vain attempt to warm them.

Seawater is pouring down their necks and into their thigh boots, but they try to ignore it. They've been wet for so long, they're past caring. The amount of water coming on board has forced the skipper to put the ship head into the wind.

'Why the hell didn't he follow the others while he had chance,' shouts Charlie.

As usual Sam has the answer. 'Fish, lad, fish,' he calls above the wind. 'That's the reason.'

At last the skipper calls to the bosun. 'Hauling time,' he shouts. 'Get the gear on board double quick. Take care now. Watch out for any big seas coming on board.'

'Go down the fish room and tell the mate,' the bosun says to Charlie.

Ted brings everyone up to the deck. Then the skipper calls him to the bridge. 'Shit,' says Bob the Bastard. 'I should've gone for a lee with everyone else. Just make sure everything's stored as best you can. Once the gear's on board, I'll dodge head to wind to make it easier for the men. You look out for them. And be careful! If I see a big sea, I'll call out over the loudspeakers.'

As Ted closes the door he can see how much ice is forming on the bridge top and the superstructure. He peers down from the verandah at the men on deck, then looks seawards. The snow is blowing horizontally into his face, almost blinding him. He's seen some bad weather but never anything like this.

'*Shit*,' he says aloud. 'God help us get through this one.'

Down on the deck a couple of men are using spanners to knock ice off the winch, trying to keep it clear. 'F*** it,' says one. 'We're flogging a dead horse here.'

'Just keep trying, lads,' says Ted. 'That's all we can do.'

Meanwhile on the bridge another trawler is calling the *Leopold*. '*Leopold, Ross Diamond*. Can you hear me, Bob?'

'*Diamond*, this is *Leopold*. Yes, Fred. Getting you OK.'

'Can't see you, Bob. Are you coming in for a lee before this bloody weather gets any worse?'

'Just hauling now but the weather's atrocious. Shit, Fred. It's freezing like a bastard and the seas are getting worse by the minute. I'm coming in as soon as the gear's on board.'

'Take care, Bob. The forecast is shocking. I don't think this'll pass over soon. It's going to be a long one.'

'Will do, Fred. Got to watch the job now. Call you later.'

The skipper peers through the window to check what's happening on deck, but the snow and ice defeat him. He pulls down the window to try and clear it, but the snow comes blowing in. He can hardly hear the winch above the howling of the wind. He drags the window back up and stands there for a moment, full of regret. *Why the hell didn't I go in while I still had time?*

Everyone is on deck now, trying to bring the gear on board. Charlie is washed off his feet and desperate hands grab hold of him and set him upright. He can't feel his hands and feet any more, but he doesn't care. The constant watch for the next sea is driving the pain from his mind. Another sea comes on board and wipes two or three men off their feet. Some disappear under the water, but as soon as it clears they're back working again.

After an enormous battle they finally manage to secure the gear as best they can. 'Get off deck while I put the ship head into the wind,' shouts the skipper. The crew all seek sanctuary in the mess to try and get warm. Charlie grabs a mug of hot tea and spots Eric rubbing his arm.

'What's wrong, Eric? What have you done to your arm?'

'I banged it on something. I went arse over bollocks when that big sea came on board. I didn't know where the f*** I was.'

Then Ted comes in. 'The ice is still forming, men. We'll have to get straight back out to chop it off. I know I always say this, but it's vital. Don't go anywhere near the radar scanner or the aerials if you're working on the bridge top. Charlie, go clear the ice off the casing at the back of the bridge. Don't go on deck, son, and don't approach the bridge top.'

Charlie nods.

'Look, it's f***ing bad out there, lads. I don't have to remind you to watch one another's backs.' He looks at all the faces, crimson with cold, then taps one man on the back. 'Come on then, lads.'

He smiles, then leads them out on deck again.

Up on the bridge the skipper is calling the *Ross Diamond*. '*Diamond*, this is *Leopold*. Can you hear me, Fred?'

'Yes, *Leopold*. I can just read you.'

'We can't make it in. The seas are too big. We'd only make more ice.'

'F***, Bob. You shouldn't still be out there. Be careful and keep in touch. We'll listen for you on the big set. Tell your operator to keep on our frequency if you can't raise us on the VHF.'

'OK, Fred. I don't think this weather's going to clear. It's not looking good. The men are doing all they can to clear the ice, but it's forming that sodding fast I'm not sure we can keep on top of it. We'll just have to wait it out. But how long for? I hope it moderates, but it's a bad one. I'll keep in touch.'

Deep down, the skipper knows there's no chance of an improvement any time soon. The forecast was dreadful. It never said anything about moderating.

'We'll listen out for you, Bob.'

Aboard the *Ross Diamond*, Fred turns to his mate. 'I'd

hate to be in their position, John. Keep listening out for them. Tell the radio operator to use the big set and not to leave the wireless room unless he has someone to replace him. If the *Leopold* calls, tell me straight away.'

'Will do, Skipper. Our lads have cleared the ice and I've sent them for a drink. Shall we start the watches or do you want us to stand by just in case?'

'Just start the watches. If anything happens I'll tell you what to do.'

The other trawlers in the area are anchored with the *Diamond*. They've all been listening in and now they're discussing the *Leopold* on another VHF channel.

'How the hell are they going to survive this f***ing weather?' says one skipper.

No one has a reply.

Back on the *Leopold*, the situation is getting worse second by second. Try as they might, the men can't keep the ice off the superstructure: there's too much water coming on board. Some of the doors are freezing over, making them difficult to open, and the accommodation can now only be reached from the back of the bridge.

After an hour or so on deck the men are completely spent. Then the skipper's voice sounds faintly over the loudspeaker: 'Get yourselves inside now.'

They all proceed to the crew's mess room and sit down dripping wet. Eric is terrified, desperately seeking reassurance. 'Don't worry,' says Charlie, putting a consoling arm around his friend's shoulder. 'We'll be fine.'

The skipper sends down a couple of bottles of rum and the bosun starts handing out drams to warm them up. Charlie loathes the stuff but he's beyond caring. The bottles are soon empty. One deckhand raises his tot. 'And a Merry F***ing Xmas to you all,' he shouts, downing it in one.

The trawler has an unfamiliar roll now. Charlie sits staring into space, scarcely registering all that is happening around him. His thoughts are with Denise and his family. The trawler is sheathed in ice and he fears the situation is getting out of control.

'Why aren't we out there clearing it?' asks one hand.

'We're flogging a dead horse, lads,' says old Sam. 'The more we chop off, the more it reaccumulates. "Men will conquer nations, mountains and skies, but never the seas." That's what mi old granddad used to tell me when I were a lad.'

As he speaks, the ship begins to lay over to one side. It takes an age to right itself, then immediately lays over the other way. Everything that was on the table is now on the floor. No one bothers to pick it up. Each time the ship rolls, the men look at one another.

Charlie remembers Denise's letter. Thank goodness he took it from his bunk earlier. It's wet, but it's still there in his pocket. He decides he wants to read it alone, difficult when the ship is laid to one side like this. Nevertheless he gropes his way to the officers' mess and sits down where he can.

He removes the letter, trying not to tear it, and opens it gingerly. Fortunately it's still legible and he starts to read, thinking all the while of Denise's smiling face.

'Darling Charlie, love of my life. Merry Xmas, darling. I'll be thinking of you on Xmas Day. I wish you were here with me now, but I feel your presence constantly. Hurry home, my darling. I hope you still love me now you know about our baby. I'll see you every time I look at him or her. No baby will ever be better loved. Our child is part of us, and you will always be part of me. I long deep down for your love and tenderness. You will always be my one true love. Hope you like the photograph, darling.'

The letter ends with a row of crosses, then a lipstick mark where Denise has kissed it. Charlie puts the mark to his lips and holds it there for some time. He blinks back a tear as he gazes at Denise's face. He can still see how beautiful she is. He closes his eyes and kisses her.

'I'll always love you, darling,' he says aloud, then puts the letter back in his pocket.

Charlie has already opened his family's card. Mam, Dad, Eileen and Howard have all signed it – even little Michael Charles! 'Merry Xmas, Charlie,' it read. 'We all love you.' He smiles at the thought of the kisses covering it and remembers his mother telling him to take care. He stands up and, grabbing whatever he can, returns to his mates.

The ship rolls heavily – first to port and then to starboard – and stays laid over. No one has moved. Silence reigns.

Charlie sits down again. Everyone is there: John the cook, Les the galley lad, the engineers, too. Charlie glances at old Sam, now concentrating intently on a piece of old newspaper. He remembers looking out to sea from Withernsea prom; then talking to Joe about the loss of his father and how it affected him. Another heavy roll to port and back, but this time the *Leopold* lays over further still.

Charlie has never been religious but now he says a little prayer. 'Please God, take care of my family, my darling Denise and our baby. Give my child a good life.'

Then comes a loud noise. Everything is moving as the ship heels over more dramatically. They hold on as best they can, staring at each other, knowing there's nowhere to run.

Back on the bridge, the skipper calls the *Ross Diamond*, but no answer. He runs to the wireless room to try again. The radio operator makes the call as the trawler heels over further still.

'*Diamond, Diamond*,' bawls the skipper. 'Mayday, mayday.'

'*Leopold*, this is *Diamond*.'

'*Diamond*! Are you … there, Fred?'

'Yes, Bob. Go ahead.'

The *Leopold* heels even further to starboard. 'My God, Fred, we're going …'

In the mess room, Charlie closes his eyes, thinking of his friends, the good times they enjoyed together, and Denise, his unborn baby and his family. He knows now he has no future. His initial sense of panic soon evaporates. Darkness washes over him and then an eerie silence. All fear has left him now. He sees a tunnel with a bright light at its end. He feels serene as the light slowly starts to fade, then nothing.

No further sound is heard.

The *Diamond* calls the *Leopold*, calls over and over again.

No answer.

The skipper of the *Ross Diamond* stands transfixed. 'My God,' he stutters. 'She's gone, she's gone.' He slumps in his chair. 'Oh my God.'

The mate shudders, face drained of all colour. 'Is there nothing we can do?'

The skipper stares at him. 'Nothing.' He shakes his head. 'They've gone.'

CHAPTER 14
XMAS STORY

Back in Hull, the Robinsons are opening their Xmas presents, laughing at the socks Mary has bought for Mike. 'What's wrong with them?' she asks innocently. 'Different coloured stripes. They're in fashion. Just right for the modern man.'

'Don't worry, love,' laughs Mike. 'I'm sure they'll grow on me. I bet Charlie will take the mick when he gets home.'

Baby Michael Charles is playing on the floor, more interested in the paper and boxes than anything else. 'Just like Charlie when he was a little one,' says Mary fondly, brushing away a tear. She takes Charlie's presents from underneath the tree, then goes to the sideboard and studies his photo. Looking at his beaming face, an unaccountable fear seizes hold of her. She shudders and turns to her family as she tries to shake the feeling away.

'All right, love?' asks Mike.

'Yes,' she says. 'Just thinking of Charlie.' She puts his presents back beneath the tree. 'I'm sure he'll like that shirt we bought him. It can stay there till he's home to open it.'

Mike comes and gives her a hug. 'He can have his Xmas then, love. You can cook him one of your lovely roast chickens with stuffing.'

They sit talking and enjoying a drink, the appetising smell of Xmas dinner drifting in from the kitchen. Just as they're about to sit down to eat, they hear a knock at the door.

'Who could this be?' asks Mike, getting up to answer it.

A man in uniform is standing there. 'Mr. Robinson?' he asks.

'That's me,' says Mike.

'I'm the chaplain at the Seamen's Mission. Could I come in, please? I need to talk to you.'

'Certainly,' says Mike apprehensively.

As soon as the family sees the chaplain, they freeze. He looks from face to face. 'I'm afraid I have some very bad news,' he says softly. He pauses. Everyone is gawping at him, open-mouthed. 'Your son's trawler … the *Leopold*. It's missing with all hands.'

Mike turns white with shock. 'No,' screams Mary, burying her face in her hands. Keening inconsolably, she runs to her husband. Eileen is crying, clinging to baby Michael until Howard grabs him from her. She goes to join her parents and the three of them stand sobbing and hugging each other.

'I can't tell you much more,' says the chaplain. 'According to the owners severe weather in the area where the *Leopold* was last reported fishing has prevented a thorough search. Several trawlers tried to go to her but the very hazardous conditions made it impossible. They'd only have been putting themselves at risk. The *Ross Diamond* was the last trawler in contact.

'Surely there must be a chance,' says Mike.

The chaplain shakes his head.

'We can't give up hope yet,' says Mike. 'We just can't.'

'I'll let you know as soon as we receive any further information, Mr Robinson. Unfortunately all I can do at the moment is offer you and your family my deepest sympathy and pray for Charlie and his shipmates. I have several other families still to visit. Please forgive me. I hate to leave you like this, but I must go.'

Mike sees him out.

'If you need anything, Mr Robinson, anything at all, please contact me,' says the chaplain, offering his hand. 'My deepest sympathy.'

'My son, my son,' murmurs Mike as he shuts the door behind him.

The house is silent. Mary and Eileen are holding each other, praying that it's all a bad dream. Mike goes up to Charlie's room and finds his son's shoes lying on the floor. Tearfully, he picks them up and sits on the bed for a while, then returns them to the floor. He wants to be strong for Mary and tries to control himself before he goes back downstairs.

'There must be something we can do,' she begs him.

'No, darling. The chaplain is right. All we can do is pray.'

'Dear Lord, let our son be safe!' says Mary. 'Please God, let it be so.'

'Say Charlie hasn't gone,' sobs Eileen. 'Say he's coming home.'

Mike is praying for a miracle but deep down he knows it's impossible. The chaplain would have said if there was any chance.

Eventually Mary has to go and lie down. 'Watch your mam,' Mike tells Eileen. 'I need some air and I must tell Denise before she hears the news from anyone else.'

Pale and trembling, he walks up the street. *What on earth am I going to say*? He hesitates momentarily, then raps sharply at the Watsons' door.

Jim comes to answer it. 'Hello, Mike,' he says. 'Come on in. What are you doing here on Xmas Day?'

Mike follows him into the house. Everyone is there. Bob is now living with Shirley but they've both come round for Xmas Day and brought the children with them. Seeing them all together like this, Mike bursts into tears.

'Sit down,' Jim coaxes him. 'What's up?'

'It's Charlie,' says Mike. He can't say any more. He raises his eyes and stares at Denise.

'What is it, Mr Robinson?' she asks anxiously. 'What about Charlie?'

'He's gone. They've all gone.'

'What do you mean?' says Jim. Nobody can grasp what Mike is saying.

'The *Leopold*,' he whispers. 'It's gone down with all hands.' Then he breaks down completely.

'No!' shrieks Denise, collapsing into her father's arms.

Mike stares blankly ahead as Barbara comforts him, while Sarah runs upstairs and grabs the teddy bear Charlie won for her at Hull Fair. She clasps it to her chest, rocking to and fro. 'No,' she sobs again and again.

'Not Charlie,' shouts Bob. 'It's not true. I don't believe it.'

Shirley rushes to his side. Eventually Barbara leaves

Mike and goes to put the kettle on, praying Denise says nothing about the baby. Mike and Mary still haven't been told and she doesn't want them to find out just now.

'Is there any hope at all?' asks Jim, going to sit with him.

'No,' says Mike. 'If only there were. The chaplain said he'd let us know as soon as he has more news. I don't know what to do. I feel so useless. My boy, my boy. How could this happen?'

Bob is struck dumb. He's lost more than just a friend. He and Charlie are like brothers.

'I must get back,' says Mike eventually. He goes to kiss Denise on the cheek. Like Bob, she hasn't spoken since they heard the news.

Jim escorts him to the door. 'I know nothing I can say will help you,' he says. 'I don't know how Denise will cope. You know how much she loves him.'

Mike nods, then turns and walks away as if in a dream.

George is home on leave for Xmas and rushes round to see Bob as soon as he hears the news.

'Oh, mate. Tell me it's not true. It can't be.'

Bob shakes his head. 'I'm afraid it is, George. Charlie's gone.'

'Them f***ing trawlers,' says George tearfully. 'He had his whole life before him. Bloody hell, Bob. Why?'

'I don't know,' says Bob. 'I'm just like you. I keep asking myself the same thing?' He puts an arm around his friend. 'He was the best mate you could ever have, and smarter than any of us. I wonder if Joe knows?'

'I'll have to go round to see the Robinsons,' says George. 'What can I say? God knows how they're taking it. I told him not to go on them bloody things. We all did.'

'We can't change anything. I wish we could. Denise is in a dreadful state. And I'll tell you now because you'll find out sooner or later. She's expecting Charlie's baby.'

George pretends to be surprised. He doesn't want to let on that Charlie told him before he sailed.

'A baby? That's going to make it even tougher for her. Bob, we've got to make sure that child never wants for anything.

We owe it to Charlie.'

'Of course, George. I just can't believe we'll never see him again.'

'Me too, Bob. It's bloody hard. I can't get his face out of my mind.'

'Do you want me to come with you to see the Robinsons?'

'Please. Say tomorrow teatime, six-ish.'

'Fine.'

George and Bob go to see the family – a visit which is very difficult for them all. Mike and Mary are absolutely devastated; they both seem to have aged overnight. All the lads can do is express their sadness and offer their condolences.

The news spreads like wildfire and within a couple of days the entire fishing community knows what has happened to the *Leopold.* Newspapers local and national carry the same headline: 'Twenty men perish on deep-sea trawler. No survivors.' Most of the dead come from the Hessle Road area, and the people of Hull show their sympathy for these brave men by collecting money for their families. Tragedy is nothing new for Hull folk, but it always hits hard. A veil seems to descend on the city. All Xmas and New Year celebrations are cancelled as the community mourns the loss of its own.

David learns about the tragedy while he's out for a Boxing Day drink. 'Hello, love,' Pat greets him on his return. Then she sees his expression. 'What on earth's wrong?'

'Young Charlie, his trawler's been lost with all hands.'

Pat covers her face with her hands. 'Oh no, not Charlie!'

At once the tears begin to flow. All she can see is Charlie's smiling face and curly black hair. She remembers how they made love. How tender he was, how thoughtful. She's never truly acknowledged the depth of her feelings for him.

Knowing nothing of Pat's relationship with Charlie, David is watching her intently. He's worried that the news will bring back memories of her late husband and make her more afraid for her son.

"What about Joe?' she asks suddenly. 'Is he OK?'

'Joe's fine,' David reassures her. 'Don't worry, his trawler isn't at Iceland. Sit down, darling. I'll make you a drink.'

Why do I bring bad luck on everyone I love? wonders Pat. *This could happen to David, too. He has to give up trawlers.*

After hearing about Charlie, Denise refuses to eat or leave the house. She can't accept that he's never coming home again. Sometimes she wakes up in the early hours thinking it's all a bad dream, then reality kicks in and she can't hold back the tears.

'You must try and pull yourself together, love,' says Barbara. 'For the baby's sake, if nothing else. You've got to eat.'

'What am I going to do, Mam? I feel as if my heart's been torn in two. I love Charlie so much.'

'I know, love, I know. But he'd want you to take care of his child.'

Denise starts crying again. 'Of course I'll take care of our baby, Mam. I'll have to tell Mr and Mrs Robinson soon, though. How do you think they'll take it?'

'I'm sure they'll understand, love. Just give them a little time.'

All Charlie's colleagues at the fish house are aghast at the news. Irish Rose is heartbroken, remembering her lost husband and her conversation with Charlie. Big Maggie, like all the girls, just can't accept that he has gone.

The Watsons too are finding it very hard to cope. In early January Denise decides that Charlie's family have to know about the baby. She goes to speak to her mother.

'I think it's time I went to see Charlie's parents, Mam.'

'I'm sure you're right, love,' says Barbara. 'Do you want me to come with you?'

'Please,' says Denise.

Denise is full of conflicting emotions as they go round to see the Robinsons. Barbara keeps reassuring her, but she's still apprehensive when they knock at the door.

'Hello, love,' says Mary, surprised. 'It's good to see you. Denise and Barbara are here, Mike.'

They all sit and talk for a while, then finally Denise plucks up the courage to speak. 'I've something to tell you, Mr and Mrs Robinson.' She bites her lip and looks to her mum for help. She just can't get the words out.

'What is it, love? asks Mike.

Denise looks down at the floor. 'I wanted to tell you earlier but it never seemed the right time. I'm –I'm ... '

She burst into tears, and Barbara steps in. 'Mike, Mary, what she's trying to say is … she's expecting Charlie's baby. It's due late May or early June.'

'You poor darling,' says Mary, taking hold of Denise's hand. 'Don't you go upsetting yourself. Did our boy know before he sailed?'

'Yes,' sobs Denise. 'We were going to tell you when he came home.'

Mary is immediately comforted by the news that Charlie has left a child for them to love, but Mike struggles for words. 'Don't worry,' he says eventually. 'We'll be here for you and the baby, just like Charlie would have been.'

'Thanks, Mr Robinson.' Denise takes a handkerchief from her pocket and wipes her eyes. 'I miss him terribly.'

'Call me Mike, love. You're part of our family now. Come on, don't be upset. I'll make us all a drink.'

In the kitchen he breaks down completely. *My lad a father without ever seeing his child.* He covers his eyes with his hands. *Why son, why?*' He pulls himself together, puts the drinks on a tray and goes to rejoin the women. Hesitantly at first, they all start talking about Charlie, laughing and crying over the things he would get up to as a child.

'You come and see us any time, darling,' says Mary.

'They're holding a service for Charlie and his shipmates next month at the Seamen's Chapel,' says Mike. 'You must come with us.'

When Denise sees the photo of Charlie and his pals on the sideboard, she starts crying again.

'Come now, darling,' says Mary. 'Dry your eyes. I can't hide that photo. Seeing Charlie smiling with his friends every day helps me to cope. Do you have a photo of Charlie, love?'

'Yes, exactly the same one. Bob gave it to me. Oh, Mrs Robinson! I can't live without him, I just can't.'

Mary takes her hand again. 'You have to, darling. We all do. I know it's hard. Our lives will never be the same again. But we have to think of the baby and all the joy it will bring.'

When Joe returns from his trip, Pat is waiting as he walks through the door. 'Have you heard about Charlie?' she asks, giving him a hug.

'Yes, Mam. I can't believe it. I've always looked up to him. He was always there for me. I should never have encouraged him to go on trawlers.'

David is watching. He knows full well what's coming next. Pat has been on at him for days to pack it in and work on shore.

'Please don't go back, Joe. Please.'

'I have to, Mam. It's my job. There are ships sailing right now with men on board just like me. We all chose the life. Dad would've wanted me to carry on.'

'But look what's happened to Charlie, so young, and all the rest of the crew.'

Joe is thinking about shaking hands with Charlie before they sailed. 'Can we talk about this later, Mam? I just want to be on my own for a while.'

David gives Pat a nudge. *Leave the lad alone*, it implies.

'OK, love,' says Pat. 'I'm sorry.'

Lying on his bed, Joe is thinking of Charlie and remembering all the good times they shared. Joe can see him walk laughing out of the chemist's shop in Withernsea, Liver Salts in hand. He smiles. Then the tears start to flow as he ponders the eternal question: 'Why?'

On the day of the service Hessle Road is packed, with only relatives and close friends allowed to enter the chapel. Charlie's family walk in together, followed by all the Watsons. Shirley is with Joe and George, and Pat and David are there, too. The chaplain begins the service by solemnly reading aloud the names of all those lost on the *Leopold*. When Charlie's name is mentioned, Mary and Eileen burst into tears. Mike puts his arms around them both, while Jim and Barbara comfort Denise.

Head bowed, George is standing between Joe and Bob. Hearing Charlie's name, he takes his friends by the hand and squeezes hard. Then he closes his eyes. 'We're all here, Charlie,' he says to himself. 'We'll miss you, dear friend. We'll always remember the good times we shared with you. Rest in peace. We love you.' He opens his eyes and looks at his friends, then closes them again.

'Like all deep sea fishermen,' the chaplain tells the congregation, 'the brave trawlermen of Hull lead a hard life. When lives are lost in a tragedy like this, still they have the strength to carry on. This is and always has been their way. We are here today as a mark of respect for these men but also to celebrate their lives. We are a strong community. We will support their families and be there for them whenever they need us.'

Prayers are said and hymns are sung. When the mourners leave the chapel they are stunned by the size of the crowd. Mrs Booth is there with her friend Mrs Brown, wiping away the tears with a big white handkerchief. No headscarves and curlers today, but heavy black coats for them both. All the fish-house workers are there, the girls are standing together crying and consoling each other, the men solemn-faced when they see their friend Mike and his family leaving the chapel.

Charlie's family and friends hug each other, still very emotional, then regather for the walk home. That's when Joe and Pat first hear the news of Denise's baby. A tear runs down Pat's cheek as she relives the moments she and Charlie spent together, picturing his handsome face, curly black hair and wonderful smile, wondering again what might have been.

After the service, the folk of the fishing community try to continue on with their lives, but it's hard for them all. The tragedy touched so many families and it's impossible for them to forget. Many exist in a permanent state of mourning, unable to accept that their husbands, sons and brothers have gone forever.

Charlie's loss is written starkly on the faces of his family and friends. Mike is a broken man, now terribly pale and fragile. Denise, too, has often been unwell. She went straight back to work, and it's given her a few moments of respite, but Charlie is constantly on her mind. Andrea and her other friends at work can see her getting bigger every day and try their best to help. Then as her due date draws near Denise leaves her job and stays at home. Her mum is always there to reassure her, trying to get Denise to prepare for the birth, hoping it might help to focus her mind on something positive.

Denise sometimes goes to sit quietly in the front room where she and Charlie so often went to be alone. She closes her eyes and thinks about his smile, his touch when they made love. She holds her stomach, telling the baby about him. Sometimes she speaks out loud, describing what a wonderful lad he was and how much they loved one another.

She promises herself that she will never ever let their baby forget him. Her family are concerned about her, but they know how much she loved her Charlie and how his loss has affected her. All they can do is give her as much support as possible.

Even the neighbours show none of the usual prejudice against girls who get pregnant out of wedlock. No one has treated Denise with anything but compassion. In the street Mrs Booth and Mrs Brown still like to stand and gossip. One day Mrs Booth sees Denise coming towards them, obviously close to her confinement.

'Hello love, how are you?' she calls.

'Not too bad, Mrs Booth,' answers Denise. 'Thanks for asking.'

Mrs Booth remembers the banter she used to enjoy with Charlie. She knew he was just teasing and always played along with him. Now just thinking of him walking past, smiling, brings tears to her eyes. She lifts up her pinny to wipe them away.

Mrs Brown puts her arm around her. Denise can see they're both upset.

'He were a nice lad, your Charlie,' says Mrs Booth. 'You take care of yourself, love. I'm sure your baby will be a smasher. You'll make a lovely mam, as well.'

'Thanks, Mrs Booth. It's very nice of you to say so.'

'God bless you, love. God bless,' says Mrs Booth as Denise walks away.

'Poor lass,' says Mrs Brown.

'Oh, Else,' says Mrs Booth. 'What a bloody cruel world we live in.'

Charlie and Denise's baby is born at home on 1 May. It's a boy, named after his father. Afterwards the Watsons and Robinsons gather round the bed to admire him amid tears of joy and sadness. Denise is holding baby Charlie. 'Look, Mam,' she says. 'He's the spitting image of his dad.'

Mary is clinging tight to Mike. 'Would you like to hold him?' asks Denise, holding the baby out to her.

Smiling, Mary takes baby Charlie in her arms and kisses his forehead. Mike is peering over her shoulder. 'He's a beauty, Mother. If only ...' But he stops himself in time. If only Charlie could have been here, he wanted to say.

'Please remember that Charlie is your grandson, too,' says Jim. 'You're part of our family. You'll always be welcome here.'

Mary doesn't want to let go of the baby, but Mike eases her towards Denise and helps her hand him back. As they leave the house he puts his arm around her. 'You all right, love?'

'Yes, darling,' she replies, tears streaming down her cheeks. 'I'm fine.'

It's nearly three years now since Charlie was lost at sea. Little Charlie is a big part of the Watson family. They love him to bits and he's a permanent reminder of their dear friend. Denise hasn't looked at anyone else since she lost her Charlie. Her family and friends keep telling her she has to live her life. 'Charlie would want you to,' they say over and over again, but she is adamant that no one could ever replace him.

Pat and David are very happily married. David is still going to sea, and Pat sees the baby every now and then. She always tells Denise how much he resembles his father.

Bob has finished his National Service, much to his relief – he didn't really enjoy his time in the army. He's back at the shoe factory, as head supervisor after getting the promotion he always wanted. He and Shirley are very happy. They're still living together and she's expecting their first child.

George finished his National Service some time ago. He joined the Musicians' Union and now earns his living as a singer and comedian in the pubs and clubs of Hull. He always did like being the centre of attention. It's difficult sometimes with Joe away at sea, and it could never be the same without Charlie, but Joe and Bob meet up with him from time to time. They talk about Charlie constantly, reminiscing about all the fun they had together.

Joe and Sarah have become very close since Charlie's death. They've been going out for a while now. He loves her very much and they're very happy together. 'Make sure you look after her,' Bob tells him. 'And don't take advantage of her.'

'Don't worry,' says Joe. 'She's bribing me. "No ring, no sex" is her motto.'

That makes them both laugh.

The Watsons and the Robinsons always go down the dock on Xmas Day. This year Denise is carrying little Charlie and they all stand in silence on the quayside while Mike and Mary throw flowers into the Humber. Mike turned grey overnight when Charlie was lost and now suffers from heart trouble, so Mary has to support him.

Then they hold little Charlie's hands as Denise tosses a single red rose into the water. She looks out over the river. 'I miss you more each day, my darling. Our son is a permanent reminder of you – your smile, your looks, everything. If only you were here to see him.'

Finally, she picks up her son. 'Come here, my little angel. Daddy's watching. You can blow him a kiss.'

Little Charlie blows a kiss into the sky, then turns to Denise with a smile. 'I can see my daddy, Mummy.'

Denise gives him a kiss. 'We all can, darling.' Jim and Barbara are weeping silently, Mary holds Mike close, and Howard hugs Eileen. 'Wave bye-bye to Daddy, my sweet.'

Little Charlie waves and Denise looks up to the heavens. 'Goodbye, my darling Charlie. I can never mend my broken heart. The pain will never fade. It will stay with me until the day

I die and we're together again at last.'

Up above, Charlie is looking down on his family, tears in his eyes. He's trying to get a message to Denise. 'I can see you and my son, my darling. I'll always be watching over you. Please God, take care of my loved ones.'

A distant voice is calling him. Far away he sees Eric and Les. 'Come on, Charlie. Our shipmates are waiting.'

Charlie takes one last long look at his family, then turns and joins the ghostly crew as they fade into the thick white mist.

****

Well, that's the story of Charlie and his friends. People never understand how fishermen could sail again after such a tragedy, but they did and still do. We can only admire them for it. All I know is that they're very brave men. I just hope the people of Hull will always remember them and continue to appreciate what they did.

EPILOGUE

My First Trip

'Ready, Charlie?' shouts mi dad. 'Time for you to go.'
Am I afraid or just excited? I don't really know.
Kitbag on my shoulder I say my last goodbyes,
My sister looking on, tears in her eyes.

Smiling at the passers-by, I try to look so tough.
'Off on trawlers?' a woman shouts. 'You don't look bloody old
enough'.
Out on deck, ready for sea, that's when the fear sets in.
My career on trawlers is about to begin.

Let go forward, let go aft. Into the murky Humber we go.
I grab my kitbag nervously, I find my bunk below.
The smell of diesel and fresh paint is making me feel sick,
Two deckhands start kidding me, taking the mick.

'Come on, young'un,' shouts the mate. 'There's work to do.
You're not here to play, you know, you're one of the crew.'
Clearing the Humber, we hear we're Iceland bound.
Three days steaming to the fishing grounds.

The next few days we roll around. The weather's very bad.
I start to think perhaps I should've listened to mi dad.
Arriving on the fishing grounds we start to tow the trawl.
Three hours later, 'Hauling time,' we hear the skipper call.

The fish all wriggling on the deck, what a sight to see.
Ten more days' poor weather. Is this too much for me?
Time drags by, the fishing's good, our ship is nearly full.
The skipper's pleased and so am I. At last we're bound for Hull.

'Get the gear on board,' the skipper calls. 'We're going home.'
My first trip is nearly over. Can't believe I've braved the storm.
I've seen the lives of fishermen. Conditions can be so bad.
I'm home now with my family from my trip as galley lad.

Danny Platten